She put up her chin.

'It would take more than your disapproval to offend me. It is immaterial to me what you think of me.'

'Is it, indeed?' said Delagarde, instantly up in the boughs. 'Then allow me to point out that it was not I who sought to place you under my sponsorship. But, since you will have it so, you had better learn to take account of my opinion.'

Maidie's brows drew together. 'Well, I will not. I have not asked you to interfere beyond what I specify.'

'Oh, indeed?' returned Delagarde dangerously. 'And what precisely do you specify? I may remind you that I have not yet agreed to anything at all.'

'Then why am I here?'

'You are asking me? How the devil should I know?'

Elizabeth Bailey grew up in Malawi, returning to England to plunge into the theatre. After many happy years 'tatting around the reps', she finally turned from 'dabbling' to serious writing. She finds it more satisfying for she is in control of everything: scripts, design, direction, and the portrayal of every character! Elizabeth lives in Surrey.

MISFIT MAID

Elizabeth Bailey

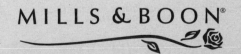
MILLS & BOON®

*First published in Great Britain 1999
Harlequin Mills & Boon Limited,
Eton House, 18-24 Paradise Road, Richmond, Surrey TW9 1SR*

© Elizabeth Bailey 1999

ISBN 0 263 81838 1

*Set in Times Roman 10½ on 11½ pt.
04-9911-83001*

*Printed and bound in Spain
by Litografia Rosés S.A., Barcelona*

Chapter One

The sensation came of stark disbelief. But Lord Delagarde was only aware of blankness invading his mind. To steady himself, he carefully gripped the mantel with neatly manicured fingers. Resting his other hand on his hip, he examined the offending apparition seated on the gilded chair at the other side of the fireplace, so boldly confronting him in his own front parlour.

She did not look like the daughter of an Earl. The green pelisse and a glimpse of some dark stuff gown beneath were frankly dowdy, and no female of distinction would be seen dead in such a bonnet. Poke-fronted and unadorned, its bilious mustard hue framed an unremarkable face, out of which a pair of grey eyes regarded him with an unblinking gaze that was, in his present delicate state, singularly unnerving.

What she had said seemed so incomprehensible that he wondered if perhaps his ears had deceived him. 'I don't think I quite understood you. Once again, if you please.'

'Certainly.' Her voice was clear and light, and free from any trace of consciousness. 'I require you to arrange my debut.'

'You require me…to arrange your debut,' he said

slowly, aware that the words must make sense, if only he could shake off this feeling of unreality. 'Yes, I thought that was it.'

'It was,' she agreed, adding in a matter-of-fact way, 'So that I may be settled in life.'

'Settled…' He put a hand to his head, conscious of a slight ache. There was, he supposed vaguely, a faint hope that the entire scene was a figment of his imagination. Perhaps he had not really been roused from his bed at a hideously early hour, been obliged to scramble into his clothes and come downstairs—unfortified by anything more substantial than a few sips of hot chocolate—to be faced with an unorthodox visit from a female of unknown origin, who threw at him this preposterous demand. She required—required!—him to arrange her debut.

Yes, he must be dreaming. Or else last night's imbibing had unhinged his brain, subjecting him to this extraordinary hallucination. It spoke again, rousing Delagarde from his abstraction.

'You are not dreaming,' it said.

Delagarde had not been aware of speaking aloud. 'I must be,' he protested, 'or else I have run mad.'

The hallucination looked him over with a wide-eyed innocence belied by its next words. 'It is more likely that you are suffering from a morning head. Be assured that my appearance here has nothing to do with the liquor in which you overindulged last night.'

Delagarde blinked, and regarded her with rising indignation. 'Are you insinuating that I was inebriated?'

'Weren't you?'

'No, I was n—' He broke off, resolutely shutting his mouth. Why was he responding to such a question? He glared at the girl. 'Even if I was, it is no possible concern of yours.'

'No,' she agreed, taking the wind out of his sails.

'Then what possessed you to mention it?' he demanded belligerently.

'To help you.'

'Help me?' Blank again.

'To show you that you are neither mad, nor dreaming,' she explained.

This time Delagarde put both hands to his swimming head. 'We seem to be going round in circles,' he complained.

'There is nothing complicated about the matter, as you will realise when you are more yourself.'

Which, Delagarde reflected, might not be for some little time. He began to wish he had not allowed his valet's disapproving comments to pique his interest. The young female, Liss had reported in fastidious tones, had announced herself to be one Lady Mary Hope, and had declared that she would not leave the premises until she had seen Lord Delagarde.

'Why the devil did Lowick let this female enter the house in the first place?' Delagarde had demanded, bleary-eyed.

It appeared that it was the porter, new to the Viscount's service, who had taken this fatal step. To his lordship's irritable inquiry as to why the butler had not then shown her the door, the valet had replied haughtily, 'The young female having been allowed in, my lord, and taking up a peculiarly intransigent attitude, expressing herself in such terms as no real lady—' He had caught himself up, and coughed delicately. 'Suffice it, my lord, that even Mr Lowick did not feel he could force her to leave without laying violent hands upon her. Which, my lord, he was loath to do, in the remote contingency that her claim of identity might be proven.'

Which it was not, Delagarde remembered suddenly. He

frowned at the girl. 'How can I be certain that you are indeed Lady Mary Hope?'

'Who else should I be?' she countered.

'How the devil should I know?' retorted Delagarde, pardonably annoyed. 'You might be anyone. An adventuress…a schemer, imposter—I have no idea.'

'Humdudgeon!' snorted his visitor in a most unladylike way. 'As a member of the peerage, you know well enough who is who. I am obviously related to the Earl of Shurland, if I am a Hope.'

'*If* you are,' Delagarde retorted, stressing the 'if'. 'And if you are Lady Mary, I suppose you to have been fathered by Shurland—or his predecessor. But I have yet to see proof of your identity.'

'Oh, if that is all,' came the airy response, 'I can furnish you with proofs enough very easily.'

'Well, where are they?'

'I can readily bring them—after we have settled everything.'

Was that a hint of challenge in her eye? Delagarde made an effort to shake off his creeping lethargy and take control of this absurd situation. Was he to be intimidated by an impertinent chit? He did not think so.

'My good girl, there is nothing to settle,' he told her in his loftiest tone. 'If this is some sort of trickery, you have mistaken your man. Whether you are, or are not, Lady Mary Hope, I have not the remotest intention—'

'Pray do not let us waste any more time on that matter,' she interrupted impatiently, not in the least crushed. 'You had as well accept my identity without further ado. However, I dare say it will be wisest for you to address me as Maidie—for everyone who knows me well uses my pet name—which will help to make people believe us to be very well acquainted.'

'I have no desire to make anyone believe it,' objected

Delagarde, refusing to avail himself of this permission. 'And I am far from accepting your identity.'

'I can't think why. You must see very well that I am indeed Lady Mary.'

'I see nothing of the kind,' declared Delagarde, losing what little patience he had. 'All I see is a strange young female, who comes to my house—at, I may add, the most unseasonable hour—'

'It is past ten o'clock!'

'—unseasonable hour, I say, for visiting. And while we are on the subject, it may interest you to know that any female with the smallest pretension to gentility would not dream of visiting a gentleman—'

'She would if she had my circumstances.'

'—in his own house, which, if you were indeed Lady Mary Hope, you would be quite aware is the height of impropriety.'

'I am aware of it,' Maidie said, 'although I have never been able to understand why.'

'It is obvious why,' Delagarde snapped. 'Quite apart from the damage to your reputation, you are alone and unprotected.'

'Do you mean to assault me?'

'Of course I don't mean to assault you!'

'Then why are we discussing it?'

'Oh, good God!'

Unable to decide which of several infuriated utterances to make first, Delagarde paced about for a moment or two until he remembered what he had begun to say. He turned on the girl.

'All this is quite beside the point. What I have been trying to impress upon you is that it is utterly unheard of for a complete stranger to walk unannounced into a gentleman's residence and throw a ridiculous demand at his head.'

Maidie raised her brows. 'What is ridiculous about it?'

Delagarde threw up his hands. 'If you can't see that, then you are the one who is mad—which I am beginning to suspect is indeed the case. Arrange for your debut, indeed! Even if I had any idea of doing so—which I emphatically do not—it would be quite impossible.'

'Why?'

'Because I am not equipped to do so. What were you thinking of? That I should launch you from this house?'

'Why not?'

'Why not!' Delagarde felt an almost irresistible urge to clutch at his hair. 'You don't mean to say you really were thinking of such a thing? Good God, girl, I am a bachelor! You need a respectable female to sponsor you—a chaperon.'

Maidie sank back in her chair. 'Is that all that is troubling you? You need have—'

'No, it is not all!'

'—no further concern,' she said calmly, ignoring his interruption. 'I have thought of all that. I have brought my own duenna. She is your cousin, so there can be no impropriety in us both staying in your house.'

'Staying in my—!' For a moment or two, Delagarde regarded her speechlessly. Then he sank into the chair on the other side of the fireplace and dropped his head in his hands.

Maidie watched him with interest. He was not at all what she had expected. She had anticipated that there might be a trifle of explanation required, but not to have her identity called in question. Why Lord Delagarde should make such a piece of work about a simple matter she failed to comprehend.

He did not look obtuse. Quite the contrary. One might not call him handsome, but it was a strong countenance—if a trifle jaded at present; she could not think he had always such a pallor—with a firm line to the jaw, a straight nose and a broad brow from which dark locks waved back into a long crop. Whether the dishevelled look of this style was deliberate, or due to the gentleman's current state, Maidie could not say. He certainly had the air of a man of fashion. She knew little of such things, it was true, but even to the untutored eye, there was an unmistakable elegance to the cut of the cream breeches and the blue coat.

From the point of view of appearances, he would certainly do, and his establishment was eminently suited to her purpose. A house in the best part of town, with a deliberate decor influencing even this small room, the simplicity of which impressed her. Nothing elaborate. Warm-shaded wallpaper, its apricot picked out in the faint stripe of the cushioned seats. Maidie approved the slim lines of the furniture, the plain brown carpet, and the sparse decoration to the mouldings about the fireplace.

She was less satisfied to have discovered Lord Delagarde to be a creature of uncertain temperament. It did not augur well for her plans. But it was possible that he was not always so. Had her timing, perhaps, been unfortunate? He had been abed on her arrival, and had kept her waiting quite forty minutes—really, could one take that long to dress?—and the traces in his face of a late and dissipated night had been evident to the meanest intelligence. Even Great-uncle had become crotchety of a morning after indulging too freely in his favourite port. Perhaps Lord Delagarde might respond more readily if his head were not aching so badly.

Maidie leaned forward a little, and addressed him in a tone of solicitude. 'Shall I send for some coffee?'

Delagarde started. God, was she still here? For a brief moment of silence, in which he had allowed his seething brain to subside a little, he had almost succeeded in forgetting her unwelcome presence. Dropping his hands, he gripped the wooden arms of his chair and braced himself to look at her again.

What had she said? 'Coffee?'

'I would strongly advise it. My great-uncle used to say that it was the best cure for your sort of condition.'

Delagarde opened his mouth to consign her great-uncle to the devil, and instead drew a steadying breath. Be calm, he told himself resolutely, be calm.

'I do not want any coffee,' he said carefully.

'I assure you—'

'No!' A pause, then pointedly, 'Thank you.'

She relaxed back. 'As you wish.'

Resolutely, Delagarde sat up. 'Now then, Lady Mary, let us be sensible.'

Come, this was an advance, decided Maidie eagerly. He had used her name at least. 'Indeed, I wish for nothing better.'

'What you wish for is quite out of the question,' Delagarde returned. 'Surely there must be some other person than myself more properly suited to the task of bringing you out?'

Maidie resolutely shook her head. 'There is no one. You, Lord Delagarde, are my nearest male relative—other than Shurland—and it is nothing less than your duty.'

'But I don't know you from Adam! As for being your nearest male relative, I have no recollection of even the remotest connection with the Hopes.'

She raised her brows. 'Who said anything about the Hopes? The relationship is on my mother's side. She was one of the Burloynes.'

'I have never heard of them,' said Delagarde, not without relief. 'Which proves they can have nothing to do with the Delagarde family.'

Maidie clicked her tongue. 'Did I say so?'

'You said…' Delagarde began, and paused, realising

that she had set his mind in such a confusion that he could no longer untangle one thing she had said from another. 'It matters little what you said. The point is—'

'The point is,' she cut in, 'that even if you refuse to recognise the relationship, you cannot escape the obligation.'

Delagarde stared at her with a good deal of suspicion. What new ploy was this? 'What obligation?'

Maidie shifted in her seat and produced the reticule that had been hidden under her pelisse. Searching within it, she brought forth a folded sheet of yellowed parchment, upon which he glimpsed the remains of a broken seal. Maidie got up and held it out to him.

'This will explain it.' As he rose automatically to take it from her and open it out, she added, 'It is from your mother. You see there the name of Mrs Egginton, to whom it is addressed? She lived nearby and very thoughtfully befriended me, and sent to Lady Delagarde after my father died. You will notice that Lady Delagarde promises to lend me countenance when I should at last come out.'

Delagarde ran his eyes rapidly down the sheet. It was indeed a letter written by his mother to this effect, for he recognised the hand. But what obligation did this constitute?

'What possible reason could this Egginton woman have for choosing to batten upon my mother?'

'Your mother was born Lady Dorinda Otterburn, was she not?'

'Yes, but—'

'Well, then. The Burloyne connection comes through the Otterburns. So you see, we are related.'

Delagarde saw nothing of the sort. The name of Burloyne had no meaning for him, although he had to admit to unfamiliarity with all the ramifications of his mother's family. But he was not going to waste time finding them out.

'The relationship,' he said firmly, 'if there is any— which I take leave to doubt—must be remote in the extreme.' He was still studying the letter. 'What is this offer my mother mentions to send someone to live with you?'

'But I told you that my duenna is your cousin. Have you not been listening?'

Delagarde found himself contemplating the desirability of boxing her ears. He restrained himself with difficulty, and once more bade himself be calm.

'Lady Mary, while it may prove to be out of my power—regrettably!—to repudiate some sort of relationship with you, allow me to draw to your attention that this letter is over ten years old. Moreover, my mother has been in her grave these many years.'

'I know that,' agreed Maidie patiently, 'and therefore the obligation devolves upon you.' She retrieved the letter and pointed to one sentence. 'You see here that your mother even states that you may be counted upon to aid the project.'

'Good God, girl, I was barely eighteen at the time!' He thrust away, throwing up a protective hand as if she might threaten him. 'Take the wretched thing away before I rip it to shreds! It has no bearing on the case. I knew nothing of the matter then, and I wish to know less of it now. In any event, my circumstances hardly make me a suitable person to lend you countenance. And if you think it escaped me that you mentioned Shurland when you gave me this cock-and-bull tale of being your nearest male relative, you are mistaken. So answer me this, if you please: why cannot he bring you out?'

'Because he is dead,' stated Maidie doggedly.

'He can't be dead,' protested Delagarde, pacing in some agitation. 'He only took over the title a year or so ago.'

'I meant my great-uncle, the fifth Earl,' she explained. 'He was my guardian.'

'Then why didn't he arrange for your debut?'

'Because he was eccentric.'

'Evidently it runs in the family.'

Maidie merely gazed at him with her wide-eyed look. She folded the letter and replaced it in her reticule. She then reseated herself and looked up at him again. As calmly as if she owned the place! Delagarde eyed her in frustrated silence for a moment or two. He had half a mind to ring for Lowick and have him forcibly remove the wretched female, but he supposed such a course was ineligible. He was, after all, a gentleman. But he was not going to accede to her nonsensical demand.

He resumed his post by the mantelpiece. 'What about this female who befriended you, the Egginton woman?'

'She died, too.'

'She would! Well, the other one, then.'

'Which other one?'

'Your duenna. Don't dare try to kill her off as well, because you have already threatened to bring her to live here.'

For the first time, a smile broke across Maidie's face, and she laughed. 'What, poor Worm bring me out? Why, she has no connections, apart from you. She is one of your poor relations. I dare say your mother had it in mind to settle her, poor thing, when she suggested that the Worm came to me.'

Delagarde was so surprised by the change that a smile wrought in her countenance that he forgot to ask for an explanation of this odd name. It was a countenance alight, the dowdiness given off by her unfashionable apparel fading into the background. He did not realise that he was staring until the smile vanished and Maidie's brows rose again, widening her eyes.

'Are you thinking that there might be some other female relative I could turn to? I assure you there is not. I am wholly dependent upon you.'

This snapped his attention back to the matter at hand, and he frowned. 'No, you are not. You have no real claim upon me at all. If all you say is true, then the charge of you falls not upon me, but upon Shurland. And don't tell me he cannot bring you out, because I know very well he is married.'

Maidie put up her chin. 'Well, I do tell you so. The plain truth is that Adela cannot abide me, and I cannot abide her.'

'Is Adela his wife?'

'Yes, she is, and we quarrelled.'

'I wonder why I am not surprised.'

'Besides,' continued Maidie, unheeding, 'Adela treated me abominably until I came of age. Only then, as if nothing had happened, she began fawning all over me, and determining to bring me out.'

'Then why the devil,' demanded Delagarde, exasperated, 'have you come to me?'

'Because,' stated Maidie in steely tones, 'I am determined never to marry Eustace Silsoe.'

Delagarde's head began to reel again. 'Who in the world is Eustace Silsoe? Why should you marry him if you don't want to?'

'He is that hateful woman's brother. Nothing will do for her but that he should succeed with me, and that is all the reason she has for offering to bring me out.'

'Just one moment,' begged Delagarde, sitting down again. 'Are you telling me that you are trying to involve me in this preposterous and impossible scheme you have concocted, when you have a perfectly acceptable alternative, only so that you can escape a marriage you don't want?'

'Yes,' Maidie said, as if there was nothing at all out of the way.

'But—' Words failed him.

'Adela and Eustace think they can trap me, but I am going to spike their guns,' she went on in a tone of gritty determination. 'And you are to help me. I have thought it all out. We will say that you are my trustee, and that I cannot marry without your consent.'

Delagarde rose again. 'We will say nothing of the kind. The whole enterprise is unnecessary, as well as ridiculous. I will have nothing whatsoever to do with such a masquerade.'

He sounded so determined that Maidie began to fear, for the first time, that her mission might be in vain. Consternation filled her, showing in her face as she got up again and took a hasty step towards him.

'But you must,' she uttered desperately. 'Your mother promised me.'

'My mother, as I have pointed out, is dead.'

'Which is why I have come to you.'

Delagarde threw up a warning finger. 'We are going in circles again.'

Maidie came a step closer, reproach filling the wide-eyed gaze. 'Lord Delagarde, I never dreamed you would refuse me!'

'Then you must be off your head—as I would be were I to agree to participate in this monstrous scheme,' he averred, retreating from her.

'But I am depending on you!'

'Well, don't,' he advised in a harassed sort of way. 'You will have to think of something else.'

'It is such a little thing to do for me.'

'Little!'

'And you will be well compensated, I assure you.'

'For living with you? Impossible! I dare say I should count myself fortunate not to end in Bedlam!'

The door opened, and a glance over his shoulder showed him a welcome interruption. Entering the room was an elderly lady, fashionably attired in a demure version of the season's new high-waisted gowns, a figured green muslin with half-sleeves overlaid with a light woollen shawl of darker hue. A lace-edged cap like a turban bedecked with ribbons and feathers did not quite conceal her hair, which was dark like Delagarde's, though streaked through with grey. She held herself well, and Maidie immediately noted a resemblance to the Viscount in her softer features, although she looked to be readier to laugh.

Delagarde seized upon her gratefully, uttering in despairing accents, 'Aunt Hes, thank God! Kindly inform this lunatic female that I cannot possibly lend her countenance and become her fraudulent trustee.'

'Gracious, what in the world do you mean?' demanded this lady in astonished accents, looking from him to Maidie and back again. 'Who is this? What is she doing here? Is she alone?'

'My own questions exactly,' asserted Delagarde, 'and if you can get any more sense out of her than I did, you may call me a dunderhead.'

Maidie found herself the target of two pairs of eyes, the one popping with questions, the other registering a grim satisfaction. She drew a resolute breath, thrusting down the most unpleasant feelings engendered by Lord Delagarde's persistent rejection. She refused to be put off. She had come this far. She was not going to be turned away from her purpose now. A sudden thought struck her. If this lady was Delagarde's aunt, and she was already living in the house, then there must be an end to Delagarde's scruples.

'But this is excellent!' she uttered, with characteristic

frankness, moving forward to grasp the elder lady's hand. 'You are his aunt?'

'Great-aunt,' amended the other, surprise in her voice.

'And you live here!' Maidie turned enthusiastically to Delagarde. 'I don't understand why you were making such a fuss. What possible objection can there be to my living here in these circumstances?'

'There is every objection. Besides, my aunt does not reside here. She is here only on a short visit.' He added on a note of sarcasm, 'Sorry as I am to disappoint you.'

'But you may prolong your visit, may you not?' asked Maidie eagerly of the other lady. 'I cannot think that the business will take very long. Indeed, I hope it won't. I am as eager to remove back to the country as Lord Delagarde is to get rid of me. But I won't go back before I am settled.'

'You see?' Delagarde said, crossing the room to take up his post at the mantelpiece again. 'Mad as a March hare!' He looked across at Maidie. 'You are wasting your time. You need not think that my aunt, who is bound to be shocked by your conduct, will support you. She will undoubtedly advise me to send you packing.'

'I can speak for myself, I thank you, Laurie,' announced the older woman firmly.

Her attention caught, Maidie's glance went from Delagarde to his aunt, who was studying her with some interest. She stared back boldly, thinking hard. Delagarde seemed to be adamant, she was making no headway there. But hope was reviving fast. If she could only bring this lady round to her side! She was not, she told herself, a schemer. Not like Adela, not in the true sense of the word. Only what else could she have done? She would have preferred to set up house on her own. It was what she had planned to do, with Worm as chaperon. But that scheme would not do, as she had been brought to realise. She had been obliged to fall back upon convention, and for that she needed help. It had not entered her head that her designated assistant would decline to give that help. Now what was she to do? She made up her mind.

Addressing herself to Delagarde's aunt, she said, 'I have not properly introduced myself. I am Lady Mary Hope, daughter of the late John Hope, fourth Earl of Shurland; and great-niece of the late Reginald Hope, fifth Earl of Shurland, and my erstwhile guardian. I am related to Lord Delagarde through my mother, who was a Burloyne.'

'Have we any relations called Burloyne, Aunt?' asked Delagarde.' 'You ought to know. She claims it comes through the Otterburns.'

The elder lady nodded. 'It does, indeed. Although it is some few generations back.'

'I thought as much. Far too remote to be of consequence.'

Maidie brightened. 'Are you an Otterburn, then, ma'am?'

'I am Lady Hester Otterburn. Dorinda—that is, Delagarde's mother—was my niece.' To Maidie's relief, Lady Hester smiled and touched her arm with a friendly hand. 'What is it you want, child?'

Drawing a breath, Maidie plunged in again. 'I want Lord Delagarde to arrange my debut.'

For a moment, Lady Hester looked at her with almost as great a blankness as had Delagarde. Then, to Maidie's bewilderment, she burst out laughing. Lord Delagarde's reluctance to oblige her was at least comprehensible. But this? She watched as the elder lady betook herself to Delagarde's lately vacated chair and sat down.

'Forgive me,' she uttered, as soon as she could speak, 'but that is the funniest idea I have heard in years.'

'I don't see why,' Maidie said, pained.

'Nor do I,' agreed Delagarde, regarding his aunt with disfavour. 'What the devil do you mean by it, Aunt Hes?'

Lady Hester bubbled over again. 'The picture of you, Laurie, in the role of nursemaid to an ingenue. Really, it does not bear imagination! What in the world possessed you to think of such a thing, child? Laurie has no more notion of how to steer a young girl through the social shoals than the man in the moon.'

'There is no man in the moon,' Maidie said, vaguely irritated.

'This is typical,' commented Delagarde, gesturing towards her. 'Her whole conversation consists of non-sequitur statements.' To Maidie, he added, 'We know there is no man in the moon. What is that to the purpose?'

Maidie tutted. 'It is a foolish expression, which only shows how little people know of the cosmos.'

Both Lady Hester and Delagarde stared at her. Maidie eyed them both back, frowning. Had she said something out of the way? She knew she had been too little in company to appreciate the niceties of etiquette. Adela was always complaining of her lack of social graces. There had been some spite in that, but perhaps there was more ground for the complaint than Maidie had thought. Well, it mattered little. She had scant interest in society, and if only she could get this business over and done with, she would not be in need of social graces.

'May we return to the point of this discussion?' she asked, her tone a trifle frigid.

'By all means,' said Lady Hester amiably. 'Do tell me why you hit upon poor Laurie for the task of introducing you.'

'It was not by chance, you know.' Maidie dug once more into her reticule, and brought out the letter, which she gave to Lady Hester. 'This is from Lady Delagarde.'

'Thank you. Do sit down, child.'

Thus adjured, Maidie resumed her former chair as Lord
Delagarde walked across and took a seat on a little sofa
that faced the fire. She eyed him surreptitiously, aware that
he was watching her. Not, she dared say, with any degree
of approval. Not that she wanted his approval. If there had
been any other option open to her, she would have felt
much inclined to abandon her scheme, for she was sure he
was going to prove difficult. He was evidently a man used
to having his own way, and all too likely to give her a
great deal of trouble.

The thought faded from her mind as Lady Hester came
to the end of the letter she was reading, and spoke.

'It is Dorinda's hand, I can vouch for that.'

'I never doubted it,' said Delagarde. 'I hope I can recognise my own mother's handwriting. What of it? You
have not heard the half of this ridiculous story. Here is
this female—'

'Lady Mary, you mean,' interpolated his aunt.

'If she is Lady Mary—'

'Oh, I think there can be no doubt of that.'

'Thank you,' put in Maidie gratefully. 'I cannot think
why he would not believe me.'

Delagarde almost snorted. 'Because your conduct hardly
tallies with the title.'

'Laurie, do be quiet!' begged Lady Hester. 'Let the child
tell her tale in her own way.'

'Her tale is imbecilic. She does not wish to marry some
fellow or other, and has thus fled her natural protector to
come here and demand that I bring her out, on the pretext
of that letter. A more stupid—'

'Hush! Let her speak.'

Maidie threw her a grateful look, and launched once
more into an explanation of her difficulties and the inge-
nious solution she had worked out. Unlike her great-
nephew, Lady Hester listened without comment, and even

managed to keep Delagarde from bursting out until Maidie had finished. Only then did she speak.

'I think I understand. There are one or two matters I should like to clarify, however. The exact relationship between us is readily discovered.'

'Readily discovered?' echoed the Viscount, incensed that his great-aunt should give the time of day to the chit's nonsensical scheme. 'If you hunted it down through half the family tree, I dare say. Besides, I am sure there must be a dozen other males closer related to her than I am myself.'

'But none of them, my dear Laurie, is a viscount.'

Maidie found herself the sudden recipient of a suspicious look from his lordship, and a questioning one from Lady Hester. What were they at now?

'Why should that weigh with me?' she asked forthrightly. 'I am an Earl's daughter.'

'And may look as high as you please for a husband? I wonder just how high you are looking to go.'

Regarding Lady Hester frowningly, Maidie shrugged. 'His rank is immaterial. It is not that which will determine my choice. I only meant that my title is bound to make it easier for me to find someone willing to marry me.'

'Undoubtedly,' agreed Lady Hester affably. 'Tell me, Lady Mary, why do you wish to be settled in life?'

A sigh escaped Maidie, as the picture of her self-imposed future formed itself in her mind. 'To tell you the truth, I had as lief not be—married, I mean. But when Eustace began plaguing me with his attentions, and then Adela must needs try to hint me into accepting him, I began to see what awaited me if I chose to remain single.'

An odd look crossed Lady Hester's face. 'Well, I do not ask why you wished to remain single, for that I can readily understand. I am single myself. But what was it that you feared?'

Maidie shifted her shoulders in a gesture of discomfort. 'To be the object of incessant suits for my hand. Once word of the legacy got out, I could see there would be no peace for me. So I thought the best solution would be to find myself a complaisant husband, who would not object to my continuing interest in other matters, and so end the nonsense at once.'

Lady Hester was regarding her keenly. 'What legacy?'

'Oh, I discovered when I came of age that my mother's fortune had been settled upon me.'

'Indeed?'

'Yes, which is why Adela suddenly changed her behaviour towards me.'

'I imagine she might,' came the dry comment.

'Of course I was glad to have such an independence,' pursued Maidie, 'for it made it possible for me to make my own choice of occupation, rather than become a companion.'

'A companion! Good gracious, why should you wish to?'

'I didn't wish to. Only I previously thought that it would have been my one path to escape from working as an unpaid drudge to Adela. But I was forced to recognise that the very independence that offered me freedom also made me a target for gentlemen seeking to marry well.'

Lady Hester was now looking very thoughtful indeed. Was she beginning to understand the motives that drove Maidie? Delagarde, on the other hand, was still frowning heavily, she noted. He caught her eye, and got up.

'Interesting though this history may be, Lady Mary, it makes no difference to—'

'Laurie!'

'What is it, Aunt Hes?'

'Pray sit down again. It happens that I find this history extremely interesting.' She turned to Maidie as Delagarde reluctantly reseated himself. 'Let us re-examine this question of our relationship.'

'But you have already admitted that the Burloynes are related to the Otterburns,' Maidie protested.

'Yes, but I am a little uncertain of your mother's parentage. I did hear that one of the Burloyne cousins married Shurland, now I think of it, but I don't recall which one. If memory serves me, there were three Burloyne brothers of my generation. Their father married into the Otterburn family, through one of the daughters of my own great-aunt.'

Delagarde blinked. 'You are very well informed, Aunt Hes.'

'One likes to keep abreast of these things.' She sounded casual, but Maidie, when the elder lady turned back to her, was surprised to encounter an extremely penetrating glance. 'Which of those three brothers was your grandfather Burloyne, child?'

'The second one, Brice.'

'Indeed?' A long sigh escaped Lady Hester, and she sank back into her chair. 'Well, well. Brice Burloyne's granddaughter. And no male relatives.'

'No, for all the Burloynes are dead now, and I have no uncles or male cousins.'

'Except Shurland,' put in Delagarde stubbornly.

'But I have told you—' Maidie began.

'Enough!' broke in Lady Hester. 'Do not fall into a pointless dispute. Now, my dear Mary—if I may call you so?'

'Oh, please don't,' begged Maidie instantly. 'No one ever calls me Mary—except Adela, and that was only to annoy. My great-uncle Reginald, when he found himself saddled with the care of me, dubbed me Maidie, and so I have remained.'

'Very well then, Maidie, if you wish it. Tell me about this Adela. She sounds a most unpleasant sort of woman.'

Maidie wrinkled her brow. 'I would not describe her as unpleasant,' she said, trying to be fair. 'Her manner is no more objectionable than Lord Delagarde's, for example.'

Delagarde's infuriated glance raked her. 'I am obliged to you, ma'am.'

Lady Hester laughed. 'She is nothing if not direct, Laurie. I don't suppose she means to insult you.'

'Why should he care? Besides, he has said worse of me.'

'And you don't give a fig, I dare say?' smiled Hester.

Maidie lifted her chin. 'I am not come here to gain his good opinion.'

'No, you are come here to gain my services,' said Delagarde. 'Not that I have the slightest expectation of your adopting a conciliatory manner! What I wish to know is, what was Shurland doing while this Adela was constraining you to marry her brother?'

'Yes, why did you not appeal to him?' asked Lady Hester.

'I did,' Maidie told them flatly. 'His answer was that, between us, my great-uncle and myself had wasted his inheritance, and I would get no assistance from him.'

'Wasted his inheritance?' echoed Delagarde. 'On what, pray?'

'It does not signify,' Maidie said hurriedly. 'The truth is that it would suit him very well for my money to come into his family, even at one remove. Were I to marry another, he could not hope to get any share of it.'

'He is scarce likely to gain directly from his brother-in-law's marriage,' objected Lady Hester.

'No, but I am sure that he and Eustace have reached some sort of agreement on the matter, for there would otherwise be no reason for him to lend his support to Adela's scheme.'

'But what drove you to take this drastic action, child? Not that I blame you, but Adela could hardly force you into matrimony with her brother. And she did, I think you said, offer to bring you out.'

'Yes, she did.' Contempt entered Maidie's voice. 'It was only for appearances' sake. She was afraid of what people might say of her, if it was seen that I married her brother without choosing him from among a number of others. And Eustace himself did not wish to figure as a fortune-hunter.'

'Then why in the world did you not allow her to bring you out, and then choose another?' demanded Lady Hester.

Maidie stared at her in frowning silence for a moment. Such a course had never even occurred to her. If it had, she would certainly have rejected it out of hand. She lifted a proud chin.

'I may not be well versed in the etiquette obtaining in fashionable circles, but I assure you, ma'am, I am not without a sense of honour.'

She thought Lady Hester looked amused, but her tone was apologetic. 'I had no intention of putting up your back, child. Are you suggesting that to have accepted a Season from Lady Shurland would have put you under an obligation?'

'Yet you are trying to put me under a false obligation,' cut in Delagarde swiftly.

'It is not false!' Maidie retorted indignantly. 'If I had not your mother's letter, I would not have involved you at all. In any event, this has nothing to do with being put under an obligation to Adela.'

'Then what?' asked Delagarde, finding himself intrigued by the workings of the wench's mind.

'I am not a cheat!' Maidie exclaimed. 'I would not pretend to one thing and mean another. Such conduct may suit Adela. It would not suit me. If I was prepared to marry

Eustace, what need was there for a Season? But I am not willing to marry him. It would scarcely be honourable in me to dupe Adela into thinking I might do so, and allow her to bring me out only in order that I could find someone else. No, no. I must arrange it for myself, or I had better not wed at all.'

'But you are not arranging it for yourself,' Delagarde pointed out. 'You are expecting me to arrange it.'

'And so you shall,' broke in Lady Hester Otterburn cheerfully.

'*What?*'

'My dear Laurie, you will hardly be outdone in the matter of honour, I should hope! It is not the part of a chivalrous man to leave poor Maidie to her fate. Besides, I know it must be an object with you to accede to your mother's wishes. I cannot think you will do otherwise than make it your business to set Lady Mary's feet upon the social ladder.'

Chapter Two

Temporarily silenced by the shock of his great-aunt's perfidy, Delagarde watched in a daze as Lady Hester Otterburn ushered the visitor out. With disbelieving ears, he heard her encouraging the wretched female to return, bringing with her the duenna and all their trunks from the Maddox Street inn where she had left them. No sooner had the front door shut behind Maidie, than his lordship came to himself with a start.

'Have you taken leave of your senses, Aunt Hes?' he demanded furiously, as that lady walked back into the parlour.

'I don't think so,' replied his great-aunt mildly.

'Well, I do! What the devil possessed you to invite her back here? If you imagine that I am to be coerced into acceding to the wench's idiotic request, you may think again.'

'Then you will be a great fool!' she told him roundly.

He stared at her. 'I beg your pardon?'

'My dear Laurie, if you cannot see what is right under your nose, I declare I wash my hands of you!'

'I wish you would,' he retorted, incensed. 'Do, pray, stop talking in riddles, Aunt.'

To his surprise, she eyed him with a good deal of speculation for a moment. Then she smiled. 'Gracious, I believe you really don't know!'

'Don't know what?'

Lady Hester laughed at him. 'How to bring a girl out, of course. No matter. You will learn fast, I dare say.'

'But I have no desire to learn it,' Delagarde stated, in some dudgeon. 'What is more, I am not going to do so.'

'Oh, yes, you are. I have quite decided that.'

'You have decided it? Thank you very much indeed. Give me one good reason why I should allow myself to have this hideous charge foisted on to me.'

'I might give you several,' said his great-aunt coolly, 'but one will suffice. You are far too hedonistic and idle.'

Delagarde fairly gasped. 'I am what?'

'I have long thought that the life you lead is ruinous. You have no responsibility, and nothing to do beyond consulting your own pleasure. It will do you good to exert yourself and think of someone else for a change.'

'Oh, will it?' retorted her great-nephew, stung. 'Then allow me to point out to you that if—if!—I agree to this preposterous idea—'

'Don't be silly, Laurie! Everything is settled.'

'—it is not I who will be exerting myself. It may have escaped your notice, Aunt, but it is usual for debutantes to have a female to bring them out.'

'Quite right,' said Lady Hester comfortably. 'I shall do that.'

'Not in this house!' objected Delagarde. 'Besides, you cannot do so. For one thing, you have no longer any position in society—'

'That can readily be remedied.'

'—and for another, your health is unequal to the strain of a London Season.'

'Nonsense, I have never been better!'

'What is more,' pursued Delagarde, ignoring these interpolations, 'I have not invited you to remain here above the few days you intended.'

Lady Hester suddenly clapped her hands together. 'That reminds me! I have not brought near enough with me for a whole Season. My abigail will have to go down to Berkshire at once. Oh, and you will have to open up all the saloons. We cannot receive morning callers in the drawing-room, and if we are to give a ball—'

'A ball! Let me tell you—'

'Or, no. It is too late to secure a suitable date. A small party, perhaps, and meanwhile we will introduce Maidie quite quietly—'

'You cannot introduce her in any way at all!' Delagarde interposed, in considerable disorder. 'Good God, I will not be sponsor to a lady looking as Maidie does! I should lose all credit with the world.'

'You are very right,' agreed Lady Hester, laying an approving hand on his arm. 'Her appearance will not do at all. I had not thought of it in all this excitement. She must be properly dressed. I shall see to that at once. Maidie cannot object to acquiring new gowns. You need have no fear, Laurie. I will make sure she does not disgrace you.'

'If her conduct today is any indication of her company manners,' Delagarde said bitterly, 'there is little hope of preventing that.'

But Lady Hester was not attending. 'We will not make too obvious a stir, I think, for that may defeat the purpose. A soirée at the start of next month will serve admirably. At first, though—'

'Aunt Hester!'

'—we shall make it our business to call upon all the leading hostesses. As Maidie's sponsor, you will of course accompany us.'

'If you think I am going to dance attendance on that cursed wench morning after morning—'

'Laurie, what am I thinking of?' interrupted his great-aunt, unheeding. 'The servants! We shall never manage with this skeleton staff. You must send to Berkshire immediately. Or, stay. Lowick may go down himself and make all the necessary arrangements.'

'Aunt Hes—'

'Gracious, there is so much to be done! I must see Lowick immediately. He and I will put our heads together, and—'

'Aunt Hes, will you, for God's sake, attend to me?'

She stopped in mid-stride, and looked at him with an air of surprise. 'Yes, Laurie?'

'Aunt Hes, stop!' he uttered desperately. 'I will not—I have no intention— Oh, good God, I think I am going mad! Aunt Hes, if you bring that wretched girl to live here, I promise you I shall remove!'

'Nonsense. Move out of your own house? Besides, we need you.'

'We!' he said witheringly. 'Why are you doing this to me?'

'Why?' A trill of laughter escaped Lady Hester, as she made for the door. 'My dear Laurie, I have your interests wholly at heart, believe me. Do not be taken in by Lady Mary talking lightly of an "independence". Brice Burloyne was a nabob.'

'What has that to do—'

But Lady Hester was gone.

Delagarde stood staring at the open door, mid-sentence and open-mouthed, hardly taking in the significance of her last utterance.

'I do not believe this is happening,' he muttered.

Was his life to be turned upside down in a matter of hours? He cursed the ill-timing that had brought his great-aunt on a visit just at this moment. She was invariably content to remain in residence on his estates at Delagarde Manor, where she had lived, courtesy of his mother's generosity, since before Laurence had been born. Her criticism rankled. Idle and hedonistic, indeed! Was he any more so than any other of his class? And what the devil had she meant by saying that he had no responsibilities? Was he not landlord to a vast estate? To be sure, he employed an agent to administer the lands, and his steward could be relied upon to keep all smooth in his absence.

Was that the burden of her complaint? That he was absent from Berkshire for a good part of the time? Good God, one could not be expected to kick one's heels in the country all year round! Who did not spend the Season in town?

Another thought struck him, and his eye kindled. If this was a dig at his continued bachelorhood—! To be sure, he had to marry some day. The line must be carried on. But there were Delagarde cousins enough for the succession to be in no immediate danger, even were he not in the best of health. Nor was he reckless in his sporting pursuits, which might put him in danger of accident. In fact, he took sufficient account of his responsibilities not to merit that criticism in the very least!

What the devil should possess her to say such an unhandsome thing of him? Aunt Hes was not wont to criticise, and he strongly suspected that she had made that up on the spur of the moment. A ploy to push him into agreeing to sponsor that dreadful girl. Well, he had not agreed! What whim should take Aunt Hes to rush to the wretched female's aid, he was at a loss to understand.

What had she said? Brice Burloyne was a nabob? One of these Indian fortunes? Oh, good God! And he was to figure as trustee, heaven help him! No doubt the creature would expect him to ward off fortune-hunters on her behalf. A vision of his hitherto ordered and pleasant existence rose up, and he could swear he saw it shatter. No! No, he would not be coerced.

Striding to the bell-pull, he tugged it fiercely, and then marched out into the hall just as a footman came quickly in through the green baize door at the back. Already he discerned an air of bustle about the house, for Lady Hester's abigail was hurrying up the stairs, accompanied by one of the maids, and the stout housekeeper, pausing only to bob a curtsy to her master as he came out of the parlour, set her foot on the bottom stair and began to puff her way up.

'Where is Lowick?' Delagarde demanded of the footman.

'Mr Lowick has gone upstairs to confer with her ladyship, my lord.'

'Oh, he has, has he? Well, go up and bring him down here to me. And send for Liss at once!'

'I am here, my lord,' said his valet, entering the hall from the green baize door, as the footman ran up the stairs. Liss had apparently held himself ready, for he was burdened with several articles of clothing.

'My coat, Liss! My hat!'

'Both here, my lord.'

Delagarde allowed his valet to help him into the greatcoat, and seized his hat. He was standing before the hall mirror, placing the beaver at a rakish angle on his head, when his butler came hurrying down the stairs.

'Ah, Lowick,' Delagarde said, turning. 'Listen to me! If that female should return here, you will—'

'Lady Mary, my lord?' interrupted the butler. 'You need have no fear, my lord. Her ladyship has given me very precise instructions. All will be in readiness to receive her.'

'But I don't want you to receive her!'

The butler bowed, and permitted himself a tiny avuncular smile. 'Her ladyship has explained that you are a trifle put out by the inconvenience, my lord.'

'Put out!'

'It is very natural, I am sure, my lord. I understand that there is an obligation which your lordship is determined to honour.'

Delagarde gazed at him. Devil take it! Aunt Hes had neatly outgeneralled him. Working on the principle, he dared say, that it was never of the least use to try to keep things from the servants. No doubt she would have the entire household duped in no time at all, everyone working to thwart him. How the devil was he to refute the obligation now, without appearing churlish or dishonourable?

'So she has drawn you in, has she?' he muttered balefully.

The butler gave him a puzzled look. 'I beg your pardon, my lord?'

'Never mind.' He received his cane from the valet with a brief word of thanks, and turned back to his butler. 'Lowick, I am going out.'

'Yes, my lord. You need not fear that every courtesy will not be extended to the young lady, my lord. The housekeeper is even now receiving her instructions to arrange for Lady Mary's accommodation.'

'I do not wish to hear anything about it! Let me out!'

'But will your lordship not take breakfast first?' asked the butler, opening the front door for him.

'The only breakfast I require is of the liquid variety—and potent!' He started out, and then paused, turning on the top step. 'And if Lady Hester should enquire for me, inform her that I have left this madhouse, never to return!'

Maidie, meanwhile, ensconced in the Hope family coach with her abigail in attendance, was congratulating herself on the outcome of her mission. To be sure, there had been a dreadful moment when she had doubted her ability to bring it off, but the entrance of Lady Hester Otterburn had changed all that. She was heartily glad of it, for she was now certain that, left to himself, Lord Delagarde would have repudiated her. It was fortunate that Lady Hester had been visiting just at this moment, for failure did not bear thinking of! What in the world would she have done?

Not having made any contingency plan—for how could she have guessed that Delagarde would dislike it?—she might have found herself at a loss. She supposed she would either have had to retreat to the Sussex house which was no longer her home, or to have continued on to the Shurland town house and revealed herself to Adela and Firmin, neither of whom had the least idea that she was in London. No, she would not have done that. Nothing would have induced her to gratify Adela with a show of willingness.

But she was not, she remembered with a resurgence of emotion, obliged to do either of those things, thanks to Lady Hester Otterburn deciding, for whatever reason, that she wished Delagarde to meet his obligation—and it was an obligation! Maidie had seen quite enough of Lady Hester to guess that she possessed sufficient influence over her great-nephew to ensure that she had her way.

Arrived at the Coach and Horses where she had passed the previous night, Maidie lost no time in relaying the story of her success to her duenna.

It had not been with Miss Ida Wormley's unqualified approval that she had set forth that morning. Indeed, having kept up an incessant discourse against the scheme throughout the two-day coach journey from the Shurland estates at East Dean—to which Maidie had paid not the slightest heed—the Worm, greatly daring, had made a final attempt to prevent her from going at all.

'I do wish you would not, Maidie,' she had begged, almost tearfully. 'It would be the most shocking imposition, and I do not know what his lordship will think of you.'

'It does not matter what he thinks of me, Worm,' Maidie had declared impatiently. 'Do stop fussing! Unless you would have me wed Eustace Silsoe, after all?'

'No, no, I am persuaded he could not make you happy,' had said Miss Wormley, distressed. 'And after the manner in which Lady Shurland has behaved towards you, I cannot blame you for wishing to seek another way.'

'Well, then?'

'But not this way, Maidie! To beard Lord Delagarde in his own home! He must think you dead to all sense of decorum. And what he will think of me for allowing you to behave in this unprincipled way, I dare not for my life imagine!'

'Have no fear, Worm,' Maidie had soothed. 'I will make it abundantly clear to his lordship that the scheme is mine, and mine alone. Do not be teasing yourself with thoughts of what he may think of you, but set your mind rather to the programme of how we are to go on once we are installed in his house. You will be obliged to take me about, you know, for we cannot expect Lord Delagarde to chaperon me. It would be most improper.'

But Miss Wormley had been in such a fever of anxiety that she had been unable to set her mind to the resolution of anything. Besides, as she had several times informed her charge, she had no idea how to set about such a programme since she had never moved in fashionable circles. Maidie knew it, and did not hesitate to set her mind at rest as she related her doings at the Delagarde mansion in Charles Street.

'I must thank heaven for Lady Hester,' sighed Miss Wormley, setting a hand to her palpitating bosom, and sinking down upon the bed.

For want of something to distract her mind, she had been

engaged, when Maidie returned with her abigail in tow, in collecting together those of Maidie's belongings that were scattered about the bedchamber they had shared at her insistence, for she could not reconcile it with her duty to allow her charge to sleep alone in the chamber of a public inn in the heart of the capital.

'But was not his lordship very much shocked?' she asked presently.

'Oh, yes,' said Maidie carelessly, removing her hat and smoothing the unruly bands that had held her hair tightly concealed under it. 'But I took no account of that.'

'No, I should have known you would not,' agreed her duenna mournfully. 'The large portmanteau, Trixie.' Rising again, she directed the abigail how to pack her mistress's clothing. Her own accoutrements were already neatly stowed in the smaller receptacle. Then she turned again to Maidie, adding, 'You never take account of me, after all.'

She spoke without rancour. A colourless female of uncertain age, Miss Ida Wormley had become inured, after near eleven years, to the knowledge that her influence over Lady Mary Hope was but sketchy. She suffered a little in her conscience, which led her to overcome a natural timidity and speak out, whenever she felt her principles to be at odds with Maidie's conduct. But, despite the fondness with which she knew her charge regarded her, she could not flatter herself that her advice and protestations were attended to.

'But I thought perhaps you might attend to Lord Delagarde.'

'Humdudgeon!' snorted Maidie indelicately. 'You know very well, dear Worm, that Great-uncle counselled me never to allow myself to be impressed by rank.'

'Yes,' agreed Miss Wormley, repressing a desire to dis-

abuse her charge of her unshakable faith in the wisdom of
the deceased fifth Earl's counsel.

'In any event,' Maidie pursued doggedly, 'Delagarde is
only a viscount.'

'Only!' sighed Miss Wormley.

'But he's ever so fashionable, m'lady,' put in Trixie
suddenly. 'Ain't that right, Miss Wormley?'

'Oh, yes. Lord Delagarde is always finding a mention
in the Court sections of the London journals, and I recognised his name often in your great-uncle's copies of the
Gentlemen's Magazine.'

'Yes, and in them scandal pages often and often! Breaking hearts left and right. Abed here, abed there—'

'Trixie!'

'Is that true?' asked Maidie, interested. 'Has he had
many such associations?'

'You must not ask me, Maidie!' uttered the Worm,
blushing. 'Trixie should not have spoken. It is all nasty
gossip.'

'But is it true?' persisted Maidie, unheeding. 'I can readily believe it, for he is certainly personable.'

'*Is* he, m'lady?' asked the maid, awed. 'What is he
like?'

'He is tall and dark, and very cross!'

'Now, Maidie—you should not! I am sure Lord Delagarde must be all that is amiable—even if it is true that
his name has been linked with a number of fashionable…oh, dear, I did not mean to say that!'

'It does not signify. You are bound to think well of him,
Worm,' said Maidie, 'for you are more closely related to
him than I. For my part, I find him excessively temperamental. I only hope he may not take it into his head to
interfere in my concerns. My dependence must be all upon
Lady Hester.'

* * *

It seemed, when the party arrived back at the Charles
Street house, that her dependence was not misplaced. She
was touched by the enthusiasm of Lady Hester's greeting,
and noted, with a rush of gratitude, that her champion en-
compassed Worm in the warmest of welcomes.

'You and I, my dear Miss Wormley, must sit and enjoy
a comfortable cose in the not-too-distant future. We call
ourselves cousins, that much I know, but I am hopeful of
pinpointing the exact relationship if we exchange but a few
of our respective forebears.'

'Oh, Lady Hester, you are too good,' uttered Miss
Wormley, quite overcome. 'And your kindness to dear
Maidie—'

'Nonsense,' said Lady Hester, brushing this aside.
'Come now, let me guide you to your chambers.'

There was a bevy of servants busy about the transfer of
the many trunks and boxes from Maidie's carriage into the
house, but they stood aside for her ladyship and her guests
to pass. Pausing only to give some final instruction to her
coachman, who was waiting in the hall, Maidie followed
her hostess, throwing a word of thanks to the various at-
tendants who were bearing her belongings upstairs.

Rooms were in the process of being prepared, and Maidie, having traversed two flights of the grand staircase and
a couple of narrow corridors to arrive there, was delighted
to discover that her allotted chamber had a southern aspect.

'Oh, is that a little balcony?' she exclaimed, moving to
a pair of French windows.

'The veriest foothold only,' said Lady Hester. 'It opens
on to the gardens, however, so you may use it to take a
breath of fresh air now and then.'

Maidie was not attending. She was tugging at the bolts,
and had pulled them back and dragged open the windows
before Lady Hester could do more than protest that she
would let in the cold. Miss Wormley, who might have

concurred, was distracted by the arrival of the luggage, and at once made it her business to inform the servants which pieces should remain in this room.

'This will do excellently,' Maidie said with approval, for the balcony extended out for quite two feet, and must be double that in width. Yes, she could set up here easily, and have an excellent view. Stepping on to the balcony, she looked up at the sky and ran her eyes around the horizon. On the second floor of Delagarde's house, there was some little disturbance to the eyeline from the tops of the surrounding buildings. The attics would have been better, but it was a temporary inconvenience. At least she might continue her work. She had been afraid that it would have been interrupted altogether.

Turning back into the room, she directed Trixie to close the windows again, and looked around for a suitable table. Ah, yes. That little whatnot over on the other side of the four-poster bed. It looked to be free of odds and ends. She might lay her charts on top, and keep it at her elbow.

'The room is to your liking, then?' asked Lady Hester.

Maidie turned to her. 'It will serve very well, thank you.' She thought she read amusement in the elder lady's eyes, and wondered if she had not been quite polite. 'I mean, it is very nice indeed.'

'Miss Wormley should be accommodated next to you, I thought,' Lady Hester said, leading the way to the adjoining room as soon as Maidie had put off her pelisse and bonnet.

Maidie noted that her ladyship's glance ran swiftly over her plain stuff gown, and settled for a moment on her tightly banded hair. She put up a self-conscious hand to smooth it, and could not but be relieved that Lady Hester made no comment.

The room next door was almost as well appointed as Maidie's own, and Miss Wormley lost herself in a stuttering speech of thanks, which Lady Hester kindly dismissed. Her own room, as she showed them in case Maidie should be in need of her, was in an opposing corridor on the other side of the house, but his lordship, it appeared, occupied one of the two principal bedchambers, the only ones located on the first floor along with several saloons.

'The other will be for his wife, when Laurie finally decides to gratify us all and make his choice.' As she led the way downstairs again, and into the drawing-room that abutted the dining-room, Lady Hester added, 'I dare say that if Dorinda had not died, she would have hustled him into matrimony years ago, though not without a battle of wills. She was as strong-minded as Laurie himself, was Dorinda. I suppose I should have made more of an effort with him in her stead, but you may have noticed that Delagarde is a difficult man to push.'

Yes, she had noticed, Maidie thought. He was a difficult man, she suspected, in every circumstance. But her interest in his possible marriage was, to say the least of it, tepid. Now, in any event. Had he had the good sense to marry earlier, no doubt her campaign would have met with less resistance. She felt it to be typical of him that he had remained a bachelor, as if he had known that it must aid him to thwart her.

They were soon installed in the drawing-room, a pleasant apartment done out in cream and straw to the walls and mantel, and to the cushioning of the light finely turned sofas and chairs that characterised Chippendale's designs.

'And now, my dear Maidie,' pursued Lady Hester, when they were all partaking of a dish of tea, 'we must make some plans. I thought, as a first step, that when you have had an opportunity to relax a little, we might make a visit to one of the discreet dressmaking establishments.'

'Discreet?' repeated Maidie.

Miss Wormley murmured something indistinguishable

but, beyond directing a brief questioning look at her, Lady Hester took no notice.

'I do not suggest a trip to Bond Street just yet, for I know you will not wish to appear where we may give rise to comment—at least, not until you have been officially presented to some of our more prominent hostesses.'

Maidie's brows went up. 'What you mean, Lady Hester, is that I am at present dressed too unfashionably to be seen.'

Lady Hester burst out laughing. 'You are very frank! I was trying to be diplomatic.'

Maidie shrugged. 'I prefer plain speaking. Besides, even had I not been made aware of my shortcomings in dress by Adela, I have sense enough to know that I cannot be so careless if I am to appear in society.'

'Lady Mary has never been one to concern herself over her appearance,' said Miss Wormley, hurrying into speech. 'And—and she has decided views of her own.'

This became apparent, when the three ladies presently arrived at the quiet premises in Bloomsbury which housed the creations of Cerisette, a French modiste who had set up in business but three years since, on her escape from the troubles in Paris. Informed that the young lady was about to make her debut, Cerisette first directed their attention to a series of made-up gowns, all created in the now popular muslins with high waists, and all of them without exception, Maidie noted, in the palest of hues, whether sprigged or plain. She gazed upon the display, which was predominantly white, with a scattering of pastels, and resolutely shook her head.

'No, no. These will not do at all!'

'My dear Maidie,' protested Lady Hester, coming up to her and eyeing the offending garments with a frowning countenance, 'these are very suitable. All young females are accustomed to wear only the most modest of gowns when they are just out. What in the world is wrong with them?'

Maidie drew a breath. 'It is not the styles, ma'am. I will be as modest as you please, only I cannot and will not wear anything made up in pastels.'

She saw the doubt in Lady Hester's face, and knew that the moment had come. She drew a breath, and told herself she was being ridiculous. What did it matter what Lady Hester thought? Or anyone else, come to that? But it would not serve. In everything else, she might shrug off criticism or rebuke, but this was her one point of vulnerability.

'What is it, child? What troubles you?'

For answer, Maidie went to one of the long mirrors with which the salon was furnished, and, with a tremble in her fingers which she could not control, once again removed her mustard-coloured bonnet. She looked at her own face, sighed deeply, and reached up to remove the pins that held the offending tresses in place.

'What in the world…?' began Lady Hester. But she was not attended to.

'Worm, take these, if you p-please,' Maidie uttered nervously, handing the pins to her duenna, who was hovering at her elbow. She took the rest of them out, and dragged her fingers through the mass of curling locks that, loosed from their moorings, sprang up about her face, forming a virulent ginger halo. She stared at her reflection in the acute misery that always attacked her when she obliged herself to look at it, and then turned, in a good deal of trepidation, but unsurprised to encounter the startled look in Lady Hester's countenance. But it was not she who spoke first.

'*Bon dieu!*' came from Cerisette, who was standing stock-still, staring blankly at that extraordinary head of hair.

Tears started to Maidie's eyes, and she felt the arm of her duenna come about her. Lifting her chin, she winked the hint of wetness away, and stared defiantly into Lady Hester's face.

'My poor child!' said that lady gently. 'It is not nearly as bad as you think.'

'It is p-perfectly h-horrid,' Maidie uttered unsteadily. 'I look just like a marmalade cat! And when L-Lord Delagarde sees it, he will undoubtedly show me the d-door.'

Lady Hester's eyes danced, but she refrained from laughing. 'He will do no such thing, I promise you. Besides, we will have you looking altogether respectable before he has an opportunity to see it.'

A faint surge of hope lit Maidie's breast. 'Can—can anything be done about it?'

'Assuredly.'

'There now, you see, my love,' said Miss Wormley comfortingly. But it was she who whisked her handkerchief from her sleeve, and fiercely blew her nose.

'A good cut will make all the difference,' Lady Hester said bracingly. 'How fortunate that you have kept the length! We will have my own old coiffeur to you this very day.'

'You don't feel that I should do better to keep it the way I have been doing,' Maidie suggested, with unusual diffidence. 'Not that I care what anyone thinks of my appearance,' she added hastily, and with scant regard for the truth, for in this aspect she was as sensitive as any young female, 'but we must not forget that my object is to attract.'

'No, we must not forget that,' agreed Lady Hester, with an amused look.

'Should we not keep it hidden?' Maidie asked, too anxious to notice the hint of laughter. 'It is far less noticeable when it is tightly banded to my head.'

'Ah, but I have always found it to be an excellent thing to make a virtue of necessity. You will not, I know, wish to dupe any likely candidates for your hand into thinking that you are other than yourself.'

'Oh. Er—no, of course not,' agreed Maidie, with less than her usual assurance.

'Since we must needs expose it, then,' pursued Lady Hester, with only the faintest tremor in her voice, 'let us by all means make the very best use of it that we can. I know that you will feel very much more confident once you see that it can be made to look quite pretty.'

Maidie was doubtful, but she bowed to Lady Hester's superior knowledge. Besides, she found the whole matter of her hair so distressing that she knew her judgement on the subject to be unsound.

'It is all the fault of my great-uncle Reginald,' she said candidly, reviving a little of her usual spirit. 'I know he could not help bequeathing me his hair, but as he was the only one of his family to catch it from my great-grandfather, it does come through him. I dare say he did not intend it, and it is the only thing he gave me for which I have any regret.'

'His lordship was very fond of dear Maidie,' confirmed the Worm helpfully. 'But he saw nothing amiss with the colour of her hair, did he, my love?'

'Yes, but he was a man. It made no difference to him.'

'It need not be a problem to you, Maidie,' Lady Hester assured her.

But Cerisette did not agree. When the customers turned to her once again, she broke into voluble protestation. Had she known in the beginning that *mademoiselle* was possessed of this so strong a head, assuredly she would not have shown her the pastels. Mademoiselle had shown good sense to refuse them. She could not risk her reputation upon *mademoiselle* appearing in anything but white. Fortunately, for the debutante, white was *comme il faut*.

'Well, it is not *comme il faut* for me,' declared Maidie stubbornly. 'I cannot possibly wear white.'

In that case, returned Cerisette, drawing herself up, she could not possibly assist *mademoiselle*.

'Dear me,' said Lady Hester haughtily. 'Then we shall take our custom elsewhere.' Turning to Maidie, she smiled warmly upon her, murmuring reassuringly, 'Come, child. I will not have you offended by this creature's whim. Do not allow her to upset you. These French modistes are prone to take pets for the least little thing.'

But Maidie had turned mulish. She might be self-conscious about her hair, but she was not going to be driven ignominiously from Cerisette's door. She resisted Lady Hester's attempt to sweep her away.

'One moment, if you please, ma'am.' She turned to the modiste. 'Perhaps you are not aware, madame, that I am the daughter of the late Earl of Shurland. I am also extremely wealthy. Since I require an entirely new wardrobe for the Season, you might reflect on how much my custom could enrich you.'

She was glad to see the shock gather in the woman's face, and turned on her heel to march out before she could reply. Not much to her surprise, the modiste ran after her with a mouthful of apologies.

Maidie cut them short. 'It makes no matter. Find me some gowns of suitable colours, and we shall say no more about it.'

The modiste made haste to comply. Clapping her hands, she scattered her assistants with a stream of instructions as Maidie turned back to Lady Hester, whose face was alight with laughter.

'Maidie, you are abominable! Don't you know that it is the height of bad taste to parade your rank and wealth?'

'So it may be,' said Maidie, unrepentant, 'but that it is effective, you will scarcely deny.'

'Her great-uncle, you must know,' put in Miss Wormley with diffidence, 'was a trifle eccentric. I am afraid he imbued her with some very improper notions.'

'Humdudgeon!' said Maidie. 'Great-uncle may have been as eccentric as you please, but I must be ever grateful for his teachings. He could not abide shams, and nor can I.'

'Well, let us not fall into a dispute over him,' said Lady Hester pacifically. 'Instead, we must bend our minds to the problem of gowning you appropriately.'

In the event, despite the new enthusiasm of Cerisette, it was Maidie and Lady Hester between them who selected the gowns most suited to her colouring. Maidie opted for a muslin of leaf-green, and a silk of dark blue. But her clever mentor bespoke a crêpe gown of pale russet that picked up highlights in her extraordinary hair, and muslins both of peach and apricot that enhanced the brightness above.

But when Lady Hester and the modiste seized upon a pale lemon gown all over silver spangles, Maidie balked again. 'Nothing would induce me to wear such a thing!'

'But you must have something suitable for a ball,' protested Lady Hester.

'That is as may be, but I refuse to parade around in a garment that would be better employed upon the stage. It looks fit for a fairy—and I am certainly not that.'

To everyone's astonishment, including her own, she fell in love instead with a creamy muslin gown covered in huge sprigs of lacy black. Despite the protestations of her elders that the *décolletage* was positively unseemly, she insisted on trying it.

'I am obliged to admit that it looks magnificent,' conceded Lady Hester, watching Maidie twirl before the mirror.

'It does take attention away from your hair,' offered Miss Wormley in a doubtful tone.

'It is hardly the garb of a debutante, but I dare say Maidie will not care for that.'

She was right, Maidie did not care. If something could indeed be done about her hair, she began to think that she might not fare so very ill, after all.

'I never thought I could look so well,' she marvelled. Drawing a breath, she turned confidingly to Lady Hester. 'I do begin to have a real hope of finding a man willing to marry me.'

'My dear Maidie,' came the dry response, 'there was never the least doubt of that. With your fortune, there will be no shortage of suitors, even had we made no change at all in the matter of your dress.'

Maidie fixed her with that wide-eyed gaze. 'Then why are we doing all this?'

Lady Hester burst into laughter. 'How can you ask me? For the purpose of bringing Laurie to heel. We cannot do without him, and he can have no objection to be seen with you looking like this.'

'Which is as much as to say,' guessed Maidie, with a glint in her eye that boded no good to the absent Viscount, 'that he would not be seen dead with me otherwise!'

It was not until the early evening that Delagarde put in an appearance. He strode into the drawing-room where the ladies had gathered before dinner, and stopped short, staring. Maidie, unable to help herself, had jumped up on his entrance, and now stood rooted to the spot, her heart unaccountably in her mouth.

She was arrayed in the dark blue silk. It had long, tight sleeves, and its folds fell simply from the high waist, but

Maidie became acutely aware that its cut across the bosom was slightly lower than it should be. Though this was as nothing to the anxiety that gripped her as she recalled her exposed locks. Until this moment, she had believed that the cleverly wielded scissors in the hands of a master had worked wonders.

The thatch of ginger had been considerably thinned, a deal of it combed forward to fall in curling tendrils about her face. The rest, behind a bandeau of blue velvet from which two dark feathers poked into the air, fell lightly upon her shoulders, with some few ordered ringlets straying down her back.

In vain did Maidie remind herself that she cared nothing for his lordship's opinion. In vain did she recall the budding resentment she had experienced upon Lady Hester's ill-considered revelation. The stunned expression in his face robbed her of all power over her emotions, until she realised that he was staring, not at her deplorable hair, but at her costume.

Delagarde found his tongue. 'What the devil is that?'

'Laurie!'

'Have you all gone stark, staring crazy?' He turned a fulminating eye on his great-aunt. 'What do you call this? She is supposed to be making her debut. Only look at that neckline! And feathers!' he uttered in a voice of loathing, his eye rising to Maidie's head. 'She looks like a matron with a bevyful of brats in her train, instead of…'

His voice died as he caught sight of her hair. For a moment he gazed in blankest amazement, the fury wiped ludicrously from his face.

'Good God!' he uttered faintly at length.

Quite unable to prevent herself from reaching up to cover what she might of her horrible locks, Maidie burst out, 'He hates it! I knew he would.'

'It is certainly startling,' he conceded. He might have been looking at a stranger!

'Well, you cannot hate it more than I do myself,' Maidie stated, resolutely bringing her hands down and gripping her fingers together. 'You may be thankful you were spared seeing it before it was styled.'

A short laugh escaped him. 'Yes, I think I am.'

Maidie shifted away, and he moved around her, his eyes riveted to the extraordinary hair. Who would have believed it? Such a little dowd as she appeared this morning—and now! He tried to recall the impression he had formed of an unremarkable countenance, but the colour of that head was so very remarkable that he could not recover it. She turned to face him again, and he could not repress a grin at the sulk exhibited in her features.

Maidie flushed. 'It's well for you to laugh. I dare say you think it excessively funny. But I must live with it.'

'So, it would appear, must I,' he returned smoothly.

'Well, it is no use supposing that I can get rid of it,' Maidie said, goaded. 'I have tried before now, and it does not help in the least.'

'You tried to get rid of it?' repeated Delagarde, amazed.

'She did,' averred Miss Wormley. 'She cut it all off.'

It was a new voice to the Viscount, and he turned quickly in her direction. One glance at the faded countenance and the discreet grey gown told him exactly who she must be. Moving to her chair, he held out his hand.

'You are Lady Mary's duenna, I think?'

'Miss Wormley, Delagarde,' confirmed Lady Hester. 'Our cousin, you know.'

'Ah, yes. How do you do?'

Miss Wormley had risen quickly to her feet, and now grasped his hand, murmuring a series of half-finished sentences, from which Delagarde was unable to untangle the references to his supposed kindness from her hopes that he had taken no offence. He cut her short with a word of dismissal.

'But you don't mean,' he went on, 'that Lady Mary really did cut off her hair?'

Miss Wormley nodded vigorously. 'Indeed, she did. She must have been thirteen at the time.'

'Worm, don't!'

'But I wish to hear it,' said Delagarde, a hint of amusement in his tone, and a smile for the duenna.

Miss Wormley succumbed. 'She appeared at the dinner table one evening, quite shorn to pieces. She might almost have taken a razor to her head, except that it was cut too raggedly for that. I was very much shocked, but Lord Shurland could only laugh.'

'Yes!' said Maidie bitterly. 'I have never forgiven Great-uncle Reginald for that. Ever since I have kept it strictly confined—until today. And I wish very much that I had not allowed Lady Hester to persuade me to do otherwise.'

Delagarde rounded on her. 'My good girl, don't be stupid! For God's sake, take off that ridiculous bandeau, and let me see it properly!'

'She will do no such thing.' To Maidie's relief, Lady Hester rose and came to stand beside her protégée. 'Leave the child alone, Laurie. You can see she is distressed.'

These words caused Delagarde's glance to move to Maidie's face. She looked not distressed, but decidedly mutinous. As well she might! What the devil was Aunt Hes playing at, to dress the girl in this fashion? His eyes raked her from head to toe and back again. It was not so much the style of the gown as the bandeau and feathers—and the colour. There was something—yes, repellent!—in the combination of dark blue and silk. Almost he preferred the dowd. This look of sophistication, of mature womanhood, he found distinctly disturbing.

He became aware of Maidie's wide-eyed gaze upon him, in it both question and—doubt, was it? He frowned. 'I didn't mean to offend you.'

She put up her chin. 'It would take more than your disapproval to offend me. It is immaterial to me what you think of me.'

'Is it, indeed?' said Delagarde, instantly up in the boughs. 'Then allow me to point out that it was not I who sought to place you under my sponsorship. But, since you will have it so, you had better learn to take account of my opinion.'

Maidie's brows drew together. 'Well, I will not. I have not asked you to interfere beyond what I specify.'

'Oh, indeed?' returned Delagarde dangerously. 'And what precisely do you specify? I may remind you that I have not yet agreed to do anything at all.'

'Then why am I here?'

'You are asking me? How the devil should I know?'

'Oh, tut, tut!' interrupted Lady Hester, laughing. 'Do the two of you mean to be forever at loggerheads?' She turned apologetically to the duenna, who was looking distressed. 'Miss Wormley, pray pay no attention. If you had been here this morning and heard them both, you would think nothing of this plain speaking between them.'

'But Maidie must not—it is quite shocking in her…' The Worm faded out as her charge's inquiring grey gaze came around to her face. Daunted, but pursuing, she took up her complaint again. 'It is not becoming, Maidie, when his lordship has been so magnanimous as to—'

'But he has not, Worm,' interrupted Maidie, moving to resume her seat in a chair next to her duenna's. 'It is Lady Hester who asked me to come. Lord Delagarde has not ceased to object—quite violently!—and he has been far from magnanimous.'

'Oh, no doubt it is churlish of me,' uttered Delagarde

in dudgeon, 'to object to my house being invaded, my peace being disturbed, and my life turned upside-down merely to accommodate the whims of a pert female who has not even the courtesy to make the matter a request. She demands—or, no, it was *required*, was it not?—that I should arrange her debut. If anyone can give me a reason why I should be magnanimous after that, I shall be delighted to hear it.'

Silence succeeded this tirade. Delagarde, having discharged his spleen, looked from one to the other in growing bewilderment. The Worm looked crushed. If Aunt Hes was not on the point of laughter, he did not know his own relative. As for Maidie herself—was that a hint of apology in her eyes? Before he could quite make up his mind, Maidie spoke.

'It is—it is quite true,' she said, in a gruff little voice. 'I had not thought of it in quite that way. I suppose I need not blame you for being so horrid.'

Delagarde was conscious of a peculiar sensation—as of a melting within him. Thrown quite out of his stride, he directed the oddest look upon her, and began, 'Maidie, I—'

She cut him short, rising swiftly to her feet. 'No, it is for me to speak now.' With difficulty, she overcame a rise of emotion that she did not recognise. 'I have been selfish. If you feel that you cannot bear to accommodate me, even for a little time, I shall quite understand.'

Before Delagarde could gather his bemused wits at this wholly unlooked-for turn of events, the door opened to admit a footman. Fleetingly, Delagarde wondered at his butler's absence, but his attention was caught by the man's words, which had nothing, as he might have expected, to do with dinner.

'Lord and Lady Shurland,' announced the footman.

Chapter Three

A sharp-featured brunette walked quickly into the room, followed more ponderously by a portly gentleman some years her senior. Both were in morning dress, and clearly in a state of some agitation. Lady Shurland cast one swift glance around, caught sight of Maidie, and flung out an accusing finger.

'So, it *is* true! Mary, how could you?'

Maidie looked briefly at Delagarde's frowning countenance, and drew an unsteady breath as she turned to face the woman. She had anticipated this invasion. It was not to be supposed that Adela and Firmin would acquiesce in her schemes. Only, must they arrive just at this moment? Nothing could have been more unfortunate. A prey to hideous indecision, she stepped forward. But before she could speak, Lady Hester intervened, rising and moving forward with hand held out.

'Good evening, Lady Shurland. We have not met, I think. My name is Lady Hester Otterburn.'

Delagarde watched the woman turn abruptly to his aunt, and shot a look at Maidie. He saw dismay in her face. Did she suppose that he meant to send her packing? It was a heaven-sent opportunity to do so. There could be little

doubt that the Shurlands had come to claim her. He looked
again to where Lady Shurland had perforce halted. So this
was the female whose machinations Maidie sought to
avoid. He had never admired angular women. Besides, she
looked to be ill-tempered, darting killing looks at Maidie
even as she exchanged greetings with Aunt Hes. His attention was drawn by the current and sixth Earl of Shurland, with whom he was slightly acquainted, and who was
evidently labouring under suppressed emotion.

'You will forgive this intrusion, I trust,' he said, addressing himself to Delagarde. 'We had been on an outing
of pleasure for the day, and returned home to be met with
the extraordinary intelligence, culled from my coachman,
that Lady Mary had arrived in town and was even now
staying in your house. You may imagine our consternation.
We lost no time in setting forth to discover for ourselves
if this were indeed the case.'

'And now that you have discovered it,' said Delagarde,
his tone so bland that Maidie's eyes flew to his face, 'what
do you propose to do about it?'

'Why, take her home, of course!' burst from Adela.

'Oh?' said Delagarde. 'But what if she does not choose
to accompany you?'

'She will do as she is told,' Shurland announced curtly,
and turned to his quarry. 'This flight of yours, Maidie, was
quite unnecessary. I do not know with what purpose you
have thrust yourself upon Lord Delagarde, but—'

'I have done it so that he may bring me out,' said Maidie, breaking in without ceremony.

'Mary!' gasped Lady Shurland in a horrified tone. 'Do
you tell me that you have had the effrontery to—to—'

'Yes, I have. But you may be easy, Adela.' For she
meant to add that Delagarde had refused to be imposed
upon. She was given no opportunity to do so.

'Lord Delagarde, I am mortified!' burst from Adela. 'She is dead to all sense of shame!'

'I believe she is,' Delagarde agreed mildly.

'And after I have shown every willingness to bring her to town myself. How could you, Mary, treat me so shabbily? To leave your home while we were absent, without a word said! And then to throw yourself upon the mercy of a stranger, as though we had behaved ill towards you. I do not know how you can look me in the face!'

Maidie was looking her very boldly in the face, an expression of distaste on her own countenance. 'Pray do not put on these airs for the benefit of Lady Hester and Lord Delagarde, Adela. I have already told them what your motive was in offering to bring me out.'

'Oh, I have no doubt that you have done your best to blacken me,' uttered Adela in a tone of deep reproach. 'You will not be satisfied until you have made me an object of censure in the eyes of society.'

'Dear me,' put in Lady Hester calmly. 'In what way, my dear ma'am?'

'Everyone will think that I was too mean and selfish to bring her out. It is quite untrue. I have done everything in my power to do the best for her—in despite of her every attempt to make an enemy of me. Only see how she repays me! Sneaking behind our backs in this unkind way.'

'Adela, leave this to me,' said her lord, and turned again to Maidie. 'I shall refrain from discussing the evils of your conduct in this company, Maidie, but I desire that you will at once stop behaving in a fashion which even you must recognise to be reprehensible in the extreme. If, as I am informed, you have indeed taken up residence in this house—'

'Pray do not speak to me as if I were a schoolgirl, Firmin,' interrupted Maidie. 'You have no authority over me.'

'On the contrary. As Head of the Family, I must consider myself responsible for you.' He swung, without warning, upon Maidie's unfortunate duenna. 'And if any further proof was needed, Miss Wormley, of your total unfittedness to have the care of Lady Mary—'

'I will not have you turn on Worm!' Maidie warned, flying to the shrinking duenna's defence. 'You may say what you wish to me, Firmin, but you may not berate my dearest Worm.'

'Oh, Maidie, pray—' uttered Miss Wormley, clutching at her bosom in an ineffectual way. 'You must not! It is perfectly true that— Oh, dear!'

'Do not be alarmed, Worm. You are not to blame.' Maidie crossed the room as she spoke, and perched by Miss Wormley's chair, putting a protective arm about her. 'Poor Worm implored me not to come, and she was even more shocked at my conduct than Lord Delagarde himself.'

'Oh, Lord Delagarde!' uttered Adela, pouncing on this and throwing out a hand towards the Viscount. 'What can I say? How can I sufficiently apologise?'

'I see no reason for apology,' said Delagarde coldly, eyeing her with a hint of hostility. 'You can scarcely be held accountable for Lady Mary's actions.'

'It is excessively tolerant in you, sir,' gushed Adela. 'But it will not do. I know, none better, how little Mary has been taught of the conventions governing the conduct of young females of her class, and I cannot but feel myself put to the blush by the way she has behaved.'

'It does you credit, my dear Lady Shurland,' put in Hester, bringing Delagarde's frowning gaze to bear on her mischievous features.

He noted the telltale twinkle in her eye, and raised questioning brows. What was she about now? She could not seriously be taking the part of a female whom he was himself rapidly taking in dislike?

'Few ladies would be so unselfish,' pursued Lady Hester

in a kind voice, 'as to offer to sponsor a female so lost to all sense of what is fitting. I would not blame you if you chose to give up the notion of bringing Maidie out.'

So that was it! Delagarde was shaken by an inward laugh. Still, from what he had seen of Adela Shurland, Aunt Hes was wasting her time. It would not work.

'Whatever my feelings might be, I conceive it to be my duty,' said Adela virtuously, and not much to Delagarde's surprise. 'I must hope to prevail upon her to conduct herself with more circumspection.' She added waspishly, 'Of course, it is no surprise to me that Miss Wormley was unable to prevent you from behaving in this inconsiderate way, Mary.'

'She has no control over the girl whatsoever,' said her spouse. 'From what I have been privileged to see, I should not think she ever has had. But perhaps she will care to explain why, if she did not approve of Lady Mary's antics, she did not see fit to inform me of what was in the wind.'

'Oh, I could not!' broke from the tearful duenna involuntarily. 'I mean, it would not be—'

'Of course you could not,' said Maidie reassuringly. 'Really, Firmin, how can you be so stupid? As though Worm would do anything so shabby as to betray me to you.'

'Naturally not,' returned Adela sarcastically. 'It is too much to expect that she might remember who is her employer.' She then turned on her husband. 'I told you to send her packing. I warned you how it would be. But no, you never listen to me. I might as well have spared my breath.'

'Adela, be silent!' snapped her lord, reddening. He turned to his hosts with an air of apology. 'My wife is in great distress. I trust you will make allowances.'

'For my part,' said Lady Hester, turning to cast a conspiratorial wink at Maidie before addressing the Earl, 'I am willing to make every allowance. Indeed, Shurland, I do most strongly advise you to leave the child with me. It is clear that she is in pressing need of guidance, and a woman of my years, who has been about the world, is far less prone to be distressed. I do sincerely sympathise with Lady Shurland, and shall be happy to take this irksome charge off her hands.'

Maidie listened to this speech with mixed feelings. She had known Lady Hester rather less than a day, but it did not need that quick little wink to tell her what her new friend was about. But Lady Hester did not know Adela. Maidie did. She was determined, and there was no hope of her voluntarily giving up the notion. There! She was arguing already. And Firmin was on her side. Not that she cared what either of them thought. There was only one thing that could induce her to leave. She had not thought that she cared for his opinion either, but if Delagarde chose to encourage the Shurlands to take her away—!

She looked across at him and found him watching her. Their eyes met. Maidie, unaccountably breathless all at once, could tell nothing from his expression. Indeed, she forgot even to try to read it, making instead the interesting discovery that his eyes were as dark as his hair. She was vaguely surprised that she had not noticed it before. It occurred to her to wonder why in the world he was still unwed. She could only conclude that those females whose interest had been aroused—not a few, she was per-suaded!—had discovered too quickly how disobliging and cross was his nature.

Then, as though to give her the lie, Delagarde abruptly smiled at her. Maidie blinked, stared at him in foolish disbelief, and was annoyed to feel herself flushing. He must have seen it, for his smile grew, and he lifted an expressive eyebrow in mute question. To Maidie's intense relief, he then turned away, stepping into the continuing discussion.

'Nothing could be further from my mind,' Adela was saying, 'than to allow Maidie to burden you, dear ma'am. Come, Shurland,' she said, turning purposefully to her husband, 'Maidie has trespassed enough. Make her come home with us, and let us have an end to this nonsense.'

'Trespass? Dear me, no,' said Lady Hester gently. 'She is here by my invitation.'

'That may be,' said Shurland heavily, 'but I am certain that Delagarde cannot wish for such a charge.'

'On the contrary,' said Delagarde, energetically entering the lists, 'you must know that my mother commended Lady Mary to my care many years ago, and I have been remiss in not honouring the promise.'

'Commended Lady Mary to your care?' echoed Shurland, gazing at him blankly. 'Why should she have done so?'

'My dear sir, nothing could have been more natural. When a young female relative is orphaned—'

'Relative? What nonsense is this, pray?'

'Surely you are aware that the Burloynes are connected to the Otterburns?' said Delagarde, in a voice of pained surprise which caused Lady Hester to choke off a smothered laugh. 'Indeed, it was my mother who sent Miss Wormley—our cousin, you must know—to look after Lady Mary when she was left without a female protector at so tender an age.'

Adela's eyes were popping, and it was evident that all this was as new to her as it was to her husband.

'How comes it about that I never heard a word of this?' Shurland demanded, casting an irritated glance at Maidie.

'Did you not? It was before your time, of course,' Delagarde said in an excusing tone. 'But perhaps the late Lord Shurland did not have an opportunity to inform you of it.'

'Reginald Hope,' said the present Earl, in a voice that very imperfectly concealed his chagrin, 'saw fit to inform me of nothing at all concerning my inheritance. If he had a thought to spare for anything other than his infernal hobby, I was not privileged to know of it.'

'How *dare* you sneer at Great-uncle Reginald?' demanded Maidie, suddenly firing up.

At the back of her mind, as she came rapidly towards the group, she took in the startled glance of Lady Hester, and the odd expression that leapt into Delagarde's features. But the spurt of anger would not be contained.

'You are not half the man he was, Firmin,' she told her cousin in a voice that shook. 'Great-uncle Reginald was the best of men, and the kindest of guardians, and as much a father to me as Worm was a mother. I will not have either of them abused. As for his preoccupation, it was a great deal more than a hobby, and of far greater worth than anything you might waste your thoughts upon.'

'Of importance to others of equal eccentricity, no doubt,' retorted Lord Shurland.

Delagarde saw Maidie's eyes flash, and was not much surprised to find that the Earl backed down. He was rather amused than otherwise by the discovery that the unshakable Lady Mary had a temper.

Shurland shifted a little, avoiding his cousin's eye, and adopted a blustering tone. 'Very well, very well. Enough said. In any event, this is no time to be arguing over what is past and cannot be mended. Go and pack your things, Maidie, for you are coming home with us.'

Maidie moved away from him, saying in a calmer tone, 'I thank you, no, Firmin. If Lord Delagarde is indeed willing to sponsor me—'

'Certainly,' broke in Delagarde. 'Not only that. I am going to figure as her trustee.'

Shurland's chest swelled alarmingly, and his cheeks reddened. 'You will figure as nothing of the kind, sir! I am perfectly aware of all the circumstances of her fortune. You have no rights in the matter at all.'

'Neither have you,' Delagarde pointed out. 'Lady Mary is of age and may do as she pleases, and I do not believe that either myself or you, Shurland, have the means to prevent her. If she chooses to come and live with my aunt and myself, there is no barrier that I can see.'

'Except,' put in Adela bitterly, 'that it makes us look like fools.'

'That cannot be helped,' said Delagarde.

'Oh! I did not look for such usage from you, my lord! It is plain that Mary has blinded you with some horrid tale against me.' She glared at Maidie, and seemed for the first time to notice her appearance, for she added in a waspish tone, 'How you suppose you might catch a husband in a get-up like that, I am at a loss to understand. You look thirty if you look a day! And if you have not sense enough to conceal that perfectly appalling hair—'

'Appalling?' echoed Delagarde, interrupting her without ceremony. 'My dear ma'am, I cannot agree with you. Lady Mary's hair is her most attractive attribute, and the gown is excessively becoming. Indeed, I was just expressing my admiration when you were announced.'

Maidie gasped at this blatant untruth, and noted that Lady Hester was struggling against a fit of laughter.

'However that may be, my lord,' said Adela sulkily, 'you will at least admit that it is hardly raiment suitable to a debutante.'

'Well, if you dislike it so much, Adela,' Maidie said before Delagarde could answer this, 'you should be happy that it is not you who will have to appear in society with me.'

'This is absurd!' Lord Shurland burst out angrily. 'I am far from accepting this faradiddle about your mother, Delagarde, but I take leave to inform you that there will be but one construction to be put upon the matter, if you take it upon yourself to interfere in this way.'

Maidie felt a sudden shift in the atmosphere, as though a chill entered the room. Glancing at Lady Hester, she was startled to find the elder lady's eyes sparkling with something other than humour. Her attention was drawn to Delagarde, who had stiffened, she thought. His narrowed eyes were turned upon the Earl, and there was a hint of ice in his voice.

'Indeed? Perhaps you would care to elaborate.'

Shurland glared at him, but blustered it through. 'Poker up, if you will, sir! You know very well what I mean. I shall not demean myself by explaining it further.'

'Very prudent,' returned Delagarde sardonically.

The Earl coloured. 'If we are to talk of prudence, let me advise you to inquire into the way things are left before you do what you may come to regret. You do not know her, Delagarde. I do!'

Maidie could make nothing of this. She saw that the Viscount's brows had snapped together, and he was now looking more puzzled than angry. Before she could request an explanation, Lady Hester had moved forward again, her calm tones dispelling the discomfort in the air.

'You quite mistake the matter, my dear Shurland. Delagarde is acting, I assure you, from motives of the purest chivalry.' She laid a hand upon Adela's arm. 'I fear you are very much put out, my dear. Never fear. We shall say that the child has come expressly to stay with me, because Delagarde's mama wished for the connection, and because Reginald Hope was my own dear friend.'

'You may say so,' answered Adela shrilly. 'I will not. No one will think that an adequate reason for Mary to come out under your aegis instead of mine. I shall be made to seem the greatest beast in nature, and I think it is quite heartless of Mary to subject me to such a horrid slander!'

Upon which, Lady Shurland burst into sobs, and rushed out of the room. Her harassed spouse turned on Maidie.

'I hope you are satisfied!' He swung round on Delagarde. 'As for you, sir, concoct what story you wish, but don't expect me to corroborate it!'

'The only thing I require,' responded Delagarde calmly, 'is that you will keep quiet about Lady Mary's fortune. Neither you nor I can wish for the sort of speculation that must arise if society should hear of it.'

'I shall say nothing, but I must point out to you that you, far more than I, are likely to be hurt by its becoming known.'

'Well, if you spread the news about, you will discover your mistake,' Delagarde said trenchantly. 'Because I will set it about that you tried to marry Lady Mary off to your brother-in-law.'

'If you imagine that Eustace wishes to marry her, you are mightily mistaken,' objected Shurland, incensed. 'The truth is that he desires nothing less—as who shall blame him?'

On this parting shot, he stalked out of the room, leaving Maidie a prey to conflicting emotions. On the one hand, she was relieved that Delagarde had perversely chosen to champion her; on the other, she was disturbed by Firmin's veiled hints. What had he meant? Her thoughts dissipated as Lady Hester gave way to laughter.

'What a dreadful liar you are, Laurie! I don't know how I kept my countenance.'

Delagarde grinned. 'You can talk, Aunt Hes!' He saw that Maidie was staring at him in frowning silence, and raised an eyebrow. 'Well? You have got what you wanted, have you not?'

'Yes, but I can't think why, when you know very well that you heartily dislike the notion,' she said frankly.

'True,' he agreed. 'But not as much as I disliked Lady

Shurland. Come to that, I am not overfond of Shurland either.'

'They are both hateful! And Firmin was lying, too. It is quite possible that Eustace does not wish to marry me—for he doesn't like me any more than I like him—but he will overcome his reluctance in order to get his hands on my money.'

'So will a great many others,' Delagarde said. 'Which is why we are going to say nothing about it.'

Maidie frowned. 'Then how am I to get a husband?'

'You will have to rely on your looks and natural charm of manner.'

'Oh,' Maidie said doubtfully. Then Lady Hester began to laugh again, and a slight flush crept into her cheeks. 'You mean to be sarcastic, I suppose, but I do not care.'

'You need not tell me that.'

'Well, but you completely agreed with Adela. You said exactly the same as she did about this gown.'

'Did I?' Delagarde looked her up and down.

Then, so suddenly that she had no time to protest, he stepped up to her and, in one swift movement, ripped the bandeau from her head. Maidie uttered a stifled cry and put her hands up to her hair. She hardly heard the shocked reactions of the other ladies, for Delagarde had seized her wrists, and was pulling down her struggling hands.

'Stand still!' he ordered. 'Do you think I am going to hurt you? Just be quiet a moment!'

Maidie stared up at him, lost in amazement, unable either to speak or move as she felt his fingers moving deftly in her hair, running through her curls, and prinking them. She followed the motion of his eyes as they flicked about together with the action of his fingers. As he finished, the dark eyes came to rest on hers. They smiled.

'There, that is better,' he said, and stepped back. 'You

look much younger, and the gown is now unexceptionable.'

Lady Hester clapped her hands. 'Well done, Laurie!' She came up to Maidie. 'Don't look so bemused. He is quite right. The bandeau and feathers were a mistake.'

Maidie blinked. 'But he hates my hair! I know he said something silly to Adela, but—'

'Whatever I may have said,' interrupted Delagarde, 'it is quite untrue that I hate it. Besides, since you are desirous of catching a husband, it will usefully attract attention. There is bound to be some deluded fool who falls in love with it! And the sooner the better.'

'At last we are of one mind!' retorted Maidie, reviving from her bemused state. She drew a breath, and smiled at Delagarde.

The effect was blinding, and his brows rose. Perhaps it was not such a far-fetched notion that someone would fall in love with her. Provided, that is, they had no opportunity to discover her character first.

'I must thank you, my lord, for having supported me,' Maidie was saying. 'I do not understand why you should have done so, but I won't tease myself about that.' She added in a confiding way, 'I was afraid you meant to encourage Firmin and Adela to take me away.'

'I know you were,' Delagarde said. 'And I have no more idea than you why I did not do so. I have every expectation that I will live to regret it!'

The better relations that had been established between himself and Maidie were not the only thing that prompted Delagarde to offer his escort when she expressed a need to visit the lawyer who dealt with her affairs. He'd had time enough since Wednesday to wonder why he had allowed himself to be dragooned into submission over her ridiculous charade. It was not, he thought, the advent of the Shurlands. He had been more or less reconciled before that. He had spent that first day smouldering over the perfidious way Aunt Hes has spiked his guns, but had arrived home without any real expectation of discovering the whole episode to have been imagined, as he had told himself might well be the case.

His resentment had flared anew at sight of Maidie in that objectionable attire, but it had fled as he took in the enormity of her ginger hair and discovered the chink in her armour. Gone was the self-possessed young woman who had driven him against the ropes in the morning! He had begun to realise that there was a good deal of bravado about Maidie's manner. She was still the most infuriating wench he had ever encountered, and he did not doubt but that she would drive him demented. But he could no more have thrown her out of his house than he could similarly have treated Aunt Hes.

He had done what he might to avert the worst consequences of her descent upon him, but he was a little disturbed by Shurland's remarks. It would be as well, he thought, to discover just how matters were left. Maidie's expressed wish to visit her lawyer was therefore opportune.

They set off in his phaeton on Friday morning, with Maidie (who had yesterday been on a further shopping spree with Lady Hester) arrayed in a new pelisse of warm brown and a matching bonnet adorned with russet satin rosettes. With her curls rioting under a wide brim, Delagarde acknowledged that she made an appealing picture.

'You look very well,' he said, as he handed her up into the carriage. 'Was it your choice?'

'No, it was Lady Hester's,' Maidie told him, giving him her direct gaze with those clear grey eyes. Well! It was moderate praise, but at least he approved. 'I have not yet learned enough to trust myself.'

'You will,' Delagarde said, climbing up into the phaeton, and disposing the heavy folds of his caped greatcoat loosely about him to free his arms before taking up the reins and his whip. He nodded at his groom, who let go of the horses' heads and swung himself up behind as the carriage swept past.

'It is very kind of you to take me to see Bagpurze,' Maidie told him, not to be outdone in civility.

'No, it isn't,' Delagarde said with a grin, glancing down at her. 'I have a very good reason for going with you.'

Maidie frowned. 'What do you mean?'

'Since I have been thrust into a position where I may well have to figure as your trustee, I had better know the true facts of your inheritance.'

'But I have told you!' Maidie protested. 'Do you suppose I have been lying to you?'

'You have scarcely told me anything at all, and you cannot expect me to have made head or tail of the rigmarole you did tell me. But at least I must get a straight story from a lawyer.'

'Do as you please,' Maidie said huffily. 'I have nothing to hide.' She thought for a moment, and then added, 'Besides, it is a good opportunity for us to come to terms.'

Delagarde glanced frowningly down at her. 'Terms?'

'Yes, of course. You need not think I should expect you to do all this for nothing. And I am sure you will find the charge less troublesome when we have agreed how much I should pay you for serving me.'

For a stunned moment, Delagarde could say nothing at all. He held in his horses with automatic skill as he guided them through the turn into Piccadilly. Then he found his tongue, throwing a quick look at the calm figure at his side.

'You wish to *pay* me?'

Maidie frowned up at his profile. 'What is the matter now? You need not be embarrassed to admit that your pockets are to let. I should have thought you would be only too glad of the opportunity to obtain some easy money.'

A choking sound from his groom behind failed to penetrate the blanket of disbelief in which Delagarde was wrapped. Was she off her head? Unable to think of a suitable response, he took up the first thing that came into his mind.

'It is evident to me that anything I received for serving you, as you call it, would be hardly earned.' He threw her a brief, but menacing glance. 'However, you have been misinformed. My pockets happen to be remarkably well-lined.'

Maidie's brows rose. 'Then I suppose you must have been winning at the tables?'

'Oh, that is what you suppose, is it? And am I to suppose that you don't then disapprove of gaming?'

'Why should I?' said Maidie, surprised. 'How else is a man to support himself in the character of a gentleman, unless he marries money? And there are few enough females of decent fortune, like myself, to assist all such gentlemen.'

'The sooner you assist one, then, the better!' Delagarde snapped. 'And let me tell you that I have not won my own fortune, and I am quite able to support myself in the character of a gentleman.' He added, as she opened her mouth to speak, 'However, I have grave doubts of being able to maintain that reputation if you are to remain for very long in my house!'

'Because of the way I behave?' asked Maidie innocently. 'Well, I may be a trifle unconventional, but I am perfectly respectable, Lord Delagarde, and I assure you I will not bring any disrepute upon your head.'

'It has nothing to do with your respectability,' Delagarde

stated flatly. 'It is I who will lose my character completely when I am dragged to the gallows for murder!'

A stifled squeal from the back of the phaeton reminded him that his groom was present. 'If you cannot control your amusement, Sampton, I trust that at least you may control your tongue,' he said, tossing the remark over his shoulder. 'If one word of this conversation is repeated—!'

'Your lordship may rely on me,' said Sampton hastily, choking off his laughter. 'I shall say nothing.'

'Well, see you don't.' Glancing down at Maidie, he discovered that direct gaze trained upon him, puzzlement writ large on her face. 'What is the matter?'

'I think you are a very odd sort of man, Lord Delagarde.'

'On the contrary, I am a very normal sort of man. The only oddity is in my having been saddled with you.'

'But you are not saddled with me,' objected Maidie. 'I don't wish you to do more than lend me countenance. Once I am introduced, it will suit me very much better if you will go on just as if I was not there.'

'Impossible!'

'But what difference can it possibly make to you? Lady Hester—'

'I will tell you what difference it makes,' Delagarde broke in, guiding his pair neatly through a narrow gap between a dray-cart and an ancient hackney coach. 'Hitherto, I have enjoyed a blameless reputation, with nothing known to my discredit beyond what may be pardoned in any man about town.'

'There is nothing to stop you going on in that way,' put in Maidie.

'Oh, isn't there just!' muttered Delagarde, well aware that in allowing himself to be persuaded into sponsoring Maidie's entry into society, he was laying himself open to

the justifiable censure of his circle should she offend
against its unwritten codes of conduct. From his limited
knowledge of her, he had every expectation of finding his
reputation in shreds within a very short space of time. But
Maidie, it was evident, had no notion of this. If she could
be brought to understand it, she would probably renew her
offer of recompense! The thought drew a laugh from him.

Maidie heard it, and wondered at it. She did not ask for
an explanation, for she was grappling with thoughts of her
own. She was beginning to suspect that her instinct about
Delagarde had been right. Was he going to prove more
trouble than he was worth? Perhaps it was as well that he
had refused to accept any payment. He could not justly
interfere if he received no remuneration. She had offered
it because she did not wish to be beholden to him. But if
he was not in need of funds, she could accept his patronage
as a discharge of the obligation put upon him by his
mother—and nothing more.

They had not a great way to go to reach the City, and
the journey was beguiled for Maidie by the interesting
sights and sounds of a part of London that she had not
been in before. There was a great deal of traffic, through
which Delagarde appeared to have no difficulty in thread-
ing his way. Maidie was much interested in the press of
persons jostling one another on the pavings. Everyone
seemed to be in a hurry, apart from a few loiterers standing
about, and street sellers crying their wares. But presently
they left a little of the noise and bustle behind, and entered
a quieter stretch where Maidie noted a rather higher pre-
ponderance of individuals with an air of slight affluence.

'We are almost there,' Delagarde said. 'This area is almost wholly given over to those of the legal profession.
That is Gray's Inn Gardens.'

Maidie looked where he was pointing with his whip,
and saw a pleasant-looking park with a walk running down

its centre. Then they turned into a smaller street, lined with tall buildings with neither beauty nor proportion to recommend them.

'Portpool Lane,' Delagarde announced, and brought the phaeton to a standstill. The groom jumped down and went to the horses' heads.

'Walk them, Sampton!' said Delagarde, leaping nimbly down and moving to assist Maidie to alight.

Within a very few moments, she found herself entering the somewhat constricted offices of Mr Bagpurze. A clerk hastened through a glazed inner door to inform the lawyer of the arrival of these noble clients, and Mr Bagpurze himself came out to usher them into his sanctum.

He was a stout man of some fifty years, who adhered to a full-bottomed wig in despite of fashion, and who pursed his lips on hearing of Lady Mary's determination to throw off the protection of Lord Shurland.

'His lordship has already been to see me, I may say,' he told his client, bending a disapproving stare across his heavy oak desk.

He had set for Maidie one of the two client chairs of latticed wood with cane seats. The Viscount had elected to stand, motioning the lawyer back to his own sturdy armchair of polished wood set between two enormous bookcases crowded with boxes, pink-ribboned files and great legal tomes.

'Firmin has been to see you?' repeated Maidie, in a voice of discontent. 'He would. I suppose he told you everything. What did he want?'

'If you mean, Lady Mary, that he informed me of your ill-considered flight from your home, you are correct. But that was not his purpose in visiting me.'

'Well, what was his purpose?'

'Lord Shurland wished to discover if there were any legal means by which he might prevent you from leaving his protection to seek that of Lord Delagarde,' said the lawyer.

'And are there?' asked Delagarde, from where he leaned against the near wall by a grimy window, arms folded across his chest.

Bagpurze looked at him. 'No, my lord, there are not.'

'A pity.'

Maidie turned on him the full force of her wide-eyed gaze, a spark darkening the grey. 'Why do you say that? I thought we were agreed that I was to remain in your house.'

'Oh, we are,' said Delagarde offhandedly. 'But that does not mean I am reconciled.'

'Well, I have offered to pay you,' Maidie pointed out. A startled sound from the lawyer turned her gaze towards him. 'I was perfectly ready to pay him, for I don't see that he should be expected to do this for nothing. But he will have none of it, which is quite his own fault. And I don't know why you should look like that, Mr Bagpurze. I can well afford to pay him, can't I?'

'Your ladyship is pretty well able to afford to do anything you choose,' agreed the lawyer primly. 'But that does not excuse the outrageous nature of your suggestion.'

Delagarde began to be amused. He strolled forward to the desk. 'Let us forget that matter, if you please, sir. What I wish to know is whether there have been any controls laid into the terms of this will.' He raised his brows as the lawyer drew in his cheeks. 'You need not look as if you suspect me of harbouring designs upon Lady Mary's fortune. If I am to consider myself responsible for her welfare, I had as well know what I am up against.'

The lawyer relaxed again, and did not see the intent look that came into Maidie's face as she glanced up at Delagarde. Was that what Firmin had supposed? Humdudgeon! He had obviously no idea of the light in which Lord Delagarde thought of her. The last thing on his mind would be to enrich himself by marrying her! The last thing on her mind, come to that. If one thing was more certain than anything else, it was that neither Delagarde nor herself could ever contemplate matrimony with one another.

'Lady Mary's fortune is left to her absolutely,' Bagpurze said. 'There is nothing to stop her spending it in any way she chooses. The only restriction that has been placed upon it is a proviso that only part of her fortune is to be passed over in settlements, when Lady Mary should come to marry. The remainder is secured at her own disposal, and will pass, at her death, to those of her issue who may not already be heir to some other property.'

'In other words,' said Delagarde, 'it is a safeguard to provide against an improvident match, and to ensure the future of any children she may have.'

'Precisely, my lord.'

'It appears that the late Lord Shurland was not as eccentric as I had supposed.'

'Oh, it was not Great-uncle Reginald who drew up the will,' Maidie said airily.

'No, my lady. The papers were drawn up by Lady Mary's father, John Hope, on his wife's becoming terminally ill. As well, for he did not long outlive her. Had it been left to his uncle and heir, the fifth Lord Shurland, I am bound to state that no such sensible arrangement is likely to have been made.'

'Oh, no,' Maidie agreed. 'Great-uncle had far more important matters to attend to.'

'Evidently,' said Delagarde, wondering what in the world these matters might be. More than one mention had been made of this gentleman's preoccupation.

'I am glad that my father had arranged everything for me, but I cannot blame Great-uncle Reginald. I am equally forgetful when I am engrossed. Indeed, I miss him dreadfully, for there is a great deal I do not yet know, and how I shall manage without him to advise me, I cannot think.'

Delagarde agreed to this, but absently. He shifted away again, and stood looking out of the window, for it had occurred to him that if Maidie's fortune was not going to prove the attraction that she had expected, then she was indeed obliged to fall back upon her personal attributes. These, it had to be admitted, were slight, and were so far outweighed by the disadvantages of her peculiar manners that he began to entertain serious doubts of getting her married off at all. Indeed, if Eustace Silsoe was informed of the restrictions—as how could he not be, situated as he was?—it was a wonder that he continued to press his suit. Just what were the sums involved?

He turned from the window to find that Maidie was arranging with Bagpurze the manner in which she proposed to draw upon her own funds. The lawyer was advising her to have all her bills sent to him for settlement, and was considering how best to provide her with pin money for her day-to-day needs. Delagarde stepped forward to intervene.

'It will be simplest for you to give me a draft on the Hope bankers, and let me draw the money for her.'

Maidie regarded him with suspicion. 'Why should you wish to do any such thing?'

'Good God, do you suppose I am going to make off with your money? I am trying to help!'

'Well, I could not be expected to guess that, could I?'

Delagarde eyed her bodingly. 'We will continue this discussion at some more convenient moment. Meanwhile, I have a question to put to Mr Bagpurze.'

The lawyer had looked with scant approval on their interchange, but he raised his brows at this. 'My lord?'

'I have no doubt Lady Mary will attribute some ulterior motive to my asking this—'

'I like that! You are the one who distrusts me.'

'—but it is of some slight interest to me to know what sort of figures we are dealing with. You may suppose, if you choose, as Lady Mary does,' he added sardonically, 'that I am motivated by pure self-interest. For you must know, Mr Bagpurze, that my pockets are to let and I am therefore solely interested in heiresses—'

'I never said that!'

'—and just in case there is enough set aside for settlements to tempt me—'

'Lord Delagarde, I wish you will be quiet!' Maidie cut in, leaping up from her chair in a state of some indignation. 'The idea never so much as crossed my mind—not even when Firmin hinted at it. I only realised this moment past just what he had meant. It is quite unnecessary for you to taunt me in that horrid way!'

'Then let it be a lesson to you not to be so suspicious!' Delagarde returned. Maidie opened her mouth to retort, and he held up a warning finger. 'Don't!'

She compressed her lips, but subsided, reseating herself. Turning to the lawyer, Delagarde discovered him with popping eyes and dropped jaw, and his temper gave way to amusement again. Really, the chit was impossible! She had the worst possible effect upon him.

'You must excuse us, Mr Bagpurze,' he said smoothly. 'Lady Mary and I have an unfortunate knack of rubbing each other up the wrong way.' He looked down at Maidie with a rueful air. 'Come, cry friends. I will apologise for the whole.'

Maidie's flush died, and she bit her lip. 'You are detestable! But I suppose I was provoking.'

Delagarde grinned. 'Very. Never mind. Will you give this unfortunate man permission to tell me the extent of your fortune, Maidie?'

Maidie nodded, conscious of a glow of pleasure at hear-

ing him use her pet name. 'Yes, of course. Tell him, Mr
Bagpurze.'

The lawyer pursed his lips, but had perforce to do as
she asked. 'The bulk is in investments, but the income
yield is substantial. Lady Mary has the benefit of several
thousands of pounds per annum—say between six and ten,
depending on the percentage returns.'

Delagarde blinked. 'But that must mean a fortune in
excess of one hundred thousand!'

'That is correct, my lord.' The lawyer's tone was non-
committal, as befit his profession.

'And the allowable settlements upon marriage?'

'Less than half. Forty-five thousand, to be precise.'

Delagarde very nearly clutched his head. *Forty-five
thousand pounds?* And he had made himself responsible
for the wench! How the devil had he become embroiled?

'Oh, good God,' he groaned, 'now we are in the suds!'

Chapter Four

Contrary to his avowed refusal to do any such thing on the day Maidie descended upon him in Charles Street, Delagarde not only accompanied his great-aunt and her protegée on an introductory round of morning calls, but, to Maidie's chagrin, stuck so close at her side that she had scarce an opportunity to open her mouth.

He would not allow her to respond to the most innocuous of questions. While Lady Hester was engaged with another visitor, their hostess this Tuesday, Lady Wingrove, inquired of Maidie pleasantly how she came to be residing at Charles Street.

'Oh, that is because—' Maidie began, and found herself ridden over by Delagarde.

'That is readily explained, my dear Lady Wingrove,' he said, with an engaging smile that successfully diverted that lady's attention. 'Aunt Hes had long been informed of Lady Mary's orphaned state, and wrote on many occasions to the late Lord Shurland—her friend, Reginald Hope, you must know—begging him to send the child to her. You may imagine how delighted she is to have the opportunity at last of introducing our little relative about.'

Lady Wingrove, murmuring suitably, expressed the

hope that Lady Hester would forgive the impromptu nature of the invitation and bring the child to her projected evening party on Thursday night. Then she promptly lost interest in her, embarking instead on a conversation with Delagarde which, to Maidie's critical eye, looked suspiciously like a flirtation. She was obliged to sit there and watch, taking no part in the interchange, wishing that the Worm had not thankfully given place to Lady Hester and rejected all invitations to make one of these social outings.

'Why did you do that?' Maidie demanded without preamble, the moment they were all reseated in Delagarde's town coach.

'Do what?'

'You would not let me speak to that woman! And I should like to know what you mean by referring to me as your "little" relative.'

'Is that what he did?' asked Lady Hester, amused. 'Depend upon it, child, Laurie is only intent upon planting the story we have concocted.'

'No, he is not,' Maidie contradicted forthrightly. 'He is afraid if he lets me say anything at all, I am bound to say something to disgrace him. Aren't you?'

'The thought had crossed my mind,' admitted Delagarde. 'However, I am far more concerned that you should not inadvertently let out any hint of your ghastly fortune.'

'Of course I shall not,' Maidie said indignantly. 'Do you think me incapable of keeping a secret?'

'I think you have a very unguarded tongue,' Delagarde said frankly. 'You don't care what you say, nor to whom you say it. I shudder to think of the possible consequences of some ill-considered remark.'

'Don't be silly, Laurie,' cut in Lady Hester, before the indignant Maidie could respond to this. 'You cannot expect the poor girl to sit mumchance through every social encounter. She must be allowed to make her own impression.'

'That is exactly what I am afraid of!'

'Besides,' pursued his great-aunt, unheeding, 'unless you mean to remain glued to her side in a fashion that can only serve to make you ridiculous, she is bound at some point to manage on her own. She may as well do so from the start.'

'Thank you, Lady Hester,' said Maidie gratefully. 'And what is more, Lord Delagarde, it is not in either of our interests for you to stay so close to me. No gentlemen will be able to approach me if they imagine you to be so strict a guardian. You had much better go away and indulge your own amusements, and leave me to Lady Hester.'

But this the Viscount would by no means agree to.

Although he refrained on the next occasion from interfering in quite so obvious a manner, Maidie was aware of him hovering in her vicinity, and felt that every utterance she made was subject to his critical scrutiny. By the time she made her first appearance at Lady Wingrove's party on Thursday evening, she was feeling so much out of charity with his lordship that her frustration could not but find expression.

As they entered on the announcement of their names into the bower of sea-green and gilt that comprised the two adjoining saloons on the first floor of the Wingrove house, Maidie was relieved to see that Delagarde was immediately hailed by two gentlemen.

'How fortunate!' whispered Lady Hester in her ear, as the Viscount went over to greet them. 'Those two are Laurie's particular friends. Let us hope that, between them, they may keep him so occupied that he leaves you alone for once.'

Maidie could only echo this sentiment, but she said nothing for the Wingroves were waiting to greet them. She underwent a number of introductions without untoward incident, remaining close by Lady Hester's side so that she was not called upon to do more than murmur a few conventional phrases as they meandered from group to group. She had begun the evening buoyed up with confidence engendered by the becoming apricot gown of Lady Hester's choosing, which had been delivered that very morning. But as she passed among Lady Wingrove's guests, it was gradually borne in upon Maidie that the colour toned too well, throwing undesirable attention upon her hair. It seemed to her that every pair of eyes that encountered her strayed upwards, and blinked a startled reaction. Maidie began to wish that she had not been persuaded into wearing her hair loose, and was thankful that the full enormity was slightly mitigated by a frivolous wisp of lace and flowers that served for a cap.

'Everyone is looking at my hair,' she imparted in a frantic whisper to Lady Hester at a moment when they were briefly alone.

'Perhaps they are admiring it,' suggested the elder lady with a twinkle.

'Do not be ridiculous, dear ma'am! How can they possibly do so?'

'Very easily. Now do not put yourself about, child. Forget your hair. They may look, but no one will say anything to put you to the blush, I promise you.'

Maidie drew a breath and tried to relax. It was perhaps unfortunate that, the very next moment, Lady Hester was accosted by an alarming female in puce satin with a feathered turban and a deal of ornamentation in gold. This gaunt creature stood tall and arrogant before them, all apparent condescension as she pried her jutting nose into Maidie's affairs.

'Lord, Hester, is it true what I have been hearing? Have you indeed come out of hiding only to bring out John

Hope's daughter? What peculiar virtue does she have to make you bestir yourself after all these years?'

'You may judge for yourself, my dear Selina,' responded Lady Hester, aware of her protegée stiffening beside her. 'Maidie, this is Lady Rankmiston, one of society's most distinguished hostesses. Lady Mary Hope, Selina, who is related to me.'

Maidie took the two fingers extended to her, and gave back look for look the interested stare that was bent upon her.

'Distantly related, I feel sure, Hester,' said Lady Rankmiston smoothly, with a significant look flashed at the ginger locks. 'I have not seen such a head in your family!'

Stung on the raw, Maidie gathered her defences. 'You are right, ma'am. The colour of my hair comes from the Hopes, not the Otterburns. It is a distinctive aberration that has made an infrequent appearance ever since the Tudors. There is a family tradition that it hails from an ancestor who was born of King Henry the Eighth on the wrong side of the blanket.'

'In-deed!' responded Lady Rankmiston, and Maidie was happy to note that she had taken her aback. But she made a quick recover. 'Your candour does you credit, my dear.'

'Well, I have no idea whether the legend is true,' Maidie admitted, the hostility fading from her voice. 'But I must say it lends one a certain distinction to be able to claim King Henry for a royal forebear. Most people, so my great-uncle Reginald told me, are only able to go back to Charles the Second, who left so many bastards in the nobility that it can only be counted a commonplace.'

Lady Rankmiston, apparently stricken to silence by these disclosures, could only stare at Maidie with a blank expression on her face. Maidie cast a questioning glance at Lady Hester, but her patroness was laughing.

'You begin to see, I don't doubt, Selina, the "peculiar virtue" that attracted me to this very unusual debutante.'

'Unusual, indeed,' agreed the other lady, finding her tongue. 'Such a happy turn of phrase, too! Am I to understand that Delagarde is sponsoring you, child?'

'Yes, but with the utmost reluctance,' said Maidie, throwing discretion to the winds. 'I am very much obliged to him, but I don't wish to impose upon him any more than I need. It is Lady Hester by whom I am allowing myself to be guided.'

'And I,' interposed that lady swiftly, 'have advised Lady Mary not to abate one jot of her refreshing frankness. I cannot bear these mealy-mouthed damsels who will never say boo to a goose, can you, Selina?'

'No, but neither am I an advocate for encouraging impertinence in the young,' said Lady Rankmiston, in a tone designed to crush pretension.

Maidie frowned. 'Have I been impertinent? I beg your pardon, if I have. My great-uncle had the greatest dislike of shams. He would not have me say anything but what was in my head, so I am not much in the way of curbing my speech. It is what Lord Delagarde particularly dislikes in me.'

'I can find it in me to pardon him.'

'Lady Mary was brought up by Reginald Hope,' Lady Hester explained before Maidie could pick this up. 'He was something of a recluse, you must know, and rarely ventured into society.'

A flash of recognition entered Lady Rankmiston's eye. 'Reginald Hope? What, that old lunatic had charge of you? Lord, you poor child!'

A tide of fury washed through Maidie. Without pausing for thought, she let fly. 'He was no such thing! He was the wisest and kindest of men, and I loved him very dearly. I think it is perfectly horrid of you, ma'am, to speak so

slightingly. Great-uncle was right. He said society was full
of old cats who had nothing better to do than to scratch
and claw at everyone around. And I see that you are one
of them!'

With which, she turned on her heel and marched away,
oblivious alike to the startled faces that followed her, and
the direction in which her feet were taking her. But she
had hardly gone a dozen steps when her arm was grasped
in an ungentle grip, and she found Delagarde at her elbow.

'Come with me!' he said in a savage undervoice.

Far too angry to do anything but obey, Maidie was
swept along, unaware that people stared as they passed and
turned to whisper behind fans. In a very short space of
time she found herself alone with Delagarde in a small
antechamber at the far end of one of the saloons, where
he released her and turned to set the door so that it was a
few inches ajar. He was fuming, but not so lost to all sense
of propriety as to go apart with a single female and shut
the door upon them both. He could only hope that they
would not be overheard. Not that matters could well be
much worse than they were already!

'What the devil do you think you're doing?' he demanded in an irate tone, keeping his voice low. 'Don't you
know better than to insult one of the queens of society?'

'I don't care who she is!' retorted Maidie. 'She had no
right to insult Great-uncle. If I insulted her, it was no more
than she deserved.'

Angry tears rose to her eyes, but she dashed them away.
Brought up short by the abrupt recognition of her distress,
Delagarde checked the hot words that rose to his tongue.
He eyed her in a baffled way, as the tears welled again,
and were as ruthlessly rejected.

'There is no need to cry, Maidie,' he said, on a softened
note.

'I am not!' Maidie protested, with a defiant sniff.

Delagarde suppressed a smile, and gave her his hand-kerchief. Maidie glared at him, sniffed again; then reluctantly took it and blew her nose.

'I am not upset, but only angry,' she insisted, tucking his handkerchief into a hidden recess in the petticoat of her apricot gown. 'So would you be, if someone told you that your Aunt Hester was a lunatic.'

'I dare say I would,' Delagarde conceded. 'But there is a time and place for a display of temperament. You cannot afford to lose the approval of such females as Lady Rank-miston, Maidie. You may not realise it, but you can be socially damned by those women.'

'Well, what if I am?' said Maidie impenitently. 'I have no wish to cut a figure in society.'

'Believe me, you won't. Society is more likely to cut you.'

'I don't care!'

'But I do!'

Maidie tutted. 'Why should you? It has nothing to do with you if I am socially damned.'

'Not you, simpleton,' Delagarde said irritably. 'I am talking of myself. It happens that I enjoy my social position, and I don't wish to see it blasted by your idiotic behaviour.'

'Don't concern yourself. I have already told Lady Rank-miston that you disapprove of me. I have no doubt that—'

'You did what?' interrupted Delagarde. 'Are you mad? Good God, girl, I am supposed to be your sponsor! Have you no sense of what is fitting? And Aunt Hes would have me let you loose to do as you please. I knew how it would be!'

'It is quite your own fault,' Maidie threw at him. 'You have put me so out of temper that I scarce know what I am doing. If only you will let me alone!'

'Yes, do let her alone, Laurie,' came from the doorway behind him.

He turned as Lady Hester entered the antechamber. It was plain from her demeanour that she was amused by the episode, and Delagarde's annoyance revived.

'What the devil is so funny, Aunt?'

'It is Selina,' Lady Hester told him, bubbling over. 'I have never seen her so put out.' She came to Maidie and patted her on the shoulder. 'Don't look so stricken, child. I have had a grudge against that woman for years, and it has done me no end of good to see her served out in her own coin.'

'I don't believe this!' uttered Delagarde, disgusted. 'If you mean to congratulate the wench on her ill manners, instead of correcting her, there is no more to be said.'

'If that means you have nothing more to say,' Maidie put in, 'then I am heartily glad of it.'

'I have a great deal more to say, but not to you,' he retorted. 'It would be useless, and I am not going to waste my breath. You might remember, Aunt Hes, that she has to succeed on her own merits.'

'And my title.'

'Which will avail her nothing,' Delagarde continued, refusing to address Maidie direct, 'if she means to conduct herself in this discourteous fashion.'

'Have no fear, Laurie,' said his great-aunt soothingly. 'I have smoothed over the lapse. Nothing could have been easier. I told Selina that the child is still raw from her great-uncle's death, which no one could wonder at, and she has chosen to be gracious.'

'That is all very well,' Delagarde said, still heavily frowning, 'but if Maidie is going to inform the world that she and I are at outs—'

Lady Hester laughed. 'My dear Laurie, there will be no need for her to inform the world of it. No one with the least degree of intelligence could fail to notice it. What do you expect, when you hustle the child away to a private room, looking like a thundercloud the while?'

'There, you see!' exclaimed Maidie. 'I said it was your fault.'

Delagarde eyed her with menace. 'If I do not end by strangling you, my girl, you may certainly count it my fault!'

'Laurie,' said Hester despairingly, 'do go away! For heaven's sake, let the child alone to find her feet. She will never do so if you are constantly growling about her like a bad-tempered watchdog.'

'Yes, but you seem to forget that everything she says and does redounds upon me. Not that I suppose anyone cares for that!'

'No, Maidie, don't answer him!'

On the point of responding with a resurgence of heat, Maidie looked at Lady Hester and thought better of it. Beyond casting Delagarde a brooding glance, she refrained from adding fuel to the flames.

'That's better,' approved Lady Hester. 'You have said quite enough, Laurie. Now, let it be. I shall keep the child here for a moment or two, so that she may have an opportunity to cool before reappearing in company.'

Delagarde hesitated. He was still smouldering, but Aunt Hes's words had recalled him to the impropriety of engaging in any further argument at a function such as this.

'Very well, do as you please,' he said. 'I wash my hands of it! And if she is quartered on us forever, don't blame me!'

'I wish I could think he meant it, but I fear there is little hope of him washing his hands of you,' Lady Hester said, laughing, once Delagarde had gone.

The Viscount had every intention of doing so, but he found it to be more problematic than he had bargained for.

To begin with, it was extremely difficult to concentrate on anything anyone said to him when his attention obstinately held on the question of what Maidie might be doing. It was impossible not to cast furtive looks about to check where she was in the room, and he could not help sighing with relief when he noted that Aunt Hes was still at her side. This state of affairs was conducive neither to his peace of mind, nor to his relationship with his intimates.

'What in Hades ails you, Laurie?' demanded his friend, Mr Everett Corringham, a gentleman much of the Viscount's age, but lacking his elegance. 'You have answered me at random no less than three times.'

His companion, a mischievous buck with a roving eye, let out a crack of rude laughter. 'Thinking of this waif he has adopted, I'll lay my life!'

'She is not a waif, Peter,' said Delagarde crossly. 'Nor have I adopted her. I am merely her sponsor.'

'A new come-out for you, dear boy, to be sponsoring young females,' pursued Lord Riseley, twinkling at him.

'No,' agreed Corringham. 'He usually avoids them like the plague. Too many matchmakers in tow.'

'Take care you don't find yourself riveted before too long, my boy,' teased Riseley.

'Don't be ridiculous!' snapped Delagarde, all but shuddering at the suggestion. 'Lady Mary and I don't deal together. As for sponsoring her, I had no choice in the matter, for it was my mother's doing a good many years ago. Besides, it is my aunt who is in charge of her.'

'From what I hear,' returned his friend teasingly, 'it was not your aunt who gave the girl a raking for standing up to the Rankmiston tabby.'

'Devil take it!' Delagarde swore. 'Is that story doing the rounds?'

'You couldn't expect it not to, old fellow,' said Corringham reasonably. 'Don't think it's done your little ginger head a mite of harm.'

'You don't?' Delagarde asked frowningly.

'Can't think of many who wouldn't want to see the Rankmiston receive a set down.'

'Yes, but it won't do. And she's not my little ginger head!'

Riseley grinned. 'She told the Rankmiston that she owed her hair to one of Henry the Eighth's bastards.'

'Good God! What next will she say?'

'Where did she get that head?' demanded Corringham. 'Astonishing colour.'

'She got it, Everett, from the man Lady Rankmiston stigmatised as a lunatic,' Delagarde told him.

'And was he?' asked Riseley irrepressibly.

'How the devil should I know?' demanded Delagarde irritably. 'I didn't know the fellow. He was evidently eccentric, but Maidie thought the world of him.'

'Who's Maidie?'

'Lady Mary, you fool! It's what he called her.'

'Oh. Well, if I were you, dear boy, I should shab off as fast as I could. You don't want to be leg-shackled to a female who is ripe for Bedlam.'

Delagarde groaned. 'Peter, I keep telling you—'

'It's what everyone will think, Laurie,' warned Everett solemnly. 'Particularly if you mean to conduct yourself like a plaster when the girl is about.'

'Well, everyone will be wrong, won't they?' responded the Viscount, incensed. 'Good God, I can't foist a girl on the town and then leave her to sink or swim!'

'Seems to me to be swimming pretty well,' observed Riseley.

Delagarde followed the direction of his gaze to where Maidie seemed to be the centre of an animated circle that no longer included his great-aunt. She was talking, that disconcertingly direct gaze of hers trained upon one of the two gentlemen who, with Lady Wingrove's daughter and a couple of other females, were grouped about her. From the smiles and laughter, Maidie appeared to be amusing them, and Delagarde became conscious of a sensation of warmth mingled, most strangely, with something that felt suspiciously like discontent—which must be nonsense. He was glad, he told himself firmly, that she was indeed finding her feet. Although he would wager any sum at all that Maidie was unconscious of saying anything comical. He was sorely tempted to go over and join them. But that, he was persuaded, could only result in Maidie's discomfiture. She would not thank him for it.

'I am relieved that she is making her way,' he told his friends smoothly. 'Which leaves me free to seek amusements of my own. Shall we go to the card room?'

Maidie watched the Viscount's departure from the saloon with mixed feelings. She was very happy to think that her demonstration of independence had not gone unnoticed. And if Delagarde supposed that she cared anything for the fact that the only time he had anything to say to her was when he had some stupid complaint to make, he was very much mistaken. The early interest in her hair appeared to have died down, and she was able to forget about it for moments together. She was actually enjoying herself a little, even if the persons with whom she was conversing were the sort that Great-uncle would have condemned as empty-headed fribbles. What should take them to laugh inanely every time she opened her mouth, she was at a loss to understand. But they had served a useful purpose. No doubt Delagarde supposed her to be happily engaged, which had at last made him relax his oppressive vigilance.

'Do tell us more about the stars, Lady Mary,' demanded

young Darby Hampford, recalling Maidie's wandering thoughts.

Maidie frowned. She was not going to recite any more names to them. The ladies, whose scanty knowledge consisted merely of the Zodiacal signs under which they had been born, were apt to shriek with mirth when the gentlemen, who had Latin, translated for their benefit. All had heard of Ursa Major, the Great Bear, but it seemed to provide delight of no common order to discover the existence of the Great Dog, the Little Dog and the Whale, while the Serpent-bearer and Watersnake produced artistic shudders. Familiarity having robbed Maidie of the ability to share in such reactions, she chose instead to discourse on stars in general.

'Well, they are at a very great distance from us. We are indebted to the Reverend James Bradley for having calculated in measurement the positions of many thousands of stars.'

'But how far are they?' asked one of the ladies. 'They do not look to be very distant.'

'That is because the light that we see appears to be close. But it is said that starlight has travelled millions and millions of miles before it reaches us. The sun is much nearer than any of the stars.'

Maidie saw disbelief mingling with awe in the faces about her. How odd to find so much ignorance of what was to her a commonplace! There was much more she might have gone on to explain, had not an interruption occurred—one distinctly unwelcome.

'My dear Mary, do not be prosing on forever about your dratted stars!' said a familiar voice cuttingly.

Maidie turned quickly to find Adela at her elbow. A false smile twisting her mouth, she simpered at Maidie's companions. 'You must not encourage Lady Mary to ride upon her hobby-horse. She will continue all night, and I dare say nothing could be more tedious.' Grasping Maidie's arm, she gave it a warning pinch, and added, 'Besides, I must drag my little cousin away. We have not had a chance to converse this age. Come, Mary.'

Reluctant, but as unable to repulse Adela's strong hold as she had been that of Delagarde earlier, Maidie allowed herself to be pulled into the other saloon which was relatively uninhabited, bar a couple in earnest colloquy, and one or two older ladies seated in desultory discussion to one side.

'What do you want with me, Adela?' Maidie demanded, but remembering—for she was learning fast!—to keep her voice low. 'You cannot pretend to be anxious for my company.'

'How you do take one up!' complained Adela. Then she smiled in what Maidie supposed she must imagine was a winning way, but which only served to increase her sense of the other's duplicity. 'Need we be enemies? I do think, Mary, that you owe me at least a semblance of kinship in public. I assure you I have been obliged to respond to several impertinent enquiries as to why you are not in town with me.'

'And what have you answered?' Maidie asked suspiciously.

Adela shrugged delicately. 'I have told Lady Hester's own tale. What else could I do? I am not so foolish as to declare my wrongs to the world.'

Maidie regarded her sceptically. 'You mean that Firmin has instructed you to behave with circumspection.' She saw the daggers leap back into her cousin's eyes and knew that she was right. 'I am glad he at least has accepted the situation.'

'Not without some qualms,' Adela said sharply. 'He places no more dependence on your discretion, my dear Mary, than I do myself—an opinion which your conduct

tonight has done nothing to alter. I can only be thankful
that it is not I who must answer to charges of your blunt
insolence. People will soon be saying that you are dis-
gracefully ill bred.'

It had needed only this to crown a singularly unpleasant
evening. Lady Rankmiston—Delagarde—and now Adela.
Ill bred? It was an insult to Great-uncle!

'Why must everyone tell me how to behave? Am I an
upstart mushroom pushing my way into a rank of society
where I have no place? No, Adela. I outrank half the ladies
here, yet I am supposed to alter my whole character to suit
their notions. If it was not for Lady Hester, I should be
much inclined to abandon the entire scheme.'

Adela gave a false laugh. 'Do not expect me to sympathise. Not that I have the remotest guess what your precious scheme may be.'

'You need not dissemble,' Maidie said evenly. 'You
know that I am here, like every other damsel, to find a
husband.'

'Then I wonder that you will insist upon foolishly ruining your own chances,' Adela returned peevishly. 'But I
do not know why I should complain of that. The more you
drive his rivals away—which you are bound to do, for
gentlemen cannot bear a female to be outspoken!—the better reason you will have to reconsider Eustace's suit.' She
added, with a glint of malice, 'Unless, that is, you have
some idea of entrapping Delagarde.'

Maidie slept badly. The notion, once instilled into her
head, took strong possession of her mind. It was a ludicrous suggestion, that went without saying. Nothing could
have been further from her thoughts. But that Adela could
say it, could even suppose it, had given her furiously to
think.

When she looked at her own actions, and realised the

construction that might be put upon them by an unprejudiced observer, her cheeks burned in the darkness. Thank heaven no one but Adela knew how she had bearded Delagarde! Thrusting herself into his life, and placing herself at his mercy. Worse, she knew she would have done it even had Lady Hester not been there.

The remembrance of that first encounter threw her into a worse case than ever. Had not Lady Hester herself hinted at her own suspicion? What had she said? Something about wondering how high Maidie might be aiming. But she had left off that theme soon enough. After Maidie had mentioned her independence. A creeping suspicion made her flesh crawl. It was not—it could not be!—that Lady Hester had supported her because of that independence?

A wash of distress almost caused her to burst into tears. Was it all false? The protestations of friendship; the amusement that had not given offence because of the kindness behind it; the care and attention, the support that had meant so much against Delagarde's impatience. All, all of it, only done for gain? She could not believe it. But then, what did she know of these people, acquainted with them as she had been for less than two weeks? Was she but a gullible fool to be so taken in? No, it must not be true. She did not wish to believe it. For if it were true, it meant not only that Lady Hester's liking for her was a sham— the unkindest of shams, too!—but it must mean also that Delagarde—

Here her thoughts clashed so strongly with her feelings that it was a moment or two before Maidie could regain the smallest control over the heaving sensations in her breast. Seizing the handkerchief that she had tucked under the pillow, she mopped her eyes and blew her nose. And then, as the image of its earlier use leapt into her mind, she sat bolt upright in the bed and flung the handkerchief from her. *His* handkerchief. No, she would not use it!

Agitation drove her to thrust aside the curtains about the four-poster, and slip out of bed. Moving to the French windows, she dragged the curtains to one side and gazed through the panes at the darkness outside. It was not a very clear night, but one or two of her friends up there winked at her between the clouds. Her tumultuous emotions began to subside. Yes, there was Betelgeuse, and there Rigel, the brightest and furthest points of the magnificent constellation of Orion. The Hunter's belt and sword were not visible tonight, but by the time she had located Aldebaran, the jewel of the Taurus stars, Maidie had recalled how unimportant were these worldly considerations, set against the wonders of the celestial sphere. Great-uncle had taught her that, and he was right.

Nevertheless, as the cold began to penetrate too insistently through her nightgown to be ignored, and she redrew the curtains and scurried back to bed, she drifted back to the uncomfortable thought that had thrown her into disorder.

What if the boot were on the other foot? She had no notion—for she was mistress of her own designs, was she not?—of entrapping Delagarde. But suppose it were Delagarde who had conceived the notion of entrapping her?

True, he had scorned the suggestion. Had even mocked at her, as if she had indeed harboured the suspicion. Which she had not. At least, not until now. She did not know yet if she truly suspected him. No one could accuse him of having the slightest fondness for her! Indeed, she dared say his distaste of her exceeded her own for him. But that would not preclude his determining to marry her. Had not Great-uncle pointed out that marriage, in the class to which they both belonged, had nothing to do with fondness—or even mere liking? Arranged marriages, Great-uncle had said, were quite the thing. It was common for couples to be wed without acquaintance, or, even if acquainted, to have met only in such restricted circumstances that they could not possibly know anything of each other's character. Which was what had persuaded Maidie to conceive of her scheme. Her marriage was to be one of convenience. It was all too likely that Delagarde felt the same—and what could be more convenient to him than to become possessed of her forty-five thousand pounds?

Maidie was disappointed. She had not thought it of him. But when she considered the way he set so much store by her public conduct—and had he not insisted that it was his own reputation for which he trembled?—she might be pardoned for supposing him to be seeking to mould her into conduct befitting his future Viscountess.

These unsatisfactory cogitations had left Maidie with a brooding headache, and an air of wary uncertainty, which caused her to shy hastily away from Delagarde when she encountered him in the downstairs breakfast parlour.

He was already at the table, but had risen on her entrance, and watched her frowningly as she scuttled to a place at the corner furthest away from him. Beyond bidding her good morning, he made no attempt to engage her in conversation until Lowick, who had returned from Berkshire, bringing with him a formidable retinue and a mountain of supplies necessary to the equipping of the London house in a manner suitable to entertaining, had served Maidie with a plate of ham supported by two baked eggs and several slices of bread and butter.

Delagarde, having laid aside his morning paper, watched Maidie sipping tea for a moment or two. He waved away Lowick's offer of a refill from the coffee pot, and signed to the butler to withdraw.

'Do you care to drive out with me this morning?' he asked Maidie, as soon as they were alone.

She cast him a suspicious look. 'Why should you wish to take me driving?'

He laughed. 'Why shouldn't I? The day is fine for March, and it is quite the fashion to be seen driving in the park. You are here to be seen, are you not?'

'Yes, but why should *you* take me?'

'Who else should take you?' Delagarde countered, frowning. 'Until, at least, you have acquired for yourself a court of beaux.'

Maidie eyed him. 'Well, I shall not do that if I am constantly to be seen in your company.'

Delagarde stared at her. 'Have it as you will! Why you should be so churlish about it, I am at a loss to understand. I was only trying to be helpful.'

'I did not mean to be churlish,' Maidie said, looking away. 'I have the headache.'

'Don't trouble yourself to make excuses. I am becoming used to your ways. I dare say familiarity will inure me to them altogether, and I shall not even notice.'

'No, it won't,' Maidie flashed, 'for you will not have any opportunity to become familiar. I shall be gone from your house much too soon for that.'

His eyes narrowed. 'Good! Though I fail to see why, having been so anxious to gain access to my house, you should now spurn it in that ill-bred fashion.'

'I am not ill bred!'

But she flushed, and looked down at her plate, biting her lip. Delagarde looked her over in a good deal of surprise. What the devil ailed the wench? He watched her picking desultorily at her food. Perhaps it was true that she had the headache. He studied her profile. Was she not a little pale? And where was that direct gaze that so much characterised her? She could scarcely look at him! He had just begun to wonder if there were anything seriously amiss, when Maidie suddenly turned. Something in her grey eyes touched him. A hint of pain? But before he could formulate a question, Maidie spoke.

'Am I—?' Uncertain, low-voiced. 'Do I indeed seem to be ill bred?' It was a plea. Delagarde was quite unable to withstand it. He smiled.

'Not ill bred, Maidie. Merely outspoken.'

'But you do nothing but complain of my conduct,' she said gruffly. 'You said I was ill mannered.'

'And so you were,' he agreed, grinning at her. 'But not intentionally. I doubt if your worst enemy could accuse you of saying the things you do say with any intent of malice.'

A little sigh escaped Maidie. 'That is something, I suppose.' In a stronger voice, she added, 'But I must say I do not see why what I do should make any difference to your reputation. It cannot, after all, be as pure as all that.'

'I did not say it was pure,' Delagarde said, laughing. 'I should be the last man to claim that.'

'Then why should you—'

'Listen, Maidie!' he interrupted in an earnest tone. 'There are unwritten rules governing the conduct of females, and I dare say your great-uncle Reginald—and I do not mean to criticise him, so you need not look daggers at me!—neglected to inform you, of a number of things that ought to have fallen to Miss·Wormley's lot to teach you.'

A wry grimace twisted Maidie's mouth. 'Poor Worm. She did try. I am afraid I was not an apt pupil.'

Delagarde looked amused. 'I can well imagine that her efforts might not meet with success.'

There was silence for a moment or two. Maidie toyed with the food on her plate, digesting the conversation. It did seem as though Delagarde was intent upon mending her manners. Whether his motive might be what she suspected, she had yet to discover, but it occurred to her that she might, with advantage, learn of him. It did not accord with her plans, certainly, to drive any suitors away (as Adela had suggested). On the other hand, it went against the grain with her to adjust her deportment merely for the sake of acceptance.

'It does not seem fair,' she said, speaking the thought in her mind, 'that, just because one is a female, one should be subject to restrictions.'

'Oh, there are quite as many restrictions for men, I assure you,' Delagarde told her coolly. 'But less subject to the censure of females than of one's own sex.'

'But it is the females whom I am obliged to conciliate,' Maidie pointed out. 'And Great-uncle told me positively that my rank and wealth would guarantee acceptance.'

'Acceptance, yes, and your fortune—were we to tell the world of it—would reconcile many to your devastating frankness. But the sort of incivility that you indulge in when you lose your temper, even in the daughter of an Earl, will not readily be forgiven.'

'I do not lose my temper,' Maidie said with dignity, adding at his sceptical look, 'At least, not often.'

'Pardon me! I have seen you lose it several times.'

Maidie's chin went up. 'That is only because you are so excessively provoking.'

'Permit me to return the compliment.'

She bit her lip on a sharp answer, and instead added, 'It is strange that I may not be forgiven for losing my temper, but everyone is ready to forgive your drinking yourself under the table, and gaming away half a fortune.'

'I rarely, let me tell you,' retorted Delagarde, 'drink to excess. And as for gaming, I have already told you that I am but a moderate gamester, if I am one at all.'

'You will not, however, dare to say the same of your *affaires*,' Maidie challenged candidly.

'My—!' Delagarde stopped, the affability wiped from his face. 'That is a disgraceful thing to say—and typical!

How dare you mention such matters? No female of true gentility would dream of referring to that part of a gentleman's life of which she should know nothing.'

'That is not what Great-uncle said,' Maidie told him with maddening calm. 'He advised me to be astute enough to judge what a husband might be up to, so that I might use it to my advantage when I particularly wished for some little service or trifle which he might otherwise be unwilling to render me.'

'Your *eccentric* great-uncle,' said Delagarde with a good deal of emphasis, pushing back his chair and rising from the table, 'gave you a singularly ill-advised education!'

'Not at all,' Maidie said tranquilly. 'He did not wish me to grow up one of these namby-pamby females who can do nothing for themselves.'

'There is nothing namby-pamby about a well-bred girl, with quiet manners and a calm disposition, who has not had her head stuffed with a lot of arrant nonsense.'

Maidie raised her brows at him. 'Then why haven't you married one?'

For a moment or two, Delagarde regarded her impotently. Then he threw down his napkin, turned on his heel, and stalked out of the breakfast parlour without another word.

Entering the re-opened green saloon upstairs some little time later, Maidie discovered both the elder ladies to have come down, having breakfasted in bed—a custom in which Lady Hester always indulged, and which Maidie knew she had encouraged the Worm to emulate. They looked to be enjoying a lively discussion, seated in two of the Chippendale chairs which they had turned to face the window in order to enjoy a little of the wintry sunshine that entered there.

'There you are, Maidie!' sang out her ladyship, throwing out a welcoming hand. 'Come and hear how we have successfully traced our relationship.'

'Oh, my love, it is too comforting! It seems that Lady Hester is my father's first cousin. I had no inkling that we were so closely tied.'

Maidie went across and bent to press a kiss to her duenna's faded cheek. 'I am so glad for you, Worm.' Turning to Lady Hester, she felt all her uncertainty rush back, and was quite unable to prevent a good deal of reserve creeping into her greeting. 'Good morning, Lady Hester.'

Her patroness instantly disconcerted her. 'Why, what is this, Maidie? You are very cool all of a sudden.'

Dismayed, Maidie stammered, 'I—I beg your pardon, ma'am. It is just—I did not mean—' She faltered to a stop under Lady Hester's questioning gaze.

'Have you quarrelled with Laurie again?'

'No! At least, yes, I have, but that has nothing—I mean, it is not because of—'

To Maidie's intense discomfiture, the Worm was now regarding her with an equal degree of astonishment. 'My love, this is not like you. What is the matter?'

Maidie turned quickly away, ashamed to have allowed the horrid suspicions she entertained to have affected her demeanour. If only Great-uncle had taught her a little of the art of dissimulation! But all forms of fakery were anathema to him, and so ingrained with his beliefs was she that it had been stupid of her to suppose that she might attempt prevarication.

Nevertheless, when she found that the two elder ladies had risen and followed her into the centre of the room, the disagreeable sensations engendered in her by the thought that Lady Hester's amiability might be feigned led her to ward off the urge to blurt out the truth.

'My dear child, what in the world is amiss?' Lady Hester was asking in a tone of deep concern.

'Dearest Maidie, what is it? What can I do?' chorused the Worm at the same time.

'Nothing, nothing,' Maidie said desperately. 'It is only that I—I have the headache!'

'Oh dear, oh dear,' clucked Miss Wormley, thrusting her into a chair and feeling her brow. 'I do trust that you are not sickening for something.'

Maidie protested, trying to push her away. But she was less happy when Lady Hester gently removed the duenna and bent over her, lifting her chin with one hand and scanning her face. Maidie could scarcely meet her eyes.

'She does not look to be in prime pin, certainly. Why don't you go and lie down, Maidie?'

Maidie nodded, and was relieved that Lady Hester moved away. 'Yes, perhaps I will.'

'Come, my love,' twittered the Worm. 'I will come up with you and—'

'No, no, Worm. Thank you, but I shall be better alone.'

'That's right,' agreed Lady Hester, sitting on a green-striped nearby sofa. 'You go and rest, child. We have no engagement this morning. Ida and I—' smiling kindly at the Worm '—will continue our comfortable cose.'

Maidie rose hastily, a rush of distress choking at her throat. 'Oh, yes,' she uttered huskily, on a most unaccustomed note of petulance, 'no doubt it will be comfortable—since I will be absent!'

She regretted her outburst instantly, for Lady Hester stared at her, surprise in her face.

'Maidie, my *dear*,' protested the Worm, throwing a distressed look at their hostess.

But the deep sense of humiliation that underlay all Maidie's fears would permit of no damping down. Her emotions welled up, and found expression.

'You need not look like that, Lady Hester! Well do I know that no one could wilfully seek my company.'

'My love!'

'My dear child, how can you think that?'

'What else am I to think, when everyone makes it plain enough?' She saw hurt enter Lady Hester's expression, and remorse bit at her.

'Am I to understand that you include me in that "everyone", Maidie?'

Maidie burst into tears. Groping her way back to the chair, she sank into it and hid her face in her hands, valiantly gulping down the rising sobs. She heard the Worm clucking about her, shrunk into herself the more, and was relieved when Lady Hester intervened.

'Dear Ida, give the girl a little space, do!'

The Worm's lamentations ceased, and Maidie, venturing to peep through her fingers, saw a handkerchief held out to her and clutched it gratefully. Presently she was able to wipe away the tearstains and, sniffing dismally, looked up to find two pairs of concerned eyes trained upon her from the sofa.

'Now, my dear,' began Lady Hester, one firm hand on the Worm's wrist discouraging the duenna from making any move towards her charge, 'what is this all about?'

The kindness of her tone struck at Maidie's pain, and thrust her into blurting out her trouble. 'Why have you befriended me, ma'am? Was it only for the sake of my fortune?' Then she looked quickly away, catching her breath on a sob. 'I do not know why I ask you. You are bound to deny it.'

'No,' said her ladyship seriously. 'No, Maidie, I will not deny it.'

Chapter Five

Maidie's eyes flew to Lady Hester's, and her chest went hollow. She had been afraid of that answer, but truly she had not expected it!

'Don't look so stricken, child,' begged Lady Hester. 'There is no need. I did, it is true, urge Laurie to sponsor you for just that reason. When I established that you were Brice Burloyne's granddaughter, I immediately suspected that what you called your independence must be substantial. I knew that Brice had been what we used to call a nabob and had made a fortune in India.'

'Yes, he did,' Maidie agreed dully, for she was sick at heart. 'I had no idea of it myself, for my mother died long before I was old enough to be told.'

Lady Hester gave a tiny smile. 'You are hurt, and I don't wonder at it. But bear with me a little, child. Of course I thought of you for Laurie. I am but human, and a little of the matchmaker is in all of us females.' The mischief leapt into her eyes. 'But I would have to be a great fool to continue to entertain such hopes in the face of your antipathy to Delagarde, would I not?'

'Yes.' It was a small voice, for a faint hope was lifting a little of the cloud.

The mischief deepened. 'Surely, dear child, you cannot truly believe that my adoption of you has remained of a mercenary nature? I cannot answer for Laurie, but you won my heart in the shortest possible order, Maidie.'

Maidie stared at her, a glow spreading through her bosom. After a moment, she became aware that the Worm was weeping softly, and her own eyes brimmed again.

'Oh, ma'am, forgive me! Pray forgive me!'

Lady Hester brushed the apology aside. 'Nonsense, there is nothing to forgive. I am only sorry that you should have been troubled by such uncomfortable thoughts.'

Maidie smiled rather mistily. 'You are very good. I am so thankful to have been wrong.'

A thought occurred to her. She had been wrong about Lady Hester. But what of her other suspicion? All desire to weep receded, and she became aware of a heightened beating in her pulse. Should she ask? She must. She had to know!

'Then it was not Lord Delagarde himself who wished to—I mean, I had a notion that—'

'Gracious, my dear, banish it!' exclaimed Lady Hester, laughing. 'Laurie never thought of such a thing. He may have guessed what was in my mind, but it must be obvious to all of us that he would be frankly appalled at the suggestion.'

Maidie, her breast swelling now with quite a different emotion, was about to announce, in no uncertain terms, that such sentiments were entirely reciprocated. She was forestalled by the entrance of Lowick, who ushered in some morning visitors: Adela, Lady Shurland, and her brother.

Jumping up, Maidie went quickly to the window, sure that the traces of her recent distress must still be visible. She heard Lady Hester exchanging greetings behind her, and trusted that she would keep these unwelcome callers occupied for a moment or two to give her time to compose herself.

When at last she turned around, she saw that Adela had seated herself and was engaged in animated conversation with Lady Hester, in which the Worm bore no part, but sat silent beside her newly discovered kinswoman as if she depended upon her for protection. Eustace had remained standing, at a little distance from the ladies, and he was surveying Maidie with a look of pained disapproval.

She put up her chin, and stared back at him. She knew that an impartial observer might suppose her to be inordinately nice in her notions to be turning down such a promising-looking suitor. For Eustace Silsoe was a personable young man, fairer than his sister, the distinct angularity of his features lending him much more countenance than was apportioned to Adela. He was above average height, slender of body, and neat in his dress. Only his eyes, which were slate blue, detracted from these attributes. They were cold, and held, for the most part, a calculating look that could not but repel a female of Maidie's openness.

He crossed over to the window. 'I am sorry to see you flinch from my presence, Maidie.'

This was so far from the truth that Maidie relaxed. A convenient supposition, were she inclined to allow him to believe it. But her innate honesty revolted.

'If you must know,' she told him tartly, 'I turned away upon your entrance because I had just been in an upset, and I did not wish you or Adela to notice it.'

He looked discomfited. 'I am sorry to hear it. No doubt your sojourn in this house is not proving as agreeable to you as you had expected?'

'Not at all. I was merely labouring under a little misunderstanding.'

Recalling that it was due to Adela's spiteful words last

night that she had taken the notion in the first place, Maidie cast a glance across at her cousin. What she saw caused her to turn back to Eustace, with suspicion in her grey gaze.

'What does Adela mean by putting on these airs of friendship with Lady Hester?'

'It would scarcely serve our cause not to remain upon good terms with this household.' Eustace smiled, but it did not reach his eyes. 'You will forgive my plain speaking, I know, being so much an advocate for it yourself.'

'So much, Eustace, that I have no hesitation in telling you that you are both wasting your time. I shall not change my mind.'

'From what my sister has been saying,' he said urbanely, 'it seems as though you may well find it in you to be glad of my continuing interest.' He threw up a hand as she opened her mouth to retort. 'No, don't rip up at me, I beg. Content yourself with your quarrels with my sister. Now I, my dear Maidie, am not at all quarrelsome. I am also perfectly ready to permit you every sort of licence. I do most sincerely advise you to think well on it.'

'I have already thought,' Maidie said flatly, 'and I re-peat. I shall not change my mind.'

The blue eyes held hers, a glint in them that sent an involuntary shiver up Maidie's spine. She wanted to recoil, but she would not let him see that. She stood her ground, a slight lift to her brows pointing a question.

'Your ambition is most praiseworthy, Maidie,' Eustace purred softly.

Maidie stiffened. 'I do not take your meaning, Eustace.'

'Oh, I think you do.' Again that surface smile. 'Pray do not imagine that I blame you. I am, after all, as ambitious as you. But you would do well to consider. Such a prize might seem tempting. Should you succeed, it would be a triumph.'

There could be no doubt of his meaning now. Maidie resolutely closed her lips, but her bosom rose and fell rather rapidly. The insinuation rekindled the tumult of emotion that had only just died down. So Eustace also believed that she was setting her cap at Delagarde! She managed to keep her voice steady.

'You are mistaken, Eustace.'

He laughed very gently indeed. 'You can't think how relieved I would be if that were so. Or is it pride that makes you say it? He does not seem to favour you, does he?'

The headache that had been nagging at Maidie all morning now thumped painfully at her temples—which must account for the sudden lump in her throat that prevented her from making any reply.

'And if he did favour you,' Eustace went on, 'you would hardly be the first to have made the attempt to turn his affection to advantage. He is said to be impregnable, didn't you know? He has been on the town for more than a dozen years, and the most resolute and beauteous of maidens has failed to catch him. He prefers, it seems, to amuse himself with a string of mistresses.'

Did he say it to dissuade her from, as he thought, an attempt to attach the Viscount? Or was his intent to destroy any glimmer of respect or liking she might have felt for Delagarde? Fortunately, since she felt neither, his words fell upon deaf ears. It was, she was persuaded, the intensity of her headache that was lowering her spirits.

'That,' Maidie managed, with an assumption of nonchalance she was far from feeling, 'is nothing to me.'

'I am relieved to hear it.' Again he smiled, and the purr was back in his voice. 'You could not, I am persuaded, wish to be an object of interest to the gossips as they follow your progress—or lack of it. Nor could you wish for a husband who would make it his business to thwart your every move. Now I, on the other hand—'

'Thank you,' Maidie interrupted evenly, 'but you have already said it.'

'And shall again. Don't forget it, Maidie. I know what you want from life, and I am willing to give it to you. Why look further?'

She put up a hand to her aching head. 'I have told you, and I will tell you no more. I wish you will give up the notion, for I mean it, Eustace.'

'Now, yes,' he agreed. 'I will wager, however, that you will be glad enough to turn to me before too long.'

Maidie could tolerate no more. She turned from him and moved back to the centre of the room, addressing herself to Lady Hester. 'If you will excuse me, ma'am, my headache is a good deal worse. I am going to my room.'

'My poor child! Yes, yes, go up at once, Maidie. I will entertain Lady Shurland.'

'Thank you,' she said gratefully, and nodded at her cousin. 'Good day, Adela.'

Reaching her room, Maidie rang for her maid. Then she sank on to her bed, grasping one of the posts for support. It must be the disturbed night that was to blame, for she was a good deal upset by the encounter with Eustace. She had never before allowed herself to be distressed by anything the hateful creature said. It must be this ludicrous idea he had taken into his head—put into it, no doubt, by Adela!—that she was one of these designing females who had foisted herself on to the Viscount only so that she might somehow force him to wed her. And Eustace must know it was humdudgeon, for he had himself pointed out—as had Lady Hester—that Delagarde would do anything in the world rather than take her to wife!

Such a resurgence of the ache at her temples accompanied this thought that Maidie gripped the bedpost more strongly, and rested her brow against it. That was what came of thinking about Delagarde! Merely because the wretch infuriated her so much. Almost as much as did Eustace. And what had that creature meant about the gossips?

The entrance of Trixie into the room put this reflection out of her mind, for her maid, on hearing of her headache, bustled about, divesting her of everything save her shift and hustling her into bed. Hardly had Maidie got between sheets than Miss Wormley arrived, bearing a steaming concoction of herbs which she obliged Maidie to sip as she lay against a bank of pillows.

'Have they gone?' she asked of the Worm, who was sitting on the edge of her bed, once Trixie had departed.

'I do not know, my love, for I followed immediately upon your leaving the room, and ran down to desire the housekeeper to make up this tisane for you.'

Maidie reached out a hand, and her duenna clutched it. 'Oh, Worm, that horrid Eustace is still determined! Will nothing convince him that I won't marry him?'

The Worm clucked distressfully. 'Yet he cannot but be convinced when once you are betrothed, Maidie. We must hope that you will soon find yourself able to accept a respectable man.'

'Yes, but I don't think I will, Worm,' objected Maidie. 'Not as long as Delagarde insists upon keeping my fortune secret. I have not attracted anyone at all!'

A hiccuping sob sent the Worm into spasms of tutting, from which she was only rescued by a knock on the door, followed by the immediate entrance of Lady Hester.

'How is your headache? I declare, I am astonished not to have one myself after entertaining that precious pair! You poor child, to have been obliged to live with that woman.'

'Oh, Lady Hester, you can have no notion!' exclaimed the Worm before Maidie could answer. 'The way she used my poor lamb when first she came to East Dean!'

'How did she use her?' asked Lady Hester with interest.

'Don't, Worm,' Maidie cut in. 'It is nothing to the pur-pose now.'

But the Worm did not heed her, and she was feeling far too unwell to expostulate. It had been a difficult time. Ut-terly cast down by Great-uncle Reginald's passing, she had allowed herself, to her shame, to be bullied for several months. Indeed, she had only roused herself from her ap-athy at the threat of losing the Worm, when she had (in the words of Shurland) kicked up such a dust that he had overborne his wife and allowed the duenna to remain. The Worm had then joined Maidie in Adela's ill graces, and the two of them had laboured to rectify all the instances of neglect that the new Countess decided was the fault of the previous incumbent—mending linen, polishing and ti-dying, sorting endless papers through drawer after over-stuffed drawer—until the place was cleared to her satis-faction.

The worst cruelty had been the enforced dismantling of Great-uncle's observatory, and Maidie had wept and wept as she began carefully to pack everything away. It was Firmin, discovering her at this task, who had stopped it. He had told her, with an amiability that astonished Mai-die—for he had been forceful in his condemnation of the waste of resources on this hobby—that she might re-assemble it all if she chose. Only when she came of age a few weeks later had Maidie understood his reason. It also accounted for the sudden access of friendliness with which Adela had been behaving ever since.

But the change had come too late. Maidie had conceived a violent dislike of Lady Shurland, and her determination to be gone from East Dean into her own establishment— by whatever means—had become fixed.

'What a very unpleasant female, to be sure,' commented Lady Hester when the Worm came to the end of her disclosures. 'You did quite right to enlist Laurie's help instead, Maidie.'

'Yes, but I am not as certain of that,' said Maidie, recalling her grievance. 'No one has shown the smallest disposition to attach me, and unless Delagarde will allow news of my fortune to become generally known—'

'My dear child, you have scarce been in society a week,' protested Lady Hester. 'Indeed, last night was the first occasion upon which you may be said to have met any eligible young men.'

'But I didn't. At least, none of them talked to me for more than a moment. Except Mr Hampford and his friend, and they only used me to make an impression upon the other ladies.'

'It does not signify,' insisted Lady Hester. 'We have secured any number of engagements over the next few weeks, and you are bound to meet a good many gentlemen.'

An unpleasant recollection seized Maidie. What was it Eustace had said about the gossips watching to see if she should succeed with Delagarde? But how would they know? Unless he or Adela were to—

'It will avail me nothing to meet these gentlemen,' she burst out on the thought, 'if Adela and Eustace set it about that I am in a plot to entrap Delagarde!'

Lady Hester stared at her blankly. 'You are what?'

Maidie flushed. Her voice went gruff. 'I had not meant to say anything about it. Only Adela said it last night, and Eustace went on about it again today. It was that which set me thinking—because I knew I had no such scheme in mind—whether the boot might not be on the other leg. It had not occurred to me until just now that perhaps those two might tell it to the world.'

'Oh dear, oh dear,' uttered the Worm. 'They might well,

dear Lady Hester. It would be so like Lady Shurland to do such a thing.'

Maidie watched the frown gathering on Lady Hester's brow. She did not think, she *could* not think—! But, catching Maidie's eye, the older woman smiled.

'Do not be imagining that I have that idea in my head, child. I know well you had no such intention when you came to us. But this must be thought of.'

Maidie hesitated. But the question had to be asked. 'Do you think Lord Delagarde perhaps harbours that suspicion?'

The elder lady's laughter reassured her. 'Gracious, no! Laurie is not such a fool.' She drew a resolute breath. 'But the same cannot be said of the world at large. Something must be done.'

'You want me to keep my distance?' said Delagarde incredulously. 'What game are you playing, Aunt? If you think it escaped my notice that you had conceived the notion of bringing about a match between us, you are mistaken.'

'Is that why you have so determinedly been trying to prove me wrong?'

Delagarde eyed her with acute suspicion, leaning against the mantelshelf in the little parlour where she had dragged him on his return to the house. It was dusk, and no fire had been lit. The room was both shadowed and cold, and he was in need of dinner. But Aunt Hes had successfully diverted his attention from these evils. He did not know what she was about, but he was too well acquainted with her not to know that she was brewing mischief.

'I have not been trying to prove anything,' he said coolly. 'Whatever I have done, it has been in reaction to that wretched girl's activities.'

'Then it cannot be anything but a relief to you to be

requested to remain out of her vicinity for a few days,'
returned his great-aunt prosaically.

'To what purpose?' he asked obstinately.

Lady Hester laughed. 'Oh, very well. I might have
known there would be no driving you without giving a
reason.'

'So you might. But as I am still in the dark, I must
request you to answer my question.'

He watched her take a seat in the chair where Maidie
had sat that very first day, and the remaining light from
the window fell on her face. She looked serious, and Delagarde was surprised. Was there something to this after
all?

'I am afraid that Lady Shurland and her brother are li-
able to prove troublesome.'

As he listened to a fluent account of the day's events,
Delagarde found, to his annoyance, that his mind dwelled
stubbornly on the absurd supposition that Maidie's whole
enterprise had been designed as a plot to entrap him into
matrimony. That she had entertained for so much as an
instant the ridiculous notion that *he* had some idea of entrapping her served only to illustrate her innocence. Good
God, only a simpleton would suppose him to be motivated
by forty-five thousand pounds! His own fortune, in investments and the income from his estates, yielded considerably more than that in the space of a year. She did
not know that, of course, but he would have supposed that
his whole attitude to her must indicate how mad she was
to think of it.

But this accusation that came from Lady Shurland and
her brother—quite as idiotic!—persisted in his head long
after he had agreed to Lady Hester's scheme to frustrate
them. She was of the opinion that they would not mention
the matter if they could see that nothing was to be gained
by it, and no one could make anything of such a rumour

if the parties concerned were rarely seen together. A period of this, and society would have formed their own views, which would render rumour profitless to the scandalmongers.

Delagarde was ready enough to fall in with the scheme, even if he still suspected that Aunt Hes had a wider purpose in mind than she had told him. It was no pleasure to him, he told himself, to be obliged to waste his time—and do violence to his temper!—in keeping Maidie from committing every kind of imprudence. There was as little hardship in giving up attendance at a Saturday concert evening, instead spending time with his cronies at Boodle's, as there was in driving out of town on Monday for a couple of nights to witness a prize fight instead of attending two insipid evening parties. Not that Delagarde would have thought of abandoning his pleasures on Maidie's behalf, had he not conceived it to be his duty to carry out the responsibility he had taken on.

He was naturally delighted to be let off his leash, so to speak, and if he once or twice found his imagination dwelling on what trouble Maidie might have got herself into without him, it was not to be wondered at. He supposed it was equally unsurprising that he should be thinking so much of that insane suggestion of Maidie's trying to entrap him, because he must wonder whether his absence had discouraged, as it was hoped, Silsoe and Lady Shurland from putting such a rumour about.

No one would believe it, now that he and Maidie had not appeared together in society for the better part of a week.

Encountering her at the breakfast table on his return to town on the Wednesday morning, Delagarde found Maidie apparently disinclined to converse with him beyond the commonplace. He had been tempted to inquire about her progress. Beginning perhaps with how she was so far enjoying the Season, and—because her looked-for departure must depend upon the question!—whether she had yet acquired any beaux. But somehow the words stuck in his throat. Maidie did not linger, and the opportunity was lost. Delagarde sought his answers of Aunt Hes.

'She is doing very much better, Laurie, now that you are not there to tease her into saying and doing the wrong thing. She is determined not to gain a reputation for ill breeding, and she tries very hard to think before she speaks. I am excessively proud of her efforts, and I believe she is settling down quite nicely. The best thing you can do, Laurie, is to leave well alone!'

'I thank you,' he said sardonically. 'I need not ask, then, whether she has gathered around her a bevy of admirers?'

Lady Hester looked mischievous. 'As to that, it would be difficult to judge. She is certainly regarded as something of an oddity, but—'

'That does not surprise me!'

'But,' continued his great-aunt airily, 'it is too early to say whether any gentleman is growing particular in his attentions.'

'But there are attentions?' asked Delagarde, despising himself for his interest, and conceiving a most disagreeable feeling of animosity towards some unknown young man. He dismissed it, realising that, in the role of guardian thrust upon him, he would wish to assure himself of the worth of any pretender to Maidie's hand.

To his intense annoyance, Lady Hester chose not to answer this, instead reiterating her desire that he should maintain his distance for a further period, possibly until their own upcoming party at the Charles Street house.

'But that is in April! Am I to hold aloof for yet two weeks more?'

Lady Hester's brows rose. 'But you said positively that you don't wish to dance attendance on Maidie day after day.'

'Of course I don't,' Delagarde snapped, irrationally annoyed by this reminder. 'But I am her sponsor. People will think it excessively odd.'

His great-aunt regarded him with a disquieting glint that savoured strongly to Delagarde of amusement. 'Dear me. We seem to be destined to make tongues wag, whatever we do. Let us leave matters as they are until next week, then.'

With this mitigation Delagarde opted to express content, and was irritated to find himself still irked by the restriction.

Early on Friday evening, however, while engaged with Corringham and Riseley at Boodle's, he received a summons from his great-aunt, asking him to return home at once on a matter of extreme urgency. Beset by a number of hideous possibilities as he walked swiftly from St James's Street to his house, Delagarde was annoyed to realise that they all involved Maidie in trouble. His pace hastening unconsciously, he arrived in Charles Street, and ran up the steps.

The door opened as he reached the top. Lowick had evidently been on the watch for him. Good God, it must certainly be serious!

'Lady Hester is awaiting you in the downstairs drawing-room, my lord.'

Delagarde crossed the hall and thrust open the door. His eyes swept the room, and took in one salient fact. Maidie was not there. He looked from Miss Wormley's agitated countenance to that of Lady Hester, both ladies having risen on his entrance and started towards him.

'What the devil is amiss, Aunt Hes?'

Lady Hester put out her hands and he grasped them strongly. 'Maidie is missing!'

'What?'

'She is missing, Laurie!'

'Good God! How can she be missing? What in Hades can you mean? You have not mislaid her, I suppose!'

She disengaged her hands. 'Don't be silly, Laurie! This is serious. We are engaged at the theatre tonight, and she knows it. But she has not been seen since early this morning.'

Taken aback, Delagarde stared at her. He took in that she was in evening dress, a turquoise silk crossed at the bosom, and a flowing lace cap on her greying locks. For a moment, he was conscious of a rise of anxiety. But common sense reasserted itself immediately.

'This must be nonsense. There might be any number of reasons why she has not been seen. Are you certain she is not in the house?'

'We have searched everywhere,' said Lady Hester positively. 'Yet no one saw her leave, and she has not taken her maid, or a footman.'

Delagarde frowned. 'But does she know that she must do so in London? Knowing Maidie, it would not surprise me if she had not even thought of it.'

He had forgotten Miss Wormley, but she broke in all at once, wringing her hands painfully. 'That is nothing to the purpose, my lord! I am dreadfully afraid that the worst has happened.'

'What worst?' Delagarde asked, unimpressed.

'Mr Silsoe has kidnapped her, I am sure of it!'

This was so ridiculous that Delagarde had to laugh. 'Not if he is in his right mind!' He saw that Miss Wormley was unconvinced, and clicked an impatient tongue. 'For God's sake, ma'am, it is a criminal offence! Do you suggest the fellow is desperate enough to take so crazy a measure?'

'There is no saying what he might do,' uttered the Worm. 'Aided and abetted by his sister, too!'

'Come, come, ma'am. Lady Shurland is scarce likely to lend herself to such a scheme. As well accuse Shurland himself! I never heard such nonsense!'

'There, Ida, you see,' said Lady Hester, leading the other lady to a chair. 'Did I not say the same? Now, sit you down, my dear, and try to compose yourself. Delagarde will at once go in search of Maidie and—'

'The devil I will!' Both the older women regarded him reproachfully, and he threw up his hands. 'This is insane! You cannot expect me to scour London for that wretched girl. Why, she might be anywhere. How the devil should I know where to start looking?'

'You are responsible for her, Laurie,' said Lady Hester severely.

'That is debatable.'

'At any rate, you have accepted responsibility for her.'

'How can you say that, when you have enjoined me to keep away these many days?'

'That has nothing to do with it,' argued his great-aunt. 'At a time like this, you must remember your obligation.'

'Obligation!' He threw his eyes to heaven. 'Oh, very well, I will go in search of her. But ten to one she will walk in the moment I have left the place.'

He stalked out to the hall just as Lowick answered a knock at the door. As he had confidently predicted, Maidie stood upon the threshold. It might have been supposed that this sudden return, relieving him of the necessity of setting out on what he had been convinced would turn out to be a wild goose chase, would have at once had a calming effect upon his ruffled temper. Instead, it threw him into such a flame that he pounced on her furiously as she entered the house.

'There you are! What the devil do you mean by it, you

impossible wretch? How dare you go off without letting
anyone know?' Seizing her arm, he marched her uncere-
moniously across the hall, pouring the vials of his wrath
upon her hapless head with unabated vigour. 'Do you realise that everyone is worried to death about you? Here have
I been dragged from my club to scour the town for you,
and you walk in, as cool as you please!' He thrust her into
the drawing-room, and let her go. 'There, you see! Did I
not say so?'

'Oh, Maidie, thank heaven!' fluttered her duenna, rushing to enfold the truant in her arms. 'I have been sick with
dread!'

'Good gracious, Maidie, what a turn you have given us!
Where have you been?'

Maidie, stunned by these unprecedented attacks, and
thoroughly unnerved to find Delagarde awaiting her, en-
dured in bemused silence until the fuss abated. It was perhaps fortunate that Delagarde chose to behave to her in
the manner which their early association had made familiar, for she recovered more readily than she might otherwise have done from a flood of consciousness at seeing
him so unexpectedly.

'I have only been to a lecture,' she said, when she was
finally able to edge in a word.

Dead silence greeted this statement, all three staring at
her blankly. The Worm was the first to recover, as though
it took her a moment or two to take it in after the absurd
fears she had been indulging.

'Oh, a lecture,' she repeated, and nodded as if that made
all right.

'A lecture!' repeated Delagarde scoffingly. 'You do not
expect us to believe that!'

'What sort of a lecture?' asked Lady Hester.

'At the Royal Society,' Maidie said, frowning. What in
the world was the matter with them? 'I am sorry to be so

late, but I got into a discussion afterwards with the speaker, and some of his colleagues—they all knew of Great-uncle Reginald, is it not wonderful?—and I lost all count of time. One of them was so kind as to find me a hackney, and I came home as soon as I could.'

She perceived that neither Delagarde nor Lady Hester seemed to understand her, and she frowned. 'But what is the matter? A lecture at the Royal Society. They hold them regularly, I understand. But it was quite by chance that I heard of this one. It was to be given by a man who is acquainted with Herschel, so of course I could not resist.'

Delagarde blinked. 'This sounds to me like pure fantasy. You are glib enough with this ridiculous explanation, but I wish you will tell us the truth.'

Maidie opened her eyes at him. 'But I have told you the truth.' She turned to Lady Hester. 'I do apologise, dear ma'am. I had forgot that we are going to the theatre. I shall run up and change this moment. Do not hold dinner for me!'

Turning, she dashed out of the room. When Miss Wormley would have followed her, Delagarde detained her.

'See if you can get the truth out of her. I am not such a fool as to be put off with this cock-and-bull tale of a lecture at the Royal Society!'

To his astonishment, the Worm nodded vigorously. 'Oh, my lord, nothing could be more likely. I wonder I did not think of it for myself. I wish she had told me. But never mind. All's well that ends well. Excuse me, my lord. I will help her to change so that she will not delay Lady Hester.'

Delagarde watched her rush off after her charge, and turned a fulminating eye on his great-aunt. 'It is all very well for you to sit there laughing, Aunt Hes. Either this is the most arrant nonsense, or the girl is quite off her head!'

Lady Hester mastered her mirth, dabbing at the corners of her eyes. 'I don't think so, Laurie. But be sure I will get to the bottom of this. I promise you, I am quite as intrigued as you are.'

But Delagarde did not inform his great-aunt of what was really troubling him. Whatever she chose to do, he was himself determined to get a sensible answer. Informing Lady Hester that his exile was at an end, and that he would himself escort them to the theatre, he went off to his own rooms to change from his topboots, buckskins and frock coat into the more appropriate raiment of black satin knee-breeches and a blue cloth coat over a Florentine waistcoat. He was seething with suspicion. For there seemed to him to be but one explanation of Maidie's extraordinary conduct. Why she should be at pains to make up such a patently false tale to cover her tracks, he could not imagine. Unless it was that the gentleman with whom she had no doubt had an assignation was one of whom she knew well he would violently disapprove!

No opportunity to get Maidie alone presented itself until the first interval, and then Delagarde's plan to detach her from the party was frustrated. First, upon the curtain's falling on the first act, by two of Lady Hester's acquaintance who descended upon them from a nearby box. Second, by the entrance of Eustace Silsoe. He had come, he said, from his sister, who requested her dear Mary to come to her box for a few moments.

There was little Maidie desired less than to leave the box on the arm of her despised suitor, but she had agreed with Lady Hester that it was politic to allow the world to suppose that good relations existed between the two households. She rose, therefore, and shook out the peach muslin petticoats to the simple gown with a plain neck and three-quarter sleeves, which was augmented only by an embroidered Norwich shawl disposed across her elbows, and a neat lace cap. Accepting Eustace's arm, she allowed him to lead her from Delagarde's box into the corridor.

She regretted it at once, for Eustace told her he had no intention of taking her to Adela's box.

'We will go out into the foyer, Maidie, and stroll up and down together.'

'Why?' she asked forthrightly.

He turned his feline smile upon her. 'Why, so that people may suppose that we are enjoying one another's company. All you are required to do is to smile, and nod, and look as if you are interested in what I have to say to you.'

'Oh, is that all?' She preceded him through a door into the open area behind the boxes that gave access to the stairs and the balconies. 'And suppose I do not choose to do any of those things?'

Eustace gave his gentle laugh, and leaned closer to speak almost into her ear. 'I shall talk to you with an earnest air, which will give an appearance of even greater intimacy.'

Maidie stiffened, and tried to pull away from him. 'You are hateful! If you think I am to be persuaded by such tactics as these—!'

'Oh, I have long given up the idea of persuading you. I am merely laying a trail for future investigation.'

'I do not understand what you can possibly mean,' Maidie told him, frowning. 'I do not wish to continue this conversation. Please take me back to Lady Hester.'

'On no account.'

Instinct urged Maidie to strike him, or to wrench herself from his grasp, and run incontinently away. But a moment's reflection told her that this would be playing into his hands. There were far too many persons standing or strolling about. Her short sojourn in town had taught her that the fracas that such a course would create could only result in undesirable attention and gossip. She cast a quick look around, hoping to see a face she recognised. Perhaps she might accost another party so that her walk with Eustace would seem less particular. But she knew none of them. She heaved a despairing sigh, and then rescue came in a familiar voice that spoke in her immediate rear.

'Ah, there you are,' said Delagarde.

Maidie turned quickly, and found the Viscount was behind her, holding out a glass. Her heart leapt—with gratitude!—for his arrival could not have been more opportune. Then she caught what he was saying, and realised it had been deliberate.

'I have procured you some water, Maidie. Are you feeling a little more the thing?' He gave Eustace Silsoe a nod. 'Kind of you, sir, to bring her out of that stuffy atmosphere. But you may safely leave her in my charge.'

To Maidie's intense admiration, he then utterly ignored Eustace, whose urbanity was so evidently shaken that he quite forgot to hide his chagrin. She felt Delagarde take her arm as he guided her to one of the straight chairs that were set here and there against the wall.

'Sit down, and drink that. Give me your fan.'

She held it out to him, and sipped at the water, watching him open her fan and gently ply it up and down before her face. Out of the corner of her eye, she saw Eustace hover for a moment, irresolute. Then, apparently accepting defeat, he turned and walked quickly away. Quite forgetting the terms upon which they had earlier parted, and the disagreeable feelings she had experienced, Maidie smiled up at the Viscount.

'That was so clever of you, Lord Delagarde! Thank you.'

He grinned. 'Duplicity, Maidie. Very useful in certain social situations.'

'I see it is,' she laughed. 'I could not think how to get away from him without making a scene.'

'Well, thank God you didn't!'

She surveyed him candidly. 'You did not expect it of me, I dare say. That I would refrain, I mean. But I have learned a great deal since I came to town. For instance, I know that if you continue to fan me, and I pretend to be faint, no one will approach us.'

'Very good, Maidie,' approved Delagarde, a quizzical gleam in his eye. 'Dare I hope, then, that it is safe to ask you any awkward questions?'

'If you mean that you expect me to lose my temper—'

'Temper, Maidie? But you do not have one.'

An involuntary giggle slipped out. 'Well, I don't—except when you say something to send me up into the boughs.'

He laughed. 'Perhaps I had better reserve my questions until we are at home.'

Maidie gave him her direct look. 'But now you have intrigued me. What do you want to ask me?'

'Shall I risk it?'

A gleam of fun lit her features. Delagarde blinked, as some unnamed emotion flitted through his chest, like a flashing fire. The thought struck him all at once that in their short acquaintance, she had rarely smiled at him.

'It might make a test, do you not think? If I can keep my temper, I must be growing more tolerant of yours!'

He relieved her of the glass and took her hand, lifting her to her feet. 'That may be too much of a test. Besides, they are calling the second act. We must go back.' He handed the empty glass to the boy who was inviting the patrons to return to the auditorium, and gave Maidie his arm.

'But what do you want to know?' she asked him as they entered the little corridor.

'The truth about your escapade today,' he said, capitulating, as his desire to find out came back—more strongly, if anything.

'But I told you—'

'Don't fob me off with this lecture,' Delagarde cut in hastily. 'Had you an assignation?'

Maidie stopped dead in the corridor, removing her hand from his arm and turning to face him. 'Had I a what?'

The Viscount tried to read her face, but the dimly lit corridor made it a pale shadow. 'You are angry already.'

'No, I am not. I just don't think I can have heard you correctly.'

'Come here!' he said, taking her arm without force, and moving her near the door of his box where a glass-covered candelabra threw light on to one side of her countenance.

Maidie stared up at him, confused by his attitude, and acutely aware of his hand still grasping her arm above the elbow. He was behaving oddly, most unlike his usual way with her. Perhaps his absence this last week had mellowed him towards her, for she knew well how provoking he found her. If she had wondered at the reason for his holding aloof, she was too much relieved to care. It was not surprising that he had loomed a trifle too large in her mind, for she was not to know when he might take it into his head to surprise her with a show of attention. She had been glad, of course she had, to be spared the sort of strictures that had been her portion earlier tonight. But this new conduct was unprecedented. She had never before supposed him to be possessed of such charm as he had just displayed. Those *affaires* became even more readily believable!

'An assignation, Maidie,' he said, quite softly. 'Don't lie to me, if you please. Did you have an assignation?'

Blankly she took in what he meant. It seemed so incredible a question that she could not think why he would ask it. Besides, as she asked in astonishment, 'With whom?'

'How the devil should I know?' But the impatience was instantly suppressed. 'Come, the truth! Did you go to meet some man?'

'Yes, I did go to meet a man,' she agreed.

His grip tightened. 'I knew it!'

'But it was not an assignation, Delagarde. I do not know anyone with whom to have one.'

'I don't know who you may have met this last week,' he objected, releasing her at last. 'I am more concerned with whom you met secretly today.'

Maidie's gaze widened. 'I think you have run mad. I went, hoping very much to meet this man—not secretly at all, but in the presence of a number of others. And, of course, to hear him talk about Herschel.'

'Herschel?'

'The astronomer. Surely even you must have heard of Herschel? He discovered a new planet.'

But Delagarde was gazing down at her in the liveliest astonishment, not unmixed with disbelief. 'You are surely not expecting me to believe that you are interested in astronomy?'

Maidie was so surprised that she merely gazed at him. 'Why are you staring at me in such puzzlement?'

Her brows went up. 'In what else but astronomy should I be interested, pray?'

With which, Maidie turned and re-entered the box, leaving Delagarde utterly mystified. He followed her into the box and shut the door just as the curtain rose on the second act. He had no more than a passing interest in what was going forward on the stage. He had seen Sheridan's comedy often before, and there was nothing exceptional about this Mr Puff's delivery to take his attention from Maidie's disclosure.

He was at first inclined to dismiss it as an attempt to throw dust in his eyes. But he recalled that once or twice there had been instances of similar oddity. To do with the great-uncle! Good God, was it that which had been the former Lord Shurland's abiding interest? But that he should have passed it on to Maidie seemed altogether too odd—even for her. What young female would choose to spend her time raking the heavens? He would not believe it!

Not one of the ladies of his set—not even those with whom he had enjoyed an intimate association—had shown the slightest inclination to take an interest in anything beyond the latest fashions, their male admirers, and those scandalous tidbits that disgraced one of their number from time to time. True, there was the blue-stocking coterie, who moved in circles other than his own. One knew them, yes, but if one had no turn for verse, nor any literary leanings, such ladies were apt to turn their shoulder all too quickly.

His experience accounted in some measure for his single state. The majority of debutantes were insipid, and very silly, and he had never been tempted to exchange a convenient bachelorhood for a life spent listening at home to the sort of inanity one met with everywhere in society. He preferred on the whole the company of his friends, who could converse sensibly on a number of topics. He had of necessity resigned himself to his eventual fate of marriage to some featherheaded creature, who would fulfil her role with taste and elegance, behave with the modesty befitting his Viscountess, and do as she was told.

But that was for the future. No, he knew too much of women to be expected to swallow this tale of Maidie's. She was unusual, had been brought up oddly. But that a girl of her years could go off to attend a lecture at the Royal Society—! No, and no again.

Delagarde resolved not to question Maidie further on the subject, for time would inevitably expose the truth.

He regretted this decision within three days when he came down to dinner on Monday evening, arrayed very correctly in a sky blue coat of satin with matching knee-breeches and a discreetly floral waistcoat of corded silk, his cravat artistically arranged and his dark locks brushed back in ordered waves, ready to escort the two ladies to a ball—Maidie's first. Naturally he could not absent himself.

In the drawing-room he found only his great-aunt, resplendent in a grey silk gown topped by a half-robe of silver netting with a scattering of feathers in her elegant coiffure. Delagarde was not surprised to find that Maidie had not yet come down. In his experience, young ladies on the eve of their first ball were generally late, their attention taken up by last-minute changes of mind, and a great deal of unnecessary titivation. Footsteps on the stairs at last signalled her arrival, and he turned to the door, not averse to seeing how she looked when tricked out at her finest.

But it was Miss Wormley who came hurrying into the drawing-room, a handkerchief held to her nose, and an unsteady hand at her brow. Broken accents assailed his ears.

'Oh, Lady Hester! Oh, my lord!'

Lady Hester rose hastily. 'What is it, Ida?'

Delagarde almost snorted. There was no need to ask what was this emergency. 'Don't tell me! Is she feeling sick or something? I suppose she is too nervous to come down.'

'No, indeed, nothing of that sort. I wish—oh, if only I had not been laid down upon my bed! I got up, you see, for I felt I must make the effort, if only to wish dearest

Maidie well. And—' The duenna transferred one hand to her bosom, drawing a painful breath.

'For heaven's sake, Ida! What is it you wish to tell us?'

The most dreadful presentiment rushed into Delagarde's mind. She could not! Not on an occasion like this! Forboding gripped him.

'You are not going to tell us she was not there?'

'Oh, not again, surely!' gasped Lady Hester.

But Miss Wormley's woeful demeanour was answer enough. She quavered into speech again. 'You may be sure I sent Trixie rushing to find her immediately. Indeed, I berated her soundly for not alerting me earlier.' She sniffed and shook her head. 'Trixie could not find her. Lady Hester, my lord, there is no concealing it from you. Maidie is not in the house.'

Chapter Six

A wave of intense emotion overcame Delagarde. He raised clenched fists to heaven. 'What did I do, Lord? Tell me, what did I do?'

'It is of no use to rail at the Almighty, Laurie.'

But Aunt Hes could not, even in this extremity, he noted with displeasure, refrain from indulging her amusement. He was still more irritated by the tendency of Maidie's Worm to behave like a watering pot, sniffing into her handkerchief.

'I wish you will not waste your tears, Miss Wormley. There is no reason to suppose that anything worse has happened to the wench than befell her the other day. She has merely a lamentable disregard for the time.'

'I am not crying,' protested Miss Wormley, energetically blowing her nose. 'Indeed, I am quite cross with Maidie!'

'Poor Ida has had the misfortune to contract a cold in the head, Laurie,' explained Lady Hester, and moved to pat the other woman's shoulder. 'I do think you ought to go back to bed, Ida. There is nothing you can do, after all.'

But Miss Wormley shook her head vehemently. 'I could

not rest, dear Lady Hester. But I dare say his lordship is quite right, and she will come in at any moment. It is too bad of Maidie, indeed it is. I shall be very tempted to scold her when she returns.'

'Save your breath,' recommended Delagarde grimly. 'I shall be only too happy to perform that office on behalf of the three of us.'

But as time passed, with no sign of the errant Maidie, he began to feel an uncommon degree of anxiety. He had refused to set off in search of her, convinced that a little patience would reward them all. Besides, where would one begin? It had been dark already when she was found to be missing. She was unlikely to be discovered in the streets, even had he taken out his phaeton and driven around in the hopes of seeing her. A footman had been dispatched at once to the Royal Society, but had returned empty-handed with the intelligence that the place was shut up and a billboard outside indicated that no lecture had been held that day. Delagarde had vetoed Aunt Hes's suggestion that they should send round to various houses to discover whether she was visiting. As far as any of them knew, she had made no particular friends as yet, and her disposition was not sociable. Why would she take it into her head to call upon any of the matrons she had met?

'Besides, we do not wish to give rise to unnecessary talk.' A sentiment with which Aunt Hes had been in agreement. For the same reason, he would not allow Miss Wormley to send to the Shurland household. The last thing they wanted was to arouse comment and question from that quarter!

'But if there is anyone who may know her whereabouts,' had argued the duenna unhappily, 'I am afraid it is Mr Silsoe.'

'You are not again suggesting that he has kidnapped her?'

'My lord, I do not know what to think! Maidie told me that he will not accept her rejection, and after his conduct to her the other night at the theatre, she did not know what she was to do to discourage him further.'

But Lady Hester had been inclined to support the Viscount. 'He would be extremely ill advised to attempt anything of that nature, my dear Ida.'

Between them, they had calmed the duenna's fears, and Delagarde had been relieved when she was at last persuaded to retire to her bed. Her cold having gained upon her, Miss Wormley had sat sneezing and spluttering in great discomfort, and had appeared relieved at last to give in to Lady Hester's pleadings.

'Have no fear, Ida. We will come to tell you the moment we have news of Maidie.'

With this assurance, the duenna had allowed herself to be contented, and she had departed, sped on her way by Lady Hester's promise that a hot brick and a soothing drink would be sent up as soon as may be.

'And I will have a tray brought to you a little later, in case you feel yourself able to swallow a few mouthfuls.'

Left alone with his great-aunt, Delagarde found himself the target of her intelligent and questioning gaze. He frowned. 'Well?'

Lady Hester smiled. 'You are hungry, Laurie, and it is affecting your temper. We will not wait dinner any longer. Ring the bell.'

He complied, but retorted acidly that it was not lack of food that was affecting his temper. 'Where can the little wretch have got to?'

'I know no more than you, my dear boy. But it will not help to starve ourselves.' She added, with something of her usual mischievous twinkle, 'Nor to pace about in that restless fashion. Anyone would suppose you to be anxious.'

Delagarde flung himself ostentatiously into a chair. 'There! Does that satisfy you? And you have very little power of observation if you suppose me to be suffering from anxiety. It is nothing to me if the wench chooses to behave in this impossible fashion. I am only irritated by the inconvenience of being obliged to arrive late at this ball.'

By nine o'clock, however, with dinner already over, it was Delagarde, unable to sit with any enjoyment over his port, who rejoined his great-aunt in the drawing-room and suggested she should send round a note to this evening's hostess.

'You had better tell her that Maidie is indisposed.'

'Thank you, Laurie, but I believe I am capable of making up an appropriate tale that will satisfy Lady Pinmore.'

Delagarde watched her seat herself at the little escritoire in the corner, and draw a sheaf of crested paper towards her. He was obliged to mend a pen for her to use, which he did with fingers that seemed not to wish to obey him. He cursed, seizing hold of the paring knife as the quill split a second time.

'Gently, Laurie,' chided his aunt, regarding him in some amusement. 'If you cannot wait with any degree of patience, why don't you change and go out to your club?'

'If you think,' said Delagarde, savagely attacking the quill, 'that I am budging from this house until that cursed wench is safely back inside it, you have a very odd idea of my character.' He handed her the mended pen. 'Here.'

Lady Hester accepted it, smiling to herself as she dipped the end in the ink-pot. Delagarde caught the smile, and swore under his breath, flinging away. How she could sit there, plainly amused, when none of them had the remotest idea where Maidie was or what she might be doing, he was unable to understand. That she had forgotten the engagement for tonight seemed incredible. What activity could possibly take her attention so thoroughly from the excitement of a first ball?

It was this thought that was fuelling his apprehension. He could not give credence to the suggestion of kidnapping, but there were other, equally unpleasant possibilities that he had no difficulty in believing. He did not give them voice, but his imagination played so upon him that he was moved to ring the bell for Lowick to bring up some liquid refreshment to fortify his mind.

It did not help. The hair-raising visions worsened as time wore on. There seemed to be no end to the fates that could overtake a young girl out on her own in the darkness: she'd had an accident—been knocked over by a carriage and taken to one of the common hospitals; she had been attacked in the street by footpads, and left to fend for herself with no money; she had found herself in a seedy quarter of town where some evil person had practiced God knew what deceit upon her—sold her into slavery, drugged her or lured her into a life of prostitution.

This last thought caused him to jerk up his wrist and swallow the rest of the contents of his glass in one gulp. Crossing the room, he seized the decanter that Lowick had brought up on his demand over an hour ago.

'Is that really necessary, Laurie?' came from his great-aunt, who had contented herself with a single glass of wine.

He turned with the brandy decanter poised over his empty glass. He glanced at the clock on the mantel. 'It is nearly midnight, Aunt Hes. That girl is out there somewhere—alone. I only hope that nothing dreadful may have befallen her, because that will make it impossible for me to strangle her when she does come home!'

He saw that Lady Hester was looking pale, her eyes troubled, and there was no trace of amusement in her voice. 'Laurie, if anything untoward has happened to Maidie, I shall never be able to forgive myself for having encouraged her to live here.'

Laying down the decanter and his glass, he crossed to her, and held out his hand. She put hers into it and he clasped it strongly.

'Don't look like that, Aunt Hes! In the morning, I shall go straight round to Bow Street.' But at that very instant, his ears caught the sound that he had been unconsciously awaiting all evening. 'Horses! It must be a carriage!'

Dropping Lady Hester's hand, Delagarde flung across the room and strode down the hall, forestalling the sleepy porter who was just climbing out of his chair. He threw open the front door. A ponderous old-fashioned coach had stopped outside the house, and a servant was in the act of letting down the steps as the carriage door opened and Delagarde caught sight of Maidie within.

He ran down as Maidie bent forward to descend. Acting on sheer impulse, the Viscount reached into the coach, seized a startled Maidie by the waist, and swung her down into the road. He took a brief look inside the carriage, found it empty, and turned, grasping her by the shoulders.

'Where have you been?' he demanded urgently. 'Whose chaise is this? Are you hurt at all?' His eyes scanned her face by the light of the carriage lamp. She was staring up at him in mute astonishment. 'Don't look at me like that, Maidie! If you knew—!' He broke off, suppressing a strong inclination to shake her, or—discovering the thought with a sensation of surprise—to pull her into a safe embrace. He did neither, instead turning her round to face the Charles Street mansion. 'Go inside! My aunt is extremely anxious.'

These words caused Maidie to run up the steps, beset by a surge of guilt that overshadowed the complete amazement that had gripped her at Delagarde's behaviour. If he had blasted her with invective, she could have understood it. But to be seized in that way! It had given her the oddest sensation of helplessness, and made her heart start up a tattoo in her chest in the most uncomfortable way. It was hammering still as she entered the house, but the sight of Lady Hester's face put all thoughts of Delagarde to flight. Oh, she was palpably to blame! Poor Lady Hester had been seriously disturbed. She blurted out a somewhat confused apology.

'Dear ma'am—so unkind of me—I am so sorry! You have been worried—Delagarde too! Truly, I did not mean to be so late. I had not realised the time, nor indeed intended to stay so long—forgive me!—but it was altogether too reminiscent of my times with Great-uncle. I forgot everything!'

She found herself enveloped in a hug, and was quite shocked to find, when the elder lady released her, that tears stood in Lady Hester's eyes. Her voice was decidedly shaky.

'Maidie, Maidie, you must not do this! Perhaps you don't realise how much violence you cause to the feelings of others, but I assure you that we have all been distressingly upset with worry over your safety.'

Maidie's brows creased with a puzzled frown as she allowed herself to be shepherded into the drawing-room without protest. 'But, dear ma'am, did not the Worm tell you?'

'My dear Maidie, poor Ida is quite ill. And she has been more concerned than either of us, I dare say, though I was able to persuade her to seek her bed.'

'I don't understand,' Maidie said in a troubled tone. 'I told Worm this morning what I intended. I did so especially because of the last time.'

'What did you tell her?' came from Delagarde, suddenly entering the room behind them. 'And who the devil is this man Wilberfoss you have been visiting?'

To Maidie's consternation, his voice speaking unexpectedly in her immediate rear caused that disconcerting race to start up again in her pulse. She tried to gather herself together, and was glad of the respite afforded by Lady Hester's question.

'Who did you say, Laurie?'

'Sir Granville Wilberfoss,' he reiterated, closing the door and walking across to take up a stance before the fireplace. 'She has just come home in his carriage.'

'Well, thank heaven she was in a carriage! I was more than half afraid that she was walking in the streets.'

'How—how did you know his name?' Maidie asked of Delagarde, frowning a little to cover her own unease.

'I asked the servant, of course. Will you have the goodness to answer my question?'

The stirrings of irritation in Delagarde's voice had the curious effect of calming her a little. 'About Sir Granville? He is a friend of my great-uncle. He heard that I was in town, from one of the fellows I met at the lecture the other day, and he invited me to visit him.'

'Did he, indeed? And the entertainment he offered you was sufficiently enthralling to induce you to miss your first ball, was it?' demanded Delagarde sardonically.

'The ball!' Conscience-stricken, Maidie's gaze went to Lady Hester. For the first time, she realised that both Delagarde and his great-aunt were in evening dress, and remembrance of the engagement came back to her in full flood.

'Oh, ma'am, I am so sorry! Lady Pinmore's ball! I had forgot all about it!'

'Never mind the ball,' answered her kind hostess. 'You are safe, and that is all that matters.'

'Is it indeed? I suppose it is nothing that she has spent the evening quite alone with God knows what sort of a fellow? Very pretty conduct, upon my word!'

Maidie found herself relaxing at this further evidence of the Viscount's rising temper. She was not in the least afraid of what he might say in this mood. It had been that strangely unpredictable conduct outside that had unnerved her. Besides, his complaint was ludicrous.

She giggled. 'Do you suspect him of making love to me, Delagarde? But I told you he was Great-uncle's friend.'

'Oh,' said the Viscount blankly. 'Then he is not a young man?'

'He is venerable, rather.'

'Even so. It is not unknown for elderly gentlemen to take advantage of very young females. You could have been in grave danger.'

'Humdudgeon! We were quite otherwise engaged.' Turning from him, Maidie pressed Lady Hester's hand. 'Dear ma'am, you have every right to be angry with me. But I did not mean to remain all the evening. I promise you I had every intention of coming back in time when I first set out. Only—' turning again to Delagarde, the light entering her face as the recollection of her activities came in upon her '—it *was* enthralling, you see! I have not enjoyed myself so much this age. At first we were merely talking, but very soon we found ourselves deep in observations. For you must know that Sir Granville has fashioned a telescope that is even more powerful than the last one Great-uncle had made.' Her eyes shone. 'We were able to see so deeply into space—such colours! So many clusters together! Stars that I thought I knew so well—and yet now I realise that I was scarcely seeing them at all. Oh, it was breathtaking! I could hardly bear to tear myself away.'

She stopped, becoming aware of the extraordinary expression on Delagarde's face. He was, in fact, staggered. Was this Maidie? She was a creature transformed. She had as well have been at the ball, and been talking of that in this fashion. But, no. There was more than enthusiasm here. Maidie was bursting with happiness! Such a pang shot through him at this thought that he was for several moments quite unable to speak. It was perhaps fortunate that Aunt Hes claimed her attention, for he was thrown into disorder. Until it occurred to him why he should experience the feeling. Here had he been, picturing to himself the most hideous disasters that might have befallen Maidie, and all the time she had been happily engaged with a—

'—*telescope!*' burst from him on the thought, in a voice of strong derision.

Maidie, in the middle of renewed apologies to Lady Hester, broke off abruptly and turned to him in surprise. 'Why, what is the matter?'

Delagarde emitted a mirthless laugh. 'You can ask that? You have been missing for several hours. No one had the slightest clue as to your whereabouts—'

'But you did! I told Worm!'

'—and quite aside from being kept waiting for our dinner for an hour and more, we have all of us been thrown into a needless agony of apprehension about your safety.'

'Humdudgeon! You should have known that—'

'So that instead of enjoying ourselves at one of the Season's most promising entertainments, we have been obliged to pace the floor all night, imagining God alone knows what hideous situations into which you might have become embroiled—idiotic as you are!'

'Well, I can't think what sort of—'

'And, to crown all, when you do finally come home—at midnight, if you please!—all the excuse you can think of is to claim that you have been looking through a telescope!'

Maidie waited a moment, meeting the fiery brown gaze with her wide-eyed stare. All remembrance of her discomfort at his odd conduct had vanished with his return to normality. She raised her brows at length. 'Have you finished?'

Delagarde was breathing rather heavily. 'I have barely begun.'

'Well, then, let me tell you—'

'Maidie,' interrupted Lady Hester hastily, 'don't allow yourself to be dragged into a pointless argument. You must expect some such reaction, after all. Laurie has been truly concerned. It is only natural that relief should produce an explosion.'

'Thank you, Aunt Hes. However—'

'Have you really been concerned?' Maidie asked him, sudden contrition darkening the grey eyes—and causing a resurgence of irregularity in her heartbeat.

'Of course I have,' Delagarde said testily. 'A pretty sort of fellow I should be if I had not! I am in some sort responsible for you.'

'Oh.' Was that all? Maidie was conscious of a drop in spirits, and her pulse steadied. What else had she expected? Not that she cared whether Delagarde had been worried about her. But need he spoil the enchantments of the evening? It was typical! Then a wave of remorse hit her. She was demonstrably in the wrong.

'I am sorry that you should have been put to so much inconvenience,' she said gruffly.

'Nonsense!' put in Lady Hester bracingly. 'One evening's worry over someone else? I wish we might all come off as lightly! The only pity of it is, Maidie, that you missed the ball.'

'I missed the ball!' struck in Delagarde. 'No one thinks of that.'

'Nobody asked you to miss it,' Maidie pointed out. 'It is not my fault if you decided it was your duty to remain here with Lady Hester and wait for me.'

Delagarde eyed her with hostility. 'It had occurred to

me to strangle you for this night's work. I cannot think why I have not done so. I must be feeling extraordinarily merciful.'

Maidie was swept with a sudden gush of merriment, and she giggled again. 'Oh, Delagarde, pray don't be so out of reason cross! You may readily go to the ball now, if you choose. I am sure it is not over.'

'Your solicitude overwhelms me,' he returned, 'but I find I have lost my appetite for it.'

She laughed, and held out her hand. 'I am truly sorry, Delagarde. There! Do let us cry friends again.'

He took her hand and held it loosely imprisoned in his larger one. 'That is all very well, but I am not at all satisfied, Maidie. What is all this about? You are not seriously expecting me to believe that you have indeed spent all this time examining the heavens?'

Maidie stared at him, withdrawing her hand. 'But this is mad! Will nothing convince you that I am wholly and exclusively devoted to the subject of astronomy?'

'You!' A disbelieving laugh escaped him. 'No, Maidie, I don't think so.'

'You will have to show him, Maidie,' recommended Lady Hester, laughing.

He turned frowning eyes upon his great-aunt. 'Show me what?'

Delagarde stared in astonishment at the small telescope fixed to a stand set at the precise centre between the French windows in Maidie's bedchamber. It was of brass, with a retractable length that she was pulling out.

'I cannot get it to its full size without opening the balcony doors,' she said, unclipping the cover over the glass end and lifting it up. 'Although this is only Great-uncle's travelling piece, which he used when we went out on what he called his expeditions.'

Delagarde was frowning heavily as he tried to take in this extraordinary new perspective on his unwanted charge. 'You went with him?'

'Always.' Maidie laughed. 'Which made it very much an expedition, for Worm would insist upon all manner of comforts for me, particularly as Great-uncle would rarely let her come. Except once when we encamped in the wilderness—like heathen Bedouins, Worm said. We turned night into day for near a week, and the whole retinue had to do the same! After that, Worm was glad to be left at home, I think.'

The Viscount watched in reluctant fascination as she turned to the whatnot, lifting up a stack of large charts—some printed, some clearly made by hand—and leafed through them, explaining their purposes as she showed them to him by the light of the heavy candelabrum he had brought in and set down upon the dresser. There were maps of the night sky, charting the stars in their constellations; crudely drawn configurations, covered over with incomprehensible jottings; tables of names and figures, neatly labelled with times, positions by degrees and places of origin; and pencilled sketches, heavily annotated, which recorded the exploration currently engaging Maidie's attention, she said.

'What are you exploring?' he asked, almost absently, for he was dazed by the evidence which proved beyond all possible doubt that she had been speaking nothing but the truth.

'I am chasing a comet.' Then she tutted, stabbing at the sketch in her hand in some annoyance. 'And this evening I find that I have miscalculated quite shockingly. By Sir Granville's telescope, I was able to perceive its true path— oh, it is quite the most beautiful object, I had no real idea of that until tonight!—and I now see that I must adjust my prognosis of its probable flight by quite a wide margin.'

Delagarde blinked. 'This is a comet? Why a comet?'

Maidie smiled. 'Well, to tell you the truth, they are not my real passion. But Great-uncle was comet crazy. Between him and Charles Messier there was nothing to choose. They were always in correspondence, and Messier wrote very kindly to me to express his sense of loss when Great-uncle died.'

'But you are not comet crazy?'

'I am planet crazy. Or rather, my fascination is with the satellites that attend them. My greatest hero is Galileo, who proved beyond all doubt—and it was by the behaviour of satellites that he did so—that it is the earth which travels around the sun, and not the other way about.'

Enthusiasm lit her features, and Delagarde gazed in dawning wonder, as he listened to the first intelligent exposition that he had ever heard issuing from the lips of a young female. Theories and counter-theories battered at his brain, and he very quickly became lost in the morass of unknown names with which Maidie littered her discourse. Whatever social inadequacies might have resulted from her peculiar upbringing, there was no doubt that Reginald Hope's encouragement of a burgeoning interest had fostered a mind that must command his deepest respect. Maidie was infuriating, yes. But she was not merely unusual. She was unique!

A burst of laughter from where his great-aunt had seated herself upon the bed, divorced from the proceedings, stopped Maidie in mid-stride. She turned to Lady Hester, and found that dame brimming with mirth.

'My dear Maidie, you will have his head off in a moment!'

Maidie looked again at Delagarde, in some dismay. She had been carried away by his questions, quite forgetting to whom she was speaking. She was prattling away like this to Delagarde, of all people! She was sure that his interest in the subject, if he had any at all, was but tepid. Most people, so Great-uncle had warned her, would be bored into a stupor by what they both found so fascinating. And Delagarde was a man of fashion—what could be more opposed?

'I beg your pardon,' she said, on a rueful note. 'You should not have asked me about it. Adela says that I lose all sense of other people when I sit upon my hobby-horse, and I dare say she is right. I do try to remember that one's passion may be of no interest at all to others.'

'Don't!' Delagarde said, smiling at her in a way that she found singularly unsettling. 'It is rather I who should be apologising for doubting you. I begin to perceive why you expressed so much reluctance to become involved in the social whirl.'

'Well, it is true that I didn't want to do so,' Maidie admitted, trying to recover her poise, 'but in fact I am quite enjoying it. Perhaps because I had only chosen to track this comet for Great-uncle's sake, so that I have not been truly averse to having my work interrupted.'

'Had you been tracking a planet, on the other hand…?' he suggested, with a questioning lift to one eyebrow.

That made her laugh. 'One does not track a planet. However, I know what you mean to say.' In a confiding manner that amused Delagarde, she told him, 'The fact is that my own work has been held up because I need a more powerful telescope. I thought it better not to attempt to have one built until I have my own establishment. They are most unwieldy, and I would not wish to have to move it once it had been erected.'

'No doubt you are wise,' Delagarde said gravely, ignoring the stifled sounds issuing from Lady Hester. 'We must trust that it will not be long before you are suitably settled, and able to command your husband's help.'

'Oh, I shan't ask him!' said Maidie forthrightly. 'That

is just why I am anxious to marry someone who is not particular about what I do. He may have his forty-five thousand pounds with my good will, if only he will refrain from interfering. Besides, I cannot think that a gentleman seeking to marry a fortune will have any interest in astronomy. He is far more likely to bury himself in cards, or sporting pursuits.'

'And you won't mind that?'

'Why should I? Provided he will not mind my burying myself in my observatory.'

Delagarde shook his head. 'You are the strangest girl. I have never heard a more absurd reason for matrimony. Why don't you look for a husband among those who attended this lecture—or some other who shares your own enthusiasm for the subject?'

Maidie sighed. 'I wish I might. But there is hardly a glut in the world of eligible astronomers.'

'Perhaps not. But I can't for the life of me see that you will be happy with anyone else.' He found himself so disturbed by this thought that he hurried again into speech. 'My good girl, you are making a great mistake. Do you really think that any man—even a fortune hunter—will be so complaisant as to allow his wife to abjure his world, to become so eccentric a recluse as your great-uncle? Is that what you want?'

She was silent, staring at him in puzzlement. Put like that, she was unable to answer him. She had thought of marriage only as a means to an end. She merely wanted to be left alone. But might this be the result of enduring life under Adela's rule, when she had been obliged to do as another bid her, and not as she wished? For she wished only for the freedom to carry on her work. Except that this taste of town life had its attractions. If she had not come, she would not have heard that lecture, or met Sir Granville Wilberfoss. There was, she found, something of greater pleasure in returning to star-gazing when one was not always able to do it. In England, with the uncertain weather, one's observing was often frustrated. She found it tedious to use the time in complicated mathematical calculations, drawing up better maps or improving one's charts. It might be a relief to while away bad weather at a social gathering instead.

She came out of these thoughts to find Delagarde still awaiting some response, and Lady Hester watching her with a twinkle in her eye. There was all at once a trace of heaviness in her chest, and she could not think why.

'Perhaps you would then advise me to remain a spinster?' she asked him seriously.

He flung away rather suddenly. 'God forbid—if it means I will have you on my hands for life!'

A dart seemed to pierce Maidie's breast. She turned away and made a business of laying down her maps and charts on the whatnot, putting them into some semblance of order. Why such a comment should hurt her, she could not imagine. No, that was humdudgeon. She was not precisely hurt. It was not as if Delagarde had not addressed many such remarks to her. Only why now, when they had seemed to be achieving a measure of understanding?

Delagarde was as much at a loss to account for his hasty remark. He could not think why he had said it. It was true, but somehow—perhaps because of this new image he had of Maidie—it seemed a hurtful thing to say to her. He turned, trying to think of some way of mitigating it. But his mind had gone blank. He watched her rearranging her papers, and the only thing that entered his brain was the obvious thought that it was going to be hard indeed for her to find a husband with whom she might share a common interest. It would scarcely lessen the damage to voice such a notion!

On the whole he was glad to be spared the necessity of

talking any further by the intervention of Aunt Hes, who rose from the bed.

'It is far too late to be entering upon such a discussion. Now go away, do, Laurie. This improper proceeding has served its turn.'

Maidie looked round quickly. 'Improper?'

'For Laurie to be in your bedchamber.'

'Oh,' said Maidie, and was annoyed to feel herself blushing.

Delagarde went to the door. 'There is nothing improper in it as long as you are here,' he said, oddly irritated by the suggestion. But he bid them both goodnight, and withdrew.

Maidie glanced at Lady Hester. 'Perhaps it is a pity that I missed the ball. I might have made some progress.' She added, on a note of melancholy, 'I believe Lord Delagarde has a poor opinion of my chances.'

Lady Hester came across and patted her cheek, smiling. 'Nonsense, my love. He does not believe the half of what he says. Pay no heed to him!' She moved to the door. 'But come! We have been most remiss. Poor Ida has not been informed of your return, Maidie. And I wish to ask her why she did not tell us where you had gone.'

But the Worm, when Maidie and Lady Hester went in to her next door, was found to be suffering from headache and a raging fever. The two ladies had too much to do in making her more comfortable to concern themselves over the duenna's lapse of memory.

'I am sure that must have been it,' Maidie whispered, when the Worm, having swallowed a dose of laudanum, was seen to be sinking into slumber. 'Poor Worm was probably too ill to heed what I said to her. I should have told you myself. Pray don't let us trouble her on the matter. Let her believe it is my fault, and that I forgot to say anything.'

Lady Hester drew her out of the room, and agreed to this, but adding a severe injunction to her not to sit up late. 'Your abigail may take the night watch, and in the morning we will call in the physician.'

But Maidie, too worried to sleep very soundly, twice awoke and went in to check on the Worm. A truckle bed had been set up for Trixie, but the conscientious maid had not used it, and was taking such good care of Miss Wormley that Maidie was able to go back to her bed with a quiet mind.

She cancelled her engagements for the next few days, spending a deal of time with the Worm, a sacrifice that induced her sponsor to harbour kindlier thoughts towards her.

'She is a good-hearted little creature, at least,' he told Lady Hester as they set out upon Tuesday evening's entertainment without her.

'Oh, it is no great hardship to Maidie to miss a party,' said his great-aunt prosaically.

Delagarde found himself irrationally annoyed by this observation. 'You think she is using Miss Wormley's illness as an excuse, then?'

'I did not say that. Maidie is very fond of Ida. Her concern is quite genuine.'

'Miss Wormley may count herself fortunate,' Delagarde said grimly. 'There are few things—outside of astronomy, of course—that rouse Maidie's concern.'

'But a moment ago, Laurie, you were extolling her kind heart,' Lady Hester pointed out. 'What are you at now?'

'Nothing.'

Delagarde was silent for a moment. He was conscious of a degree of dissatisfaction for which he could not account…had been conscious of it for some days. That it had to do with Maidie's descent upon him he could not doubt: the disturbance to his ordered existence; the unsettled state of his mind, always in some way or another concerned with the wretch's activities; the discomfort of an uncertain temper, for Maidie had the unhappy knack of arousing it. But it was none of these things that was at the root of his discontent. How could it be, when he had felt it so much aggravated by the discovery of Maidie's all-consuming crusade with the heavens?

'I do not know what to make of her!' he announced suddenly, as if unable to keep his thoughts any longer to himself.

'In what respect?'

He turned, trying to see his great-aunt's features in the semi-darkness. 'You have a fondness for her, have you not, Aunt Hes? But can you truthfully say that you understand her?'

Delagarde thought she smiled, but he could not be sure. 'Don't you?'

The response, enigmatic as ever, infuriated him. 'Have I not just said that I do not? This star-gazing, for one thing.'

'What about it?'

'One must admire her grasp of the subject. It argues a strong intelligence. But…' He paused, grappling with his thoughts, struggling with a rising emotion to which he could put no name. 'I cannot like the—the *obsession*. Excluding all else. It is not natural. It is unfeminine. It makes one feel—yes, shut out.' The phrase, for some unfathomable reason, laid fuel to his ire. 'She will never get a husband. No man will bear it!'

'Then I dare say Maidie is right to insist upon a marriage of convenience,' said Lady Hester calmly.

'Possibly,' conceded Delagarde stiffly, and by no means soothed. 'I wish her joy of it. And pity the poor fool who must spend his nights in a cold bed while his wife warms herself purely by starlight.'

Resuming an active part in the social round, Maidie found herself possessed by a certain lethargy. A tiny hope, largely unformed, that Delagarde might truly have been interested in her talk of astronomy, that it might have become the basis of a growth in mutual understanding, died quickly. He would not now concern himself at her absences from the house—apparently the only thing that had concerned him.

Had he not kept very much out of her way for some considerable time? Only the to-do over her disappearance had made him pay attention to her. Now, it appeared, he considered himself free to let her make her own way. For, on Thursday evening, once having given his escort to the ladies during the short journey in his town carriage to a soirée held by Lady Riseley, the mother of his close friend, he kept his distance. It was not, as might have been supposed, because he felt himself obliged to give attention to his friend, for Lord Riseley made it his business to see to Maidie's comfort, and introduced her also to Mr Everett Corringham.

'Another of Delagarde's cronies, you must know,' said Riseley with a grin, wafting a hand at his other friend.

He had guided Maidie to a chair set into one of the alcoves formed in the window embrasures of the large saloon, a pleasant room done out in warm shades of brown and cream with gilt edging. The two gentlemen stood before her, effectively barring her view of the rest of the guests.

'Most remiss of our friend not to have presented us to you before this,' said Corringham.

'Yes, he would keep saying that you don't care for anyone who is not interested in astronomy.'

Maidie could not but be intrigued to meet those friends who knew Delagarde best, but at this patent falsehood, she gave Lord Riseley one of her wide-eyed looks.

'He cannot have been saying so for long, because he has only known of my interest in astronomy these last few days.'

'And, I am prepared to wager, has expressed no interest in it whatsoever,' pursued his lordship, a teasing light in his eye. 'Corringham, on the other hand, is agog. Are you not, Everett?'

'Utterly,' agreed the other, hand on heart. 'You must tell me all about it.'

'I cannot,' said Maidie frankly. 'It is a vast subject, and I am myself still ignorant of many aspects. Besides, my great-uncle Reginald warned me on no account to bore others who do not share the interest.'

'But Everett does share it,' protested Riseley, mock-indignant. 'At least, he is sure that he will, if you are willing to introduce him to it. Come, Lady Mary, you must be able to cover the essentials in one little evening.'

Maidie stared at him, perplexed. She could no more understand what was his motive than she could believe Mr Corringham entertained a serious interest in her hobby. At any other time, she would have been glad to have pursued a natural curiosity to probe, in order perhaps to discover something more about Delagarde. But a nagging suspicion of a headache was making her edgy, and she lost a little of her newfound decorum.

'Lord Riseley, pray do not trifle with me in this way, for I am not in a mood for it. What is it you want of me?'

The two gentlemen exchanged glances—of amusement, Maidie thought. Then Riseley turned back to her, his grin decidedly sheepish.

'You are too shrewd, Lady Mary. I will leave Everett to explain.' He held up a hand as his friend cast him a glance of reproach. 'No choice but to rat, old fellow. My mother's party, you know. Must circulate.'

He winked at Maidie, and withdrew, leaving her to cast her questioning look upon Corringham. 'Well, sir?'

Corringham cleared his throat, and pulling forward another chair, took his seat beside her. 'It is all too obvious, I am afraid. We have heard a great deal about you.'

'From Lord Delagarde?' asked Maidie, before she could stop herself.

'And others. Don't be alarmed. A new face in town is bound to be the subject of great interest.'

Maidie glanced about the room, as if to verify this statement, and was a little dismayed to find that her vision seemed a touch blurred. She brought her gaze back to Mr Corringham's face and was relieved to find it in focus. She was scarcely aware that she spoke.

'I am not new anymore.'

'Perhaps not, but you are still something of an enigma. To Riseley and myself especially, for we had not met you. We have both been consumed with curiosity to find out what sort of a girl might attract—' He broke off, coughed again, and resumed, 'I mean, what would *induce* our friend Delagarde to take a young lady under his wing in this way.'

Maidie's eyes remained fixed upon him, while a rather painful restriction seemed to clutch at her chest. She had not missed the change of word. Clearly, Mr Corringham realised he had made an inappropriate choice at first. It could not have been a slip—could it? Her head felt curiously light, but a ring of discomfort encircled it. She frowned, finding it hard to think of what she must say.

'There was no attraction.' No, she had not meant to say that. 'Of course not. Delagarde does not even like me.' She had not meant to say that either. 'He was induced, you are very right. Between myself and Lady Hester, he found himself with little choice.' Should she have said that? Mr Corringham was looking most oddly at her. 'I should not have told you that, I dare say.'

The constriction in her chest tightened, her nose pricked suddenly. Then she sneezed.

'I beg your pardon,' she uttered, groping in her petti-coats to find a pocket handkerchief. The pressure about her brow increased, and she narrowed her eyes, finding the light in the room too bright. 'Lord Delagarde does not approve of me. I thought we were becoming f-friends at least, but—' To her consternation, she felt a stinging at her eyes, and quickly put up her handkerchief to cover them. Then she was seized by a fit of sneezing. Vaguely she heard Mr Corringham say something about Lady Hester, but could not take it in.

In a moment or two, as the sneezing died away, she was able to think a little more clearly. She knew what had happened now. She had caught Worm's cold. Lord knew what she might have said to Mr Corringham, her head ached so! Looking up at last, she saw Lady Hester coming towards her.

The next bustling moments passed as a vague blur, but Maidie forced her senses alert when she found herself in Delagarde's carriage, with his lordship for escort.

'Where is Lady Hester?'

'She could not come away just at this moment,' he an-swered. 'She is engaged with old friends. I shall return to fetch her when I have seen you safely home.'

Maidie was beyond understanding this. It seemed most odd of Lady Hester to abandon her, quite unprecedented. Especially when she was obviously ill. That Delagarde should be obliged to bring her home seemed altogether disquieting.

'I am sorry to give you so much trouble,' she produced.

'Don't be stupid.'

Maidie gave a little laugh. 'I seem to be fated to make you miss parties.'

'I know. How shall I survive it, I wonder?'

'Well, I did not mean to interfere in your life,' Maidie said, a little aggrieved by this sarcasm.

'That,' said Delagarde flatly, 'is past praying for.'

Maidie sneezed, caught her handkerchief to her face, and announced in muffled accents, 'You do not seem to me to be unduly discomposed.'

'I beg your pardon? If I heard you aright, it is obvious that you have no notion of the life I led before you thrust yourself into it.'

'Then go back to that life,' Maidie threw at him. 'I am sure I have no wish to prevent you.'

'It may have escaped your notice, but at this precise moment that is exactly what you are doing.'

Maidie sniffed back threatening tears. Her headache had assumed vast proportions. She put up her fingers to her temples, and kneaded at them.

'Had I known that you had the intention of coming with me,' she managed to say, 'I would have told you not to trouble. I could quite well have gone on my own.'

'In this state? I do not think so.'

Another fit of sneezing prevented her from making any immediate reply. It so much exhausted her that she was only able to groan afterwards, sinking her aching head against the squabs.

'You will do better not to talk,' Delagarde advised. 'We will be at Charles Street in a moment.'

'It's well for you to say that,' Maidie returned, making a valiant effort to sit up straight again, 'after you have succeeded in making me feel guilty. It is not my fault that I have caught a cold.'

Delagarde pushed her back. 'For God's sake, lie back

and rest! And you are palpably to blame. You were bound to catch a cold if you hung about your duenna's bedside.'

Maidie sniffed, and clapped the handkerchief to her nose again, retorting in muffled accents, 'Oh, and I suppose you would have had me leave poor Worm to fend for herself?'

Delagarde was silenced. He could not think why he was behaving in this fashion. He was as sulky as a schoolboy, and all for no reason at all. Of course it was not Maidie's fault that she had caught cold. And it was no trouble to him to come with her—in fact, he had offered to do so the moment his great-aunt had expressed, very mildly, a slight disappointment in having to leave just then. What should take him to carp at the poor girl?

To his relief, the carriage began to slow down, and he saw that they were negotiating the turn into Charles Street. In a moment, the horses had drawn up outside his house. He did not wait for the steps to be let down, but jumped out as the door opened and turned to assist Maidie.

She seemed to have difficulty in getting to her feet. But as he reached in to help her, she struck his hands away.

'I can manage, thank you.'

He stepped back, a flame of anger shooting through him. He watched her struggle up, holding fast to the doorframes at either side. She wavered a little, caught his glance, and reached out blindly.

'I think I am going to…'

Delagarde leapt forward as her eyes rolled shut, and she collapsed into his ready embrace.

Chapter Seven

Maidie had not quite lost consciousness and, as she felt herself lifted, she dragged her eyes open again.

'You n-need not c-carry me,' she tried to say, focusing on the odd angle of Delagarde's face. 'I am sure I can very well w-walk.'

'You may as well save your breath,' he advised, moving swiftly up the steps and into the house. 'Lowick, send someone up to warn Miss Wormley!'

Maidie subsided somewhat thankfully, and rested her head against his convenient shoulder. In her current state, for a blissful few moments, it felt like the most comfortable position in the world. But all too soon the journey was ending, and she was released to the ground and made to sit upon a chair while the Worm and Trixie hastily prepared her bed, clucking the while.

Realising that Delagarde's supporting arm was still around her, Maidie roused herself to try and thank him.

'Be still!' he ordered, shushing her. 'You can talk again when you are comfortably between sheets.'

Maidie was indeed still so faint with the sudden onset of fever that she hardly noticed him leave, and was only half aware as the new muslin gown of leaf green—put on for the first time that night—was removed and she was put to bed. But after some minutes of rest upon the softness of her banked pillows, she began to revive a little, and was able to open her eyes and give an account of herself to the Worm.

'To think that it is my fault you are laid low!' mourned this worthy, shedding tears even as she bustled Trixie into turning the bedchamber into a sick-room, with a plethora of cordials and comforts collected from her own chamber next door.

'Don't fret, Worm,' Maidie told her. 'Lord Delagarde says I was bound to catch it if I hung about you, so it is quite my own fault.'

But this Miss Wormley would by no means allow, and she continued to upbraid herself at each of Maidie's intermittent sneezing fits, until the unexpected re-entrance into the room of Lord Delagarde himself.

'Oh, my lord!' exclaimed the duenna, shocked. 'It cannot be right—I do not think you should—oh, dear.'

'I thought you had gone back to the party,' Maidie said, ignoring the Worm's protestations, and sniffing away the streaming fluids that had accompanied her last bout of sneezing. 'You had better keep your distance. I do not wish to be blamed if you catch it.'

'Well, I am not going to keep my distance.' Delagarde sat on the edge of the bed, equally unmindful of the duenna's squeaking. He was holding a cup in one hand, which he held out to Maidie. 'I have brought you a remedy.'

Maidie took it, sniffing gingerly at the brew inside, from which emanated an aroma that was strange to her. 'What is it?'

'Hot lemon and sugar.' He grinned wickedly, adding, 'And a measure of strong navy rum.' Maidie nearly dropped the cup, but Delagarde reached out and grabbed it. 'Take care!'

'I can't drink that!' Maidie gasped, and thrust it back into his hands as she began again to sneeze.

'Rum, my lord!' came from the scandalised Miss Wormley. 'Oh no, no, no!'

'My dear Miss Wormley, it is a highly effective restorative for colds, and will help her to sleep besides. It is, I promise you, far less harmful to the system than laudanum.'

'Delagarde, have you run mad?' asked Maidie, when she had blown her nose. But she could not help smiling, for a warm softness had entered her at this unprecedented mark of thoughtfulness.

'Drink it!' he ordered, and keeping his fingers on the cup, encouraged her to raise it to her lips.

Maidie took a wary sip, and her eyes widened. 'It is not unpleasant.'

'Of course not. It is liberally dosed with sugar.'

'Oh dear, oh dear,' muttered the Worm distressfully, but ineffectually, for neither of the principals paid her the least heed.

Maidie was engaged in taking a few more concentrated sips of the hot thick liquid, which tasted more pleasant every moment. Soon she began to feel a rosy glow in her chest and a heady sensation wreathing her brain. She looked up to find Delagarde watching her, amusement in his eyes. She tried to speak, and found difficulty in enunciating the words.

'I h-hope I shill…shall not tomorrow, s-s-su—'

'Suffer a morning head?' supplied his lordship, grinning at her. 'Well, if you do, I hope it may prove a lesson to you not to plague defenceless viscounts with unreasonable demands when they have barely had a chance to open their eyes.'

Maidie giggled uncontrollably, and hiccuped. She heard the Worm tutting away, and opened wide her eyes. 'D'you mean that I am in-in-inee…drunk?'

'I should not so describe it. A trifle foxed, perhaps.'

Maidie sneezed. She felt the cup removed from her hand, and heard faintly the murmur of voices as the violence of her sneezing took all her attention. When she was once more able to take account of what was happening, she found that Delagarde had gone and the Worm was sitting in his place. The rosy glow dissipated, and Maidie discovered that she wanted to weep. But a drowsy feeling was stealing over her and, instead, she began to drop asleep. Her last thought was a conviction that Delagarde had not been there at all, and the whole episode was a figment of her fevered imagination.

'How is your protégée, Laurie?' demanded Mr Corringham, coming up to the Viscount at their friend Riseley's house.

Delagarde had escorted Lady Hester thither, so that she might at once apologise for Maidie to her hostess of the previous evening, and set it about that her indisposition would keep her in bed for a day or two.

'She has only taken a cold. It is not serious.' He found himself being regarded with a quizzical eye, and frowned. 'Well?'

'Nothing, my dear fellow, nothing at all.'

But the gleam persisted, and a surge of irritation threw Delagarde into speech. 'Everett, I know that look. What do you mean by it?'

From behind him came Lord Riseley's voice, filled with frank laughter. 'My boy, you had much better ask me. Everett will never bring himself to say it.'

Delagarde turned on him. 'Well, I do ask you. What are you at, the pair of you?'

'Don't fly up into the boughs with us, dear boy,' advised Riseley. 'Ain't our fault that you felt compelled to dance attendance on the chit merely because she caught a cold.'

'Dance attendance? That is ridiculous.'

'Is it?' returned his irrepressible friend. 'Then what came over you to persuade Lady Hester to stay while you escorted her home?'

'It is what anyone would have done,' Delagarde protested, but uneasily aware of the creeping memory of the sum of his activities last night. He repressed it, arguing, 'In any event, it was Aunt Hes who asked me to do so.'

'Oho, was it, indeed?' chimed in Mr Corringham.

Delagarde threw up his hands. 'Will you make something of that as well, Everett?'

'I should dashed well think he might!' said Riseley. 'What, is the old lady planning to parcel you off at last?'

'Parson's mousetrap looming, old fellow?' teased the other. 'And what is Lady Mary's thought upon all this?'

'Now, how should he know that?' demanded Lord Riseley of his friend, mock-indignant. 'That was your mission, Everett, and you failed it most miserably.'

'How could I help but fail, when my subject would do nothing but sneeze?'

Delagarde eyed them both with a degree of hostility. There was too much truth in their banter for his comfort. That Aunt Hes had conceived of a union between himself and Maidie he could not deny, although he was reasonably sure that she had given up the notion. That Maidie might entertain the idea for one moment was inconceivable—as inconceivable as that he would do so himself. Or was it? He was uncomfortably conscious of a wish that Everett had succeeded in his mission to discover her sentiments— if such had been his intention. It was unlikely, but suppose Maidie was developing some sort of *tendre*? He would wish to know of it—if only to teach him to be more circumspect! One did not, if a gentleman, knowingly raise expectations. He was not tenderhearted, but one would not wish any female to suffer the pangs of unrequited affection.

The oddest sensation attacked him in the chest. Revulsion? No, not that. Compassion? Yes, compassion. So vulnerable as she had seemed last night! Familiarity was damping his antagonism. He could laugh at her oddities. Was it possible that he had even begun to like her? Decidedly, he was conscious of more friendliness towards her. But how long could it last? Maidie was—

The thought escaped him as he found that both his friends were silently watching him. Striving to shake off his abstraction, he turned the subject. He was succeeding admirably in deflecting the conversation, when it was thrust back into the same channel by Adela, Lady Shurland, who boldly accosted him.

'Lord Delagarde, may I speak to you for a moment? I am anxious to hear news of my poor cousin.'

There was nothing to be read in the angular countenance other than an anxious concern but, at the back of her eyes, Delagarde read something more. Faintly intrigued, he discarded his first impulse, which was to return a polite answer in the company of his friends. Bowing acquiescence, he stepped aside with her and, as he supposed, out of earshot.

'What is it you wish to know, ma'am?'

Adela gave him a limpid smile. 'How Mary is, what else? I hear that you were obliged to take her home from this house last night, upon a sudden onset of illness.'

Delagarde shrugged. 'It was nothing very much. Miss Wormley has had a cold these few days and Lady Mary has caught it from her, that is all.'

'I am so glad,' sighed Adela. 'But it is all of a piece. Mary is giving you a deal of trouble, I believe.'

There was no gainsaying this, but Delagarde was not about to admit the fact to Lady Shurland. 'Not at all. The house is enlivened by her presence, and my aunt takes great pleasure in Lady Mary's society.'

'But you don't?' cut in Adela shrewdly.

Delagarde compressed his lips upon an exclamation of annoyance, and said, at his most suave, 'I cannot imagine why you should make such an assumption.'

The Countess smiled archly. 'You have no need to pretend with me, Lord Delagarde. Remember that I am well acquainted with Mary. She is bound to rub against you. Indeed, I must suppose any man would find her impossible to live with.'

He eyed her frostily. 'Indeed? Then it seems to me extremely odd that you should encourage your brother in his pursuit of her.'

If he had hoped to put Adela out of countenance, he was disappointed. She gave a laugh that rang a little false.

'There is no accounting for taste, sir. What would you? My poor brother is smitten. I conceive it to be my duty to do what I may to oblige him.'

Delagarde was so much disgusted by the disingenuity of these remarks that he almost walked away from the woman without another word. He was stayed only by her hand reaching out. It was placed upon his arm and she leaned towards him with an air of confidentiality.

'Lord Delagarde, it is for that I wished to speak with you, to be truthful. You cannot, I am persuaded, desire the continued burden of Mary's presence in your house. She has been, I must guess, nothing but a source of trouble and annoyance to you. Why do you not use your influence?'

What new ploy was this? What influence was he supposed to have with Maidie? And how dared the woman take it upon herself to make these wild suppositions about his state of mind? Whatever trouble and annoyance he might have felt because of Maidie's presence in his house had nothing whatsoever to do with Adela, Lady Shurland. He would not demean himself by quarrelling openly with her, but his smile was as false as her own.

'According to your reading of our relationship, Lady Shurland, I cannot imagine how you deduce that I have any influence with Lady Mary.'

'Oh, not with Mary,' she uttered impatiently. 'With Lady Hester. No one could doubt that she has influence with Mary, and she is a guest in your house, besides being your aunt.'

Delagarde raised incredulous eyebrows. 'Are you suggesting that I should intercede with my aunt to petition Lady Mary on behalf of your brother, ma'am?'

Adela sighed gustily. 'I only wish you might. Between you, I am persuaded you could induce Mary to accept Eustace. He is a respectable man, and personable—though I speak as his sister, I cannot but notice how he is admired. And he cares for her, Lord Delagarde. Surely that must count for something?'

'Yes, you mentioned that he was smitten,' Delagarde said smoothly. His eyes narrowed dangerously. 'But I, Lady Shurland, am no fool. If he is smitten, it is not with Maidie, but with her forty-five thousand pounds.'

With that, he turned his back upon her, and moved to rejoin his friends, such a blaze of anger in his chest that it was a moment or two before he realised that Lord Riseley was speaking to him. He blinked and brought his friend into focus.

'I beg your pardon, Peter?'

'I asked you what Lady Shurland has said to put you in a miff, dear boy?'

The fury was too raw to be contained. He gave a mirthless laugh. 'The woman takes me for a simpleton! As if I could be fool enough to believe for one moment—even had I not already Maidie's word for it—that her obnoxious brother has any other end in view than to get his hands upon Maidie's fortune.'

'Fortune!' echoed Mr Corringham blankly.

'You mean the girl has expectations?' asked Riseley.

Delagarde cursed. 'Now, not a word, either of you! If that cat of a female had not put me in such a flame, I would never have mentioned it.'

'But, my dear boy, you can tell us,' protested his friend.

'No reason why he should,' argued Corringham.

'He already has. Might as well give us a round tale now.'

'Yes, very well, Peter, but you had better not set it about. I wish neither to be obliged to discourage an endless stream of fortune-hunters, nor to be accused of coveting her substance myself.'

His friends whistled when they heard the sum of Maidie's inheritance, and teasingly complained of their own inability to make a play for it. Corringham was already the father of a hopeful family, and Riseley had become betrothed at the end of the previous Season. To Delagarde's chagrin, they immediately engaged upon a light-hearted encouragement to him to snatch Maidie up before any other fellows got wind of the matter.

'I thank you, and I shall now leave you both,' he said trenchantly. 'And if you dare to bring up the subject again in my presence, you may count upon my forsaking your company altogether.'

Returning on Monday night from Boodle's in the early hours, Delagarde had just sent the sleepy porter who had been waiting up for him to bed, when a sound from the downstairs drawing-room alerted him. He had shrugged off his greatcoat, and he threw it, together with his hat and gloves, on to one of the hall chairs. Lifting high the candle that had been left for him on the table, he crossed the hall and opened the door.

Light glimmered in a corner, and he saw the outline of a shrouded figure standing near the escritoire. He was a trifle above par, but not so far gone that he would take it for a spectre. Nearing, he discovered, with a sensation of startled surprise, that it was Maidie. It was the first time he had seen her in three days. Even in his elevated state, he knew her appearance here was abnormal. Since Thursday night, when he had brought her home, she had remained confined to her room, making, so Aunt Hes had told him, a steady recovery. But she was not yet officially up.

She was clad only in a dressing-robe, her hair loose about her shoulders, and engaged in thrusting about inside one of the drawers of the little desk. It was evident that she had not seen him, for she gasped, turning her head as he spoke.

'What in the world are you doing?'

'Oh, it's you,' she muttered, sighing out her breath. 'You quite startled me.'

'So you did me,' he returned. 'Why aren't you in bed? What are you looking for?'

Maidie had resumed her scrabbling search. 'I have lost my pencil. I dropped it somewhere on the balcony, and I cannot find it.'

'The balcony?'

Maidie held a quill up to the light, and tutted. 'This is no use. Even if I had some, there is no sense in writing up the chart in ink. What if I should make an error?'

Light dawned on Delagarde. Cursing, he set down his candle and grasped her wrist, removing the quill from her fingers and replacing it in the drawer.

'Do you tell me you are star-gazing at this hour? Have you run mad, girl?'

She blinked dazedly at him, and he could see even in the dim light of their candles the frown that creased her forehead. Her voice was a trifle husky, but there was no other trace of her late illness.

'But there is nothing out of the way in that. I often observe until dawn.'

'Not in your current state of health! Good God, what are you thinking of?'

'I know, but it is the clearest night we have had in several weeks. Besides, I am feeling quite well, Delagarde, I promise you.'

'Not for much longer if you have been exposing yourself to the raw night air. Do you wish to catch your death? Go back to bed at once!'

Maidie was engaged in opening another drawer, and completely ignored the command. 'Don't you have any pencils in this house?'

Delagarde was in no condition to tolerate idiotic questions. Seizing her by the shoulders, he pulled her round to face him. 'Maidie, don't trifle with me! You are going to bed, if I have to pick you up and carry you there.'

He picked up her candle and thrust it into her hand, then retrieved his own and began to draw her towards the door.

'But why can I not have a pencil?' Maidie pleaded, resisting. 'It is not much to ask.'

'Oh, good God!'

Releasing her, Delagarde moved back to the escritoire and made a rapid hunt through the contents of the drawers, holding his candle close. He found a pencil and handed it to her.

'There! Now, come.'

Clutching the indispensable pencil, Maidie allowed herself to be guided into the hall and up the stairs, talking all the while.

'You cannot imagine how frustrating, Delagarde. I had

just located that comet again—for it has moved considerably and I have not had an opportunity to change its path in the charts since I saw it through Sir Granville's telescope—and then I dropped the pencil. I have an idea it must have fallen through the railing because I crept about on my hands and knees and searched thoroughly.'

'On your hands and knees on the cold stone floor of the balcony? Exactly what any doctor must recommend,' commented Delagarde sardonically.

'But I promise you I did not notice the cold in the least. I was trying to hold the configuration in my head.'

'Well, you may write it down,' Delagarde conceded, 'but then you are to go to bed.'

She halted at her bedchamber door, turning with her candle held up. 'It is no use now. I have forgotten it. I must hope that the telescope has not shifted in my absence.'

'Maidie—' he began warningly, and paused as she smiled at him all at once.

'Would you like to see it? The comet, I mean.'

He was about to veto the suggestion in no uncertain terms, and insist upon her shutting the telescope up and going to bed, but Maidie opened her door, and grasping his wrist in a markedly unselfconscious manner, drew him into the room.

'Do look, Delagarde! It is the most beautiful thing.'

Delagarde found himself quite unable to repudiate her. Perhaps it was the lingering effects of the wine, but he felt delightfully elated by her amiability. There was a chill in the air of the room, which he had no hesitation in ascribing to the wide-open balcony doors. Maidie seemed not to notice it, but released him and went quickly across to seat herself on the stool before her telescope, setting the candle and pencil down on the whatnot beside her.

Delagarde hesitated by the still-open door. He retained

enough sanity to know that this was extremely improper, but he must make sure that she left off star-gazing and went back to bed. He did not want her death on his conscience. It must, he supposed, be the liquor, for there was something disturbing about the whole proceeding.

'You do realise,' he found himself saying casually, 'that the nature of this invitation of yours is quite shocking.'

Maidie turned on the stool. He could not see her face properly from here, but her voice was free of embarrassment.

'What do you mean?' she asked innocently.

'Come, come, Maidie. This is your bedchamber, and we are unchaperoned. If you get into the habit of inviting men to star-gaze with you,' he said on a deliberately humourous note, 'your reputation is unlikely to survive it.'

'Oh, yes,' she agreed blithely, returning to her telescope. 'But you are not a man.'

'I beg your pardon? Let me tell you that I take strong exception to that remark, ma'am!'

Maidie giggled. 'Oh, well, you know what I mean.'

'Yes, and you know what I mean. You in your dressing-robe, alone with a bachelor, at a disastrously late—or, if you will, disastrously early hour. I must have taken leave of my senses!'

Intent upon her telescope, Maidie did not acknowledge this. He doubted that she had even heard him. He watched her put her eye to the piece, and then moved to the dresser where a candelabrum stood. He lit the candles from his own and a fresh light sprang up into the room.

Maidie looked round. 'Oh, shade that, if you please. Or put it further away.'

Delagarde saw that she had extinguished her own candle, and complied. Then he went to stand behind her, looking up into the night sky. It was indeed sparklingly clear, and the stars shone brightly. He wondered how Maidie

managed to distinguish her comet from all the others. She
rose from the stool and he looked down at her face. It
gleamed palely in the starlight, plainly lighting her features. It dulled her bright hair, the curls falling untidily
about her face, and made of it a halo that caressed her
cheeks. A kind of hush fell over Delagarde's mind.

'Show me your comet,' he said softly.

Maidie ushered him on to the stool, and he looked
through the telescope's eye. At first he could only make
out a fuzz of light, but at Maidie's instruction, he looked
to one side and caught the shape of the comet in the pe-
riphery of his vision. At least, he took her word for it that
it was a comet, for to his untutored eye it appeared only
as a large blob. She talked. He listened, and looked. After
a while, it began to make more sense, and he admitted to
a certain fascination.

But he rose soon, and politely thanked her, insisting that
she close up all her apparatus. She did so, discoursing at
some length on the phenomenon he had been examining.
Then she went off at a tangent, talking of Tycho and Kep-
ler, and the age-old debate about the planetary paths in
relation to the sun. Delagarde was quickly out of his depth,
but found himself making a supreme effort to keep track,
putting a question where his own scanty knowledge prod-
ded an incomplete memory. He closed the French windows
when she had shut up the telescope, and remained standing
by them, watching the animation in her face as she stood
talking, the features still clear by the starlight that came in
through the glass.

In some vague corner of his brain, he heard what she
said, but the words passed over his comprehension as that
hush once more invaded his mind. He stared at her as if
mesmerised, and the intent absorption of his look penetrated at last through Maidie's concentration.

'—not fully established until Isaac Newton's *Principia*,

and people continued to believe the Ptolemaic theory for quite centuries, even after Copernicus…'

Her voice died, the thread of what she was saying slipping away from her. She stared back into Delagarde's face, softened by some trick of the light, and her bones melted. A memory flashed into her head. 'You are not a man.' She had said it. When had she said it? Only tonight? She took in his slightly dishevelled air—cravat half untied, both coat and waistcoat unbuttoned, revealing the silk shirt beneath and the veriest glimpse of flesh. His black locks fell forward on to his lean cheeks. As she stared, the depths of his brown eyes seared her, and she felt him very much a man. She had the strangest notion that something—she did not know what—must surely happen now. And then he spoke.

'What about Copernicus?'

It was a soft whisper, barely penetrating the silence that dragged between them like a blanketing mist. Maidie felt her throat dry, and she swallowed.

'I have forgotten.'

Delagarde reached out, but his hand stilled, poised in the air. His face changed, as if some recognition broke into his head. He snatched his hand back, and his voice cut harshly across the dreamy atmosphere.

'I should not be here!'

He turned abruptly and walked quickly out of the room.

Maidie watched him go, stricken with a savage sense of loss.

April dawned two days later, and Maidie reappeared in society for Lady Hester's own party in Charles Street. The first intimation of change came when she found herself still standing at the head of the stairs, alongside her hostess and Delagarde, some fifteen minutes after the last arrival might have been expected.

'What in the world does this mean, Laurie?' demanded Lady Hester during a temporary lull. 'I am sure I did not send out as many invitations as this.'

Delagarde was frowning. 'I thought it was odd. Didn't you say this was to be a small party?'

Maidie had her own puzzlements. 'What I should like to know is why everyone is being so friendly towards me.'

'Why should they not be?'

'But, Delagarde, I do not know the half of these people. And neither Lady Wingrove nor Lady Pinmore has before taken the least notice of me.'

Lady Hester was about to answer, when she was distracted by a new arrival. 'Lord, it is Selina! You are perfectly right, Maidie. Something very peculiar indeed is going on.'

Astonished, Maidie watched the ascent up the staircase of Lady Rankmiston, magnificent in bronze satin, accompanied by her youngest son—'the only one unmarried', whispered Lady Hester out of the corner of her mouth. Maidie heard a muttered curse from Delagarde, and turned to look at his suddenly grim profile. What he meant by it she could not begin to guess—and she was certainly not going to ask.

She had awoken yesterday to the memory of the Viscount's visit to her bedchamber, and had suffered a severe attack of embarrassment. That it might all have been a dream she knew to be a vain hope, and she could only ascribe her conduct to the fact that she was not yet quite well. How could she have been so lost to all sense of propriety and decorum? She shuddered to think of the Worm's reaction, and had not dared to mention the matter to Lady Hester. She had met Delagarde but briefly since, hideously conscious of the blush mantling her cheeks, and had been relieved that he neither referred to the incident, nor lingered in her company. It had taken all her resolution to appear as normal tonight—a betrayal of Great-uncle's code that she felt deeply but could not help. She was becoming the most adept of shams! Only the fear that Lady Hester might question and probe if she faltered had enabled her to face the Viscount with an assumption of poise.

But this unprecedented surge of visitors to the house succeeded in driving the memories to the back of her mind, and she forgot them altogether as she received the most gracious of greetings from Lady Rankmiston.

'That settles it,' said Lady Hester, when Delagarde was escorting that lady on to the saloons. 'There can be but one explanation.'

Maidie looked expectantly at her. 'What is it, dear ma'am?'

Lady Hester turned to her, her countenance expressive of a measure of exasperation. 'Word of your fortune must have got out, Maidie.'

'Oh, no!' Then she thought about it. 'Or—well, perhaps it is not such a great matter. I always meant for it to be known. It was only Delagarde who insisted upon secrecy.'

'I fear, my dear, that you will very soon be regretting such an accident, if I am right.' Lady Hester tutted. 'Three of our most inveterate fortune-hunters have managed to secure an entry, for I know that I did not invite them.'

Maidie frowned, conscious of a lowering feeling in her stomach. Why, she had no notion, for it had always been her intention to allow one of that fraternity to win her hand. Somehow, the prospect of being pursued by interested suitors no longer seemed so desirable.

'But how is it possible for them to come if they were not invited?' she asked, with a touch of irritation.

Lady Hester laughed. 'Nothing could be easier. They have only to find an interested matron—perhaps an aunt or a sister, or merely some friend of the family—and offer their escort to our party. I imagine we have quite doubled the number of people expected.'

Maidie was apprehensive when they abandoned their posts soon after, and joined the guests who had spread through all three saloons. It was as well, as Lady Hester remarked under her breath, that she had instructed Lowick to open up all the rooms.

It was a new sensation to be the centre of attention. Maidie doubted that it had anything to do with her appearance, although she had been pleased with the effect of the round gown of pale russet hue, with its three-quarter sleeves and neckline plain enough to induce her to allow her ginger locks to curl upon her neck, unadorned. She was besieged, person after person coming up to her, without exception exuding goodwill, until they were ousted by the next.

A very little of this sufficed Maidie. She longed for the days of her first appearance, when she was treated to condescension, but was at least able to move freely through the press of persons. She hailed the arrival of Darby Hampford, whom she had previously met, with relief at first.

'Oh, yours is a face I know, thank heaven!'

It smiled unctuously. 'And will become better acquainted with, I trust. Dear Lady Mary, how I have longed since that night to hear more from you about the heavens. Never have I been so enthralled.'

Maidie eyed him, her cordiality waning. 'Indeed?'

'Can you doubt it? You must, indeed you must, give me the pleasure of listening to you.' He leaned closer, saying in a tone far too intimate for Maidie's comfort, 'But not here! Let us meet somewhere—in private.'

'In private!' Maidie echoed blankly.

'Yes, yes, I must have you to myself. One cannot converse with any degree of comfort at a party. You are new to London, I know, but there are places where one may safely ignore the proprieties.'

'Mr Hampford, are you out of your senses?' demanded Maidie forthrightly.

'Utterly, Lady Mary!' He came closer, as if he would whisper in her ear, but she drew away. He murmured, 'Don't retreat! I would I could say what is in my heart, but I cannot. Not where anyone might hear.'

Maidie was stunned. Was she supposed to take this seriously? Did he imagine her to be flattered? She could harbour no illusions. Lady Hester was obviously right.

'You must take me for an idiot, Mr Hampford,' she said flatly.

He smiled in what she supposed he must imagine to be a winning manner. 'Far from it. I think you a perfect angel.'

'Humdudgeon! I will not be talked to in this fashion. Please go away—or I shall be obliged to request Lord Delagarde to have you removed from the party.'

She turned her shoulder, uncaring of the titters that broke out around them, ill concealed by those who had overheard by a hand over a mouth or a lifted fan. She could only trust that Darby Hampford would retire, discomfited, and that her reception of his outrageously insincere approach might serve to discourage others.

Her trust proved to have been misplaced, for she was subjected to several further attempts to engage her interest, and, although none was quite as blatant as that of Hampford, Maidie was in no doubt about what must have prompted them.

'This is intolerable!' she told Lady Hester, when the announcement that refreshments had been laid out belowstairs afforded a brief respite.

Her hostess was lingering as the throng of guests made its slow way out of the saloons. Later, Lady Hester would be obliged to go down and make an appearance, but she trusted Lowick to ensure that the needs of each guest were catered for, despite the highly augmented nature of the gathering.

'Are you having a difficult time of it, poor child?' she asked sympathetically.

'Ma'am, it is dreadful! I have never heard such a collection of falsehoods and duplicity as I have been obliged to listen to tonight. Great-uncle warned me that society is full of deceit. I now learn how right he was. But what infuriates me the most is that they imagine me to be ignorant of their intentions. As if I were the veriest nincompoop!'

Lady Hester had to laugh. 'That is very bad, certainly. Don't despair, my child. I think you will find that these attentions will die down in a few days.' She bubbled over again. 'Particularly if you mean to snub the pretensions of like-minded gentlemen in the way you handled Hampford.'

'Lady Hester, you should have heard him! I was quite nauseated. I see that I must be grateful to Lord Delagarde for having kept the matter secret at first. I should otherwise have taken this sort of attitude to have been normal, and not been put so much upon my guard as I am now.'

'Are you indeed grateful to his lordship?'

It was a new voice, entering upon the discussion so suddenly, and with so tart an inflection, that Maidie was startled. She turned quickly, and noted that Lady Hester did likewise. Adela! She might have known.

'This is a private discussion,' she said instantly. 'You should not be listening.'

Lady Shurland produced a coy smile. 'Far, far be it from me to pry into what does not concern me, dear Mary, but in this instance I feel I am in honour bound.'

About to speak, Maidie felt Lady Hester's restraining hand on her arm, and subsided. She watched her hostess glance about the saloon in which they were standing, and herself noted that it was almost empty. Satisfied, Lady Hester addressed the intruder.

'What is it you mean, Lady Shurland?'

'I would not wish to be the instigator of any trouble, but I do think that Mary ought to be informed of Lord Delagarde's part in this.'

'In what precisely?'

'Come, come, Lady Hester. You are both wondering how it comes about that the world has got hold of Mary's secret.'

Maidie snorted. 'You are not suggesting that Delagarde put it about? Humdudgeon! He was the one who insisted that we should tell no one.'

'I acquit Lord Delagarde of any malice. It was not intentional. Merely carelessness—or stupidity.'

Again, it was the pressure of Lady Hester's hand on her arm that kept Maidie from bursting out. Why her instinct should prompt her to fly to Delagarde's defence, she did not know. But she found she could not bear Adela's criticism.

'Do enlighten us, Lady Shurland,' invited Lady Hester.

'It was on the day after you fell ill, Mary. You were there, I think, Lady Hester—at Lady Riseley's. I wondered at the time if he had been overheard.'

'But what happened?' demanded Maidie impatiently.

Adela smiled again, clearly enjoying this evidence of anxiety. 'We were talking of you, Mary. I had asked after your health, for I was truly concerned. I happened to mention Eustace, and his continued desire to press his suit. Lord Delagarde made a most cutting and unforgivable remark with regard to my dear brother's motives.'

'Mentioning my fortune, you mean?'

'Inadvertently, I am persuaded. But that is not all.'

'Then what is "all", Lady Shurland?' prompted Lady Hester.

'Lord Delagarde must have forgotten his own decree of secrecy, for I distinctly overheard him discussing the matter of Mary's fortune with those friends of his.'

'Corringham and Riseley?'

'Yes, Lady Hester.' This time Adela's smile was malevolent. 'It is obvious by tonight's showing that I could not have been the only person to overhear their conversation.'

Maidie stared at her. She did not doubt the story's truth, but she was ready to swear that the spread of it owed more to Adela, and perhaps Eustace, than to Delagarde. Adela might have felt some advantage to her brother in being only one among a number of fortune-hunters. He would thus escape notice. But that Delagarde had let out the truth could not but affect Maidie. She remembered all at once his grim look earlier. He must have recalled the meeting.

'It is to be hoped,' Adela continued sweetly, her sly mission apparently incomplete, 'that it will not now be rumoured that Lord Delagarde kept the secret of your fortune from the world because he wants you for himself, Mary.'

'It is certainly to be hoped not,' said Lady Hester, with more steel in her voice than Maidie had ever heard.

Looking at the older lady, she thought her eyes were sending a warning to her cousin. She lost no time in voicing it herself.

'If you spread such a tale about, Adela—'

'I? What have I to gain?'

'Perhaps nothing,' said Lady Hester softly, 'but then again, it might suit you to ensure that such a rumour was "overheard". It could only be to Delagarde's discredit. Fortunately, his reputation is so well established that I doubt if anyone would believe it.'

'They would not believe it, in any event,' Maidie chimed in, her voice a trifle unsteady, 'if they have seen Delagarde and myself together. Only an idiot could be so blind as to suppose anything of the kind, and if it was suggested to Lord Delagarde himself, I am sure he would laugh.'

A little of Adela's assurance left her, and she frowned. 'I do not understand you.'

'Delagarde is too polite to let you see it,' Maidie said recklessly, 'but the truth is that he was utterly averse to bringing me out.'

'Maidie, hush!' warned Lady Hester.

'Why, ma'am?' Maidie pursued, flushed and bright-eyed. 'It is as well to have the truth, if people are going to talk. He did not want me, Adela, and he does not want me now. He has been brought to tolerate my presence in his house, but I assure you that he cannot wait to be rid of me. There! Now what have you to say?'

She was near to tears, hardly understanding herself what had prompted her to tumble it all out. Somewhere inside her a voice was crying out at the ghost of a memory of Delagarde's dark eyes, which had caught hers so compellingly in a dream of starlight.

Delagarde looked unseeingly through the window in the little downstairs parlour, his back to Lady Hester. He was dressed with his usual impeccable elegance, in a green frock-coat over buckskins and topboots, his cravat neatly tied, but he had not yet breakfasted, and it might be hunger that was causing the hollow within him. Aunt Hes, unusually, had risen before he did, although they were both late following last night's evening party. The last guests had departed at some time after one in the morning.

'I have not told you in order to upbraid you, Laurie,' said his great-aunt gently.

He turned his head. 'If you had, it would be no more than I deserve. Do you think I had not realised all this last night?'

Aunt Hes's explanation of the change in attitude towards Maidie had been unnecessary, for he had immediately seen its significance for himself. Recalling that conversation with Adela, Lady Shurland, his first thought was that his friends had betrayed him. Indeed, he had sought them out there and then.

'You know better than that, old fellow,' had said Corringham coolly.

'If I supposed you seriously believed it, dear boy, I should feel compelled to call you out!' had protested Lord Riseley.

Delagarde had at once apologised, and his friends had sympathised with his situation, supposing, as he had himself, that someone had overheard their conversation. That someone he had not, until this morning, thought to be Lady Shurland.

'She denies having helped the rumours,' said Lady Hester. 'But the murder is out, and there is nothing to be done about it now.'

He moved to the mantelpiece and leaned his arm along it. 'Is Maidie distressed? She looked to be coping well enough last night.'

He saw the familiar twinkle enter Lady Hester's eye. 'She is more disillusioned than distressed. Great-uncle Reginald, you must know, has proved to be right once again.'

Delagarde laughed. 'The devil he has! What must we do, I wonder, to convince her that every fashionable fribble is not necessarily a hypocrite?' To his surprise, his great-aunt became serious. He frowned. 'What is it, Aunt Hes?'

She threw out a hand. 'Oh, don't look like that. I am persuaded it will not amount to anything—at least, I hope not. But that woman means mischief, I am sure of it.'

'Lady Shurland? Come, Aunt Hes, what is the matter?'

Lady Hester sighed deeply. 'She will brand you a hypocrite, if she can, Laurie. She as good as told us that she
will set about the rumour that you kept Maidie's fortune
secret because you want her for yourself.'

Delagarde was so surprised that he let out a peal of
laughter. Of all the nonsensical notions! What, was he supposed to rate his attractions so low that he would stoop to
so petty a trick? He might not have any better personal
attributes than the next fellow. But with his title and position, he had been sought after for so many years that he
would have to be a perfect fool to so belittle his own
chances. If, that was, he'd had any idea of attempting to
attach Maidie.

Why then should Aunt Hes be regarding him in so dis-
satisfied a fashion? 'You don't believe that yourself, Aunt
Hes, surely?'

'Of course I don't believe it,' she responded tartly. 'It
is only that I have realised that Maidie was quite right.'

'What the devil do you mean?'

'She said you would laugh at the idea.'

Delagarde raised an eyebrow. 'Did she, indeed?'

'She also told Lady Shurland that you never wanted her
here, and could not wait to be rid of her.'

Delagarde frowned. He may have expressed some such
wish on occasion, but she must know he did not mean it.
On the contrary, he was growing quite used to having Maidie about the place. And the other night…no, it was better
not to think about that, perhaps. He could only ascribe his
questionable behaviour to the unfortunate effect of liquor
on his inhibitions. Though he had meant well. Starlight,
he decided, was deceptive. She had seemed different, not
at all the Maidie who infuriated him so readily. She had
inspired quite different sensations within him—and he cer-

tainly did not wish to think about those. He hurried into speech.

'That is nonsense. Why the devil should she tell Lady Shurland any such thing?'

'To dissuade her from setting about that absurd rumour, I imagine,' Lady Hester suggested calmly. 'I am inclined to agree with Maidie. No one who has seen you together could suppose you to be contemplating matrimony.'

'Good God, I should hope not!' exclaimed Delagarde involuntarily. 'Marry Maidie? I do not think so.'

He was brought up short by Lady Hester's next remark, delivered as calmly as if she were talking about the weather.

'You could do worse, Laurie.'

Delagarde stared at her blankly. She returned the look steadily.

He drew a breath. 'Aunt Hes, you cannot be serious! I know you had some such idea at the outset, but that was before you properly knew Maidie.'

She nodded. 'Yes, I know her now. And I do seriously believe that you ought to consider marriage, Laurie.'

Chapter Eight

Delagarde gazed at her, a mixture of emotions churning within him. Disbelief warred with some other thrust of energy. Not anger, he was too shocked to be angry. He felt—yes, betrayed! Aunt Hes had been his ally, had never attempted to push him into matrimony. He had thought she had given up this notion of his making a match with Maidie. He could not marry Maidie! She must know that!

'You can't have thought,' he uttered in a voice that sounded strangely hollow, even in his own ears. 'She would drive me crazy. Do you have any idea how disrupted my life has been? Even my thoughts are no longer my own. It is not to be thought of! Do you think I could endure this confusion, this disorder, this—this, yes, *discomfort*. I have not had a day's peace of mind since that girl entered this house. If I have to endure much more of it, there will be nothing for it but to put a period to my existence!'

Lady Hester laughed gently. 'That bad? Dear me.'

'Of course it is that bad! Well, perhaps not that bad. But I tell you, I am positively glad that the secret is out. At least I stand a chance of being rid of the wench!'

'I thought you said you did not wish to be rid of her.'

'That was before I knew that you are still harbouring this ridiculous notion that I should marry her.'

'Have no fear,' recommended his great-aunt cheerfully. 'I will harbour it no longer. I quite see that I have been entirely mistaken in my ideas.'

'You have, yes,' Delagarde told her, feeling absurdly unbalanced by his own agitation.

'You may be easy, my dear boy. I shall not mention the matter again.'

Delagarde eyed her suspiciously, but could discern no trace of that telltale twinkle in her eyes, which appeared, on the contrary, to be unusually grave. He elected to be satisfied with her assurance, and his blood began to cool.

At this inauspicious moment, the door opened and Maidie herself peeped into the parlour. Conscious of a resurgence of feeling, Delagarde only managed to stop himself retreating to the window by a strong effort of will. Good God, this was absurd! Must he now be so conscious that he could no longer endure her presence? He forced himself to speak.

'Good morning. I trust you did not find last night's revels too much for you?'

Maidie looked blank, but Lady Hester intervened. 'He refers, I think, to the fact that you are only just out of your sickbed. Did you sleep well?'

'After last night?' She laughed mirthlessly, coming into the room. 'No, ma'am, I did not. I cannot imagine how I should be supposed to sleep well after last night.' She turned to Delagarde, and he discerned distress in her features. 'I feel dreadfully culpable, my lord. I never intended that you should be pilloried for my actions.'

Delagarde could not allow this to pass. 'Don't be stupid, Maidie. You should rather be censuring me, for this whole sorry situation is quite my own fault.'

'Yes, for allowing me to badger you into bringing me

out,' Maidie said remorsefully. 'I have brought all this trouble down on your head, and I don't know how Adela is to be kept from casting aspersions upon your character.'

Delagarde found himself laughing, the consciousness quite dissipated. 'She may try. Don't concern yourself. Even if anyone believes it, they will not mention the matter to any of us, so why should we allow ourselves to be troubled by it?' He was disconcerted to receive one of Maidie's wide-eyed stares. 'Don't you believe me?'

She looked away. 'I don't think you can wish anyone to suppose that you want to marry me.'

A tide of heat flooded Delagarde, and he cast an involuntary glance at his great-aunt. To his relief, she was looking rather at Maidie than at him. He moved swiftly towards the door.

'Don't let it worry you,' he managed to say, and made to leave the room. Her voice detained him.

'Lord Delagarde!'

He turned. 'Yes?'

'Now that I have so many suitors, I will do my best to choose someone quickly, and then you may be easy. I don't wish to be more of a burden to you than I have been already.'

Delagarde did not know what to say. Her manner was so different to what it had been in the past. Was this change of heart prompted solely by what had occurred last night? Unease filtered into his breast, and he did not know why. He said the first thing that came into his head.

'Take care to choose wisely. Remember that, whomever you marry, you must live with them for the rest of your life.'

He was gone from the room on the words. Maidie stared after him, struggling with the sensation that beset her. It was akin to what she had felt that never-to-be-forgotten

night after he walked out of her bedchamber. She felt—
yes, *bereft*.

She was at a loss to understand herself. She had slept
badly, it was true, tossing and turning while those pointless
questions went round and round in her head. What should
she do? How could she right Delagarde against the rumours? Would Adela spread the lie, or the truth? Which
was worse? Maidie could not think what had prompted her
to speak out, to say those things. It must have been near
dawn before she slept, and she had woken very little refreshed.

It had not helped that she had been obliged to give the
Worm an account of what had occurred at the party, for
Lady Hester had seen fit to warn her duenna of what was
going forward. Poor Worm had been very much shocked.
But it was she who had suggested the solution that Maidie
had presented to Delagarde. Though not quite in a manner
that recommended itself to her charge.

'Dearest Maidie, I do believe it may be the hand of
providence.'

'Providence? What in the world do you mean, Worm?'

The duenna had seized her hand and clasped it warmly.
'Do you forget your purpose in coming to town, Maidie?
You said yourself that you have not so far encountered
many eligible gentlemen. But now here you are, finding
yourself quite surrounded by the most suitable *partis*.'

Maidie had been moved to protest. 'You cannot mean,
Worm, that you would have me marry someone like Darby
Hampford?'

'Was he the one who pressed you so uncivilly?' had
asked the Worm anxiously. 'Of course I could not wish
you to marry him. But were there not others to whom you
would not object?'

But Maidie had discovered that she could not think of
one to whom she would not object. Somewhat resentfully,

she had conjured up the images of those gentlemen who had proved to be on the catch for a rich wife.

'Lord Bulkeley, perhaps?'

'What is he like?' had asked the Worm eagerly.

Maidie had shuddered. 'He is old—five and fifty at the very least! And he is quite gross, Worm. I do not think I could bear to marry him.'

The duenna's face fell. 'Some other, then?'

Another countenance had swum into Maidie's memory. 'I suppose I might endure Sholto Lugton,' she had suggested with a marked lack of enthusiasm. 'At least he is young. Too young, in fact! Why, he is barely nineteen, I believe.'

'It need not be a barrier, Maidie,' had offered the Worm diffidently. 'A very young man is easily led, you know, and less likely to offer you much opposition.'

'You mean I could mould him?'

'Dearest Maidie, it cannot be denied that you have a strong personality.'

'No,' Maidie had agreed. It had crossed her mind that it would be more appropriate to be matched with a man who was equally strong, or stronger, but she had refrained from saying so. She could think of only one man in this connection, and he would not do at all!

'In any event,' had pursued the Worm with determined hope, 'it is likely that there are others whom you have not yet considered. Only think, my love! You will have quite your pick of them, and may choose precisely whom you wish.'

Only…what if the one she wished for did not wish for her? That was a possibility that had apparently not occurred to the Worm. It occurred forcibly to Maidie. Not that she had anyone particular in mind, but it had been borne in upon her that she must possess so little degree of attraction, outside of her fortune and title, that she would do well to think no more of expecting to marry someone who might care for her, let alone someone who might touch her own heart. Really, it mattered little whom she married. Worm was right. She must make a choice as soon as may be, and so free Delagarde from her irksome presence in his house.

She was recalled from her wandering thoughts by Lady Hester. 'A penny for them, child.'

Maidie went to the window. 'Oh, nothing, ma'am. I was merely wondering how quickly I can settle my affairs.'

'I wish you will not do anything hasty, Maidie,' said her ladyship.

Turning to face her, Maidie forced a smile. 'I don't think Lord Delagarde would agree with you.'

To her surprise, Lady Hester gave a sigh that appeared filled with melancholy. 'Drat the boy! I had begun to have some hopes of him.'

Maidie came back into the room, standing in the spot that Delagarde had lately vacated by the fireplace, and staring down in perplexity at her hostess.

'What can you mean, ma'am? What has Delagarde done?'

'It is what he has not done,' said Lady Hester mournfully. 'I quite thought he was beginning to be fond of you, my dear.'

Maidie felt her throat go dry. 'F-fond? Of me? I think you must be mistaken, ma'am.'

'Perhaps.' A straight look was directed at Maidie. 'Not that I expected anything to come of it. There are your feelings to be taken into account, after all.'

'Well, I have never—' Maidie broke off, quite unable to put into words the conflicting experiences of her dealings with Delagarde. She looked away, conscious of heat in her cheeks, and then drew a breath and looked back boldly. 'Ma'am, I must be truthful. I do not know what to think of Delagarde. I feel horribly conscious of what I have done to bring him censure. He—he has a most unsettling effect upon me, that I know.'

'Yes, I had noticed,' said Lady Hester, a laugh in her voice.

'But he can be kind. He makes me laugh—on occasion. If he had not such an uncertain temper—! But I do not know why I complain of that, for mine can be quite as bad.'

'Very true,' agreed the elder lady, smiling. 'You have a deal in common, in fact.'

Maidie's eyes widened. 'Are you mad, ma'am?' Recollecting herself, she added quickly, 'I beg your pardon, but I think you must be. A deal in common with Delagarde? Why, we are poles apart!'

Leaving the mantel, she swept back and forth, as narrowly as the little parlour would allow, the jerking movement of her hands registering the agitation of her spirits.

'We can scarcely agree on anything, he and I. His notions are nearly all of them diametrically opposed to my own. Where I see common sense and practicality, he complains of eccentricity. All his enjoyment is to be found in this fashionable whirl of engagements, which I heartily despise. Perhaps not that—but I can derive only a modicum of pleasure from it. And he is far too autocratic! He must have his will, no matter what. Really, I cannot conceive how I have been able to inhabit the same house with him. The sooner I find myself a husband and set up my own establishment, the better.'

'Yes, Laurie seemed to be of the same opinion,' said Lady Hester drily.

Maidie's eyes flashed. 'Did he? Did he, indeed? He need not concern himself. Now that I have the luxury of choice, I shall do my best to oblige him—as soon as possible.'

Her perambulations had halted, and she stood in the

middle of the room, defiant and determined. Why she had fallen into that moping melancholia, she was at a loss to imagine. Great-uncle would have been grieved to see it. She knew what she wanted, she had come here only for this, and now it was within her reach. Why should she hesitate?

She became aware that Lady Hester was eyeing her with an amused expression, and her colour rose.

'Oh, don't poker up, child!' said the elder lady quickly, forestalling her with a lifted finger. 'Dear Maidie, of course you are quite right to pursue your goal. As well that you have made the decision, for I fear you will have no peace from your would-be wooers.'

'Well, I have the advantage of them, ma'am,' Maidie said, her flush dying down.

'True enough. But here I must echo Laurie. Take care whom you choose, child, for you know nothing of the world. Fortunately Delagarde does know, and he will, I am persuaded, at least discharge his duty honourably.'

Conscious of a resurgence of feeling, Maidie poised on the edge. There was a hollow in her chest, but at the same time, a flicker of resentment.

'Precisely what does that mean, ma'am?' she demanded ominously.

Lady Hester shrugged a little, as if the matter was of small account. 'Why, only that Laurie will do what he can to prevent you from marrying to your own disadvantage.'

'I beg your pardon?' Maidie could hardly believe her own ears. Was it possible? 'Delagarde will prevent me?'

'If he can. I am sure he will feel himself in honour bound to discourage you from an imprudent match.'

Maidie cast a quick glance about Lady Wingrove's crowded saloon, and noted with satisfaction that several pairs of male eyes had already spotted her. Leaving Lady

Hester's side, she moved to seat herself on a small sofa, determined to encourage every gentlemen who came within six feet of her.

The suggestion that Delagarde could feel himself called upon to object to her choice of husband had thrown her into strong indignation. Delagarde to be a judge of what might suit her! Her marriage to be subject to Delagarde's approval! Had she not told him at the outset that she required nothing more from him than his sponsorship? Of course, she saw that he was bound to interfere. Had he not done so upon every possible occasion? He would not marry her himself, oh, no. But he apparently reserved to himself the right to arrange her marriage to another! Not, of course, that she wanted to marry him—who would?— but it was the principle of the thing. What right had he to dictate to her upon her choice of husband? Well, he would not get the chance. She would get herself betrothed in the shortest possible order.

In accordance with this determination, and in unconscious challenge to Delagarde, she arrayed herself in the blue silk gown of which he had so much disapproved that first evening. She did not go so far as to wear the riband and feathers, instead instructing Trixie to dress her hair high, in a knot of ringlets from the crown, with a tendril or two curling down her cheeks. For the first time taking a serious interest in her appearance, Maidie examined her features closely in the mirror. It was not an encouraging exercise but, recollecting that she was no longer dependent upon her looks, she dismissed the despised image from her mind, disposed a lace shawl about her elbows, and went down to dinner.

If she had looked for some reaction to the blue silk gown from Delagarde, she was disappointed. His manner was as cool as her own, and he exchanged more conversation with her puzzled duenna, seated on his right, than with either

Maidie or his great-aunt. Lady Hester kept up a steady flow of cheerful small talk throughout, to which Maidie responded somewhat at random, for it was difficult to concentrate when the object of one's annoyance would keep intruding upon one's attention. Maidie could not withstand a flutter of apprehension at the thought of how he might react to what she intended to do.

The first recipient of her newfound graciousness was Lord Bulkeley. His grossness and his advanced years were alike forgiven, as Maidie smiled a welcome and patted the seat beside her. His lordship, taken aback but nothing loath, sat himself down and proceeded to display his charm.

'Lady Mary, how do you do? I have only just learned that you recently suffered from a nasty head cold. I do beg of you to take better care of yourself!'

'Thank you, I am quite well now,' Maidie told him, adding involuntarily, 'You need not suppose that I am going to prevent you seeking your fortune at my hands by dying.'

The full features before her reddened, and a pendulous chin dropped. 'Lady Mary, I protest! You mistake me, I protest.'

'Do I?' Maidie said, frowning. 'Are you not then desirous of wedding me? I thought I had been reliably informed that your pockets were to let. But perhaps that is wrong?'

The unfortunate Bulkeley sat champing, apparently unable to think of any suitable reply to make. Puzzled, Maidie raised her brows. But before she could speak, another voice intervened.

'There's for you, Bulkeley! Come away, there, and allow others place!'

Maidie looked up into a merry face that she vaguely recalled, but could not put a name to. 'Sir?'

'Lady Mary, send him about his business, I beg of you!'

uttered the gentleman. He was graceful, not at all hand-some, but with a jovial air that certainly attracted Maidie more than Bulkeley.

'Lord Bulkeley, pray go away for the present,' she said. 'I do not know who this gentleman is, but I should like to talk to him for a little.'

The discomfited Bulkeley rose, bowed stiffly, and walked off without another word. The newcomer took his place, disposed his limbs gracefully upon the sofa beside Maidie, and held out two fingers.

'Wiveliscombe. Very much at your service, Lady Mary.'

Maidie lightly touched the fingers. 'I do not think I have heard your name. Have you a title?'

'Alas, no,' he said mournfully. 'I am a humble mister, ma'am. Humble, and shockingly poor. I commend myself to your charity.'

Laughing, Maidie protested, 'I am not disposed to be charitable, Mr Wiveliscombe.'

'Oh, surely. I am persuaded you cannot mean to bestow your largesse upon Delagarde, despite what the vulgar may say.'

'No, I do not mean to,' Maidie said tartly. 'Nor, I may add, does he have any such hope or expectation.'

The gentleman grinned. 'There, now. I see I need have no scruple in putting myself forward for your inspection.'

Maidie was quite unable to help laughing. She liked this frank, open manner. A trifle of mischief lit her eyes. 'Will you submit to a catechism, then? I should require to know everything about you.'

'You may ask anyone,' returned Wiveliscombe, throwing one hand to his heart. 'My life is an open book. But I am too modest to answer any questions you may have—I would be bound to sound like a coxcomb!'

'You are a coxcomb, Wiveliscombe,' announced Darby Hampford.

Maidie looked up quickly, and caught his eye. He was standing before them, his air very much that of a dog who was doubtful of his welcome.

'My dear Hampford,' cut in Wiveliscombe in a pained tone, 'have you not grace enough to accept defeat? Lady Mary, you will not allow this fellow to oust me!'

'She will, because she is too good a creature to deny me the opportunity to redeem myself.'

This was really too much. It was easy enough to adhere to her resolve with such a man as Wiveliscombe. But on the other hand, Maidie could not make a decision about him on the spur of the moment, or on so short an acquaintance, and she did not wish him to suppose that she favoured him more than another. It was quite a different matter, however, to wilfully subject herself to the company of Darby Hampford.

Before she could make any move, the decision was taken out of her hands. Wiveliscombe rose.

'Never let it be said that I took an unfair advantage. Do your worst, Hampford! I am persuaded that Lady Mary has good taste enough to prefer my pretensions to your own.'

This outrageous speech was said with such a merry look that Maidie felt unable to take umbrage. Besides, he was perfectly right. Darby Hampford was a sham, which Wiveliscombe was not, and Great-uncle would certainly have disapproved of him. As the latter bowed and departed, Maidie caught sight of a shy young man hovering a few feet away. With a swift movement, she thrust Hampford away as he made to sit down.

'There is Mr Lugton! Don't sit down, for I wish to speak to him.' She beckoned, and the young man approached.

'But, Lady Mary—' protested Darby Hampford. 'You will not send me away in favour of Sholto Lugton?'

'Yes, I will,' Maidie said impatiently. 'Oh, if you wish it, we can talk another time. Only go away now, do.'

In deep offence, Hampford left the field. Maidie turned to the boy—for he was little more—and smiled encouragingly. He was a gangling youth, a trifle tongue-tied and self-conscious, with an anxious pallid face topped by a thatch of bright red hair that had at once commanded Maidie's sympathy.

'Sit beside me, Sholto. You do not mind if I call you Sholto, do you?'

The youth shook his head, stammering a little. 'N-not at all, Lady M-Mary.'

Maidie did what she could to put him at ease, quite forgetting for the moment that he was a suitor to her hand. Not that he had made his aspirations clear for himself, but Lady Hester had numbered him among the fortune-hunters, with a passing comment on the unfortunate nature of his circumstances. His father was dead, his mother sickly, and a very modest competence was inadequate to cope with the need to dispose suitably of two sisters. He must marry money, or take up an occupation of some kind. He was ill equipped for either, but hung about every heiress with all the air of a forlorn hope. Maidie was sorry for him.

She had just succeeded in getting him to talk a little about his aspirations, which appeared to consist of finding something he could set his hand to without any very clear idea of what that might be, when there was a further interruption.

'Lady Mary, may I request a word with you—alone?'

Maidie jumped, her heart leaping into her mouth. Delagarde's voice was icy, and his eyes, when hers flew to meet them, were smouldering. Too much discomposed to recall her fury with him, Maidie took the imperative hand he was holding out and allowed him to pull her to her feet. He drew her hand within his arm, but maintained his grip on her fingers. Then he turned to Sholto Lugton, who had risen, a look of alarm in his face.

'You must excuse us, Mr Lugton.'

'Y-yes, sir. Of c-course.'

Her heart thumping painfully, Maidie tried to protest as Delagarde drew her inexorably to the door of the saloon, and into the gallery beyond.

'What do you think you are doing, Delagarde?'

'I was about to ask you the same question,' he returned in a low tone, but with a thread of vibrant passion running through it. 'We will wait, however, until we are safely out of earshot of the saloon.'

Maidie said nothing, for she was glad of the respite as he walked her towards the far end of the long narrow gallery that ran down one side of Lady Wingrove's mansion. By the time Delagarde halted, she had sufficient command over herself to meet his eyes steadily as he released her imprisoned hand, and turned to confront her.

'May I ask what that revolting exhibition was in aid of?'

His blighting tone instantly drew Maidie's temper. 'No, you may not!' she snapped. 'In any event, I don't in the least understand what you mean.'

'Then I will tell you,' said Delagarde, almost through his teeth. 'To sit in ceremonial state and interview one fortune-hunter after another, as if you were passing each of them under review—'

'Which is exactly what I was doing!'

'—is hardly conduct to be expected from any female with the smallest pretension to gentility.' He stopped, drawing a breath as he took in her remark. 'Do you dare to stand there and tell me that you had the effrontery, the…the indelicacy…the tastelessness—?'

'Yes, I do tell you so,' Maidie returned. 'Pray, how else am I to know which of them will make me a suitable husband?'

'In the same way that every other young lady discovers it. By discreet enquiry, and by getting to know them over the course of the Season. A female does not bring up the subject herself!'

'This female does,' declared Maidie, adding somewhat balefully, 'And what is it to you, Delagarde?'

He uttered a curse and seized her by the shoulders. 'I will not stand by and watch you make a fool of yourself! What the devil do you suppose people must think of you if they see you flirting with such a fellow as Wiveliscombe?' The very name appeared to enrage him still further. 'Good God, but Wiveliscombe, of all people!'

'What do you have against him?' Maidie demanded, trying vainly to thrust his hands from her shoulders. 'I thought him altogether amusing and amiable.'

'Amusing and amiable?' Delagarde uttered a short bark of laughter, and released her. 'I'll warrant you did!'

Maidie unconsciously rubbed her shoulders, frowning. 'I do not know what you mean. And I was not flirting!'

'Oh, indeed? What then do you call it? Simpering and giggling—'

'I would scorn to simper! What is more, if I choose to flirt with him in future, I shall!'

'Not if I have anything to say to it, you won't!'

'Well, you don't have anything to say to it!'

There was a moment of silence as they glowered at each other. Maidie's bosom rose and fell rapidly with the tumult of emotion. She had never felt so angry in her life. She wanted to beat Delagarde's chest with her fists! Shocked at the ferocity of her own thought, she drew a little away from him, as if she feared she might carry out that unlady-like action.

The small movement she made pulled Delagarde up sharply. Good God, what the devil was the matter with him? Remembering all at once where they were, he glanced swiftly down the gallery, and was relieved to see that they remained in sole possession of it. He let his breath go, and stepped back.

'I have never been closer to striking a female,' he uttered, in a spent voice.

'Let it console you to know that I wanted quite as badly to hit you,' Maidie told him gruffly.

Another silence fell. Maidie stole a glance at him, and found that he was looking away. He felt her regard, and turned his head. The faintest of smiles flickered across his face.

'I could strangle you, Maidie!'

She gave him one of her wide-eyed stares. Her heart was behaving very oddly, seeming to jangle inside her. She wished he would not smile at her in just that way. Why his expressing a desire to murder her should have this effect, she was at a loss to understand. But then, it was beginning to be difficult to understand anything in her dealings with Delagarde. She looked away from him again.

'What is your objection to Mr Wiveliscombe?' she asked, as coolly as she could.

Delagarde did not mince his words, and his voice hardened again. 'He is a wastrel and a libertine. I doubt of his getting to the point of offering marriage to anyone.'

Maidie's gaze came back to his, puzzlement in her face. 'Then what does he want with me?'

Delagarde did not answer for a moment. He was regretting his hasty denunciation, for the tale of Wiveliscombe's activities was not one for the ears of a young female. On the other hand, Maidie was unlike any other female, and if he did not warn her, who would? Her naivety posed too great a risk. He could not reconcile it with his conscience to allow her to fall unchecked into the hands of that scoundrel.

'Wiveliscombe lives off his mistresses,' he said bluntly.

Maidie stared at him, an odd blank look in her eyes, and he wondered if she understood. When she did speak, what she said was not at all what he might have expected.

'Then you mean he really is an unsuitable prospect?'

Delagarde frowned. 'Did you suppose I did not mean it seriously?'

'I thought—' Maidie broke off, for she could not say what she had thought. It had occurred to her—blindingly!—that she had suspected Delagarde of *jealousy*. The notion stunned her. Could it have been? Impossible! But his fury had been out of proportion, had it not? Only if Wiveliscombe was truly as bad as he said, then Delagarde might be pardoned his anger, for he believed himself to have a responsibility towards her. A responsibility. Her heart sank. Of course he could not have been jealous. He would have to care for her to feel that.

It became suddenly oppressive to be in his company. Murmuring an excuse which Delagarde barely heard, she left him a prey to conjecture.

Did it matter to her so much that Wiveliscombe proved unsuitable? It was not possible that she had formed a *tendre* for the man in so short a period. Was it? His spirits dropped, unaccountably. Except that of course he must pity the wench, if she had indeed felt the stirrings of an attachment. Had he known, he would have dealt with her more gently. Indeed, he was hard put to recall without abhorrence his earlier conduct. What had possessed him? A burning sense of resentment had overcome him at the nauseating sight of Maidie encouraging such an unworthy collection of *partis*. She deserved better! She ought to value herself a little more highly.

He became aware that his great-aunt was coming towards him, and stiffened at her approach. Had she talked to Maidie? Anticipating a reproach, he braced himself. But he was hardly prepared for what Lady Hester did say.

'Really, Laurie, what a fool you are!'

A frown descended on his brow. 'What the devil are you at, Aunt Hes?'

'My dear boy, if you will behave in this nonsensical dog-in-the-manger fashion, you will only serve to foster these stupid rumours.'

'Dog-in-the-manger? I did nothing of the sort!'

Lady Hester twinkled. 'Laurie, you swooped upon the child like an avenging fury, swept her away from her suitors, and dragged her down here where anyone might have been privileged to witness your fight.'

Delagarde shifted uncomfortably. 'It was not a fight.'

She regarded him sceptically. 'Whatever it was, I advise you to refrain from a repeat encounter—in public, at any rate.'

'Did Maidie say anything to you?'

'Just now? She had no chance to do so. She was pounced upon by Adela and that cold-hearted brother of hers the moment she stepped through the door.'

Delagarde felt an odd frisson shake him. 'Why do you call him cold-hearted?'

'He has calculating eyes.' She sighed a little. 'The pity of it is that I fear Maidie will end by feathering his nest for him, after all.'

'*What?*' Delagarde blenched. 'She could not possibly do so! Why should you think it?'

'My dear Laurie, only look at the alternatives! Besides, there is always something to be said for the devil you know.'

At this instant, it was not a saying that found any favour with Delagarde. He surprised himself with the discovery that he disliked the notion of Maidie marrying Silsoe only one degree less than that of her marrying Wiveliscombe!

* * *

'My poor Maidie,' Eustace was saying unctuously at that very moment. 'I do sincerely feel for you, believe me.'

It was bad enough to have been forced into company with Adela and this hateful creature, without having to fathom the devious nature of his remarks. Maidie sighed wearily.

'I am sure you are going to tell me why.'

'He is talking of Lord Delagarde's attitude towards you, Mary,' put in Adela, with a pitying look.

The exchange was taking place in a window alcove set into the little corridor between one of the two grand saloons. Weakened by her quarrel with Delagarde, Maidie had felt powerless to prevent herself from being coerced, quite gently but inexorably, with Adela and Eustace either side of her, into passing through the saloon with an appearance of being deep in conversation as she went. That they had witnessed the late encounter, she could not now doubt.

'Like everyone else, we saw him all but kidnap you,' said Eustace smoothly, confirming her thought. 'It could not but set up speculation in the public mind.'

'If you think I care what anyone—'

'Ah, you don't, Maidie, of course we know that. But has not Delagarde given everyone to understand that he cares?'

A pulse began to beat in Maidie's throat, and she stared at him. 'Delagarde—cares?'

The thin smile spread mockery over Eustace's countenance. 'About what people may think of you,' he explained softly.

Maidie felt herself go hot, and avoided the cold understanding of his gaze. He had hit upon precisely the burden of Delagarde's complaint. Was it possible that their argument had been overheard? She tried to gather her self-command. It was stupid to allow this creature's unkind hints to discompose her. She looked instead at Adela.

'What is this about?'

'Consider it a cousinly warning.' Adela smiled in a way that made Maidie itch to slap her. 'You cannot be aware of the truth about Delagarde's intentions, or you would not have remained in his house.'

A sense of bewilderment began to creep over Maidie. What were they implying? She looked from one to the other. 'I do not understand you.'

Eustace tutted. 'Do you not, poor Maidie? And you are usually so quick of wit.'

'Do stop calling me "poor Maidie",' she snapped irascibly. 'If you have something to say to me, then say it, or go away.'

The cold eyes gleamed. 'Very well. Tell her, Adela, in plain words.'

'Mary, open your eyes!' urged Lady Shurland. 'Read into Delagarde's conduct towards you what is obvious to the world.'

Maidie frowned, conscious again of confusion. She clutched at the idea that she had felt herself obliged to dismiss. 'Are you saying that he is jealous?'

'Of his marked-out property, nothing more,' Eustace said bluntly. 'Your ambition—or your wishes—might blind you, but you must know, deep down, how little Delagarde could desire you for yourself alone.'

'You are scarcely fitted to take your place beside him in the position which he occupies in the world of fashion,' added Adela on a waspish note. 'He must know that well enough.'

'But you, Maidie,' Eustace continued smoothly, 'do not dream of social success. You will be contented enough if he will but provide you with an observatory at his country home. He needs an heir, yes, and trusts that you may be persuaded to give him one.'

'What could be more convenient for him?' demanded Adela. 'He may have all the advantage of your fortune, and none of the inconvenience of your presence in his life.'

It was all Maidie could do to command her features as the full import of these suggestions sank in. She felt sick. There was a thudding at her temples. And why should there be this desolation at her heart? They had outlined a programme that she would, some few weeks earlier, have seized upon eagerly. Was contemplating still—but with any man other than Delagarde!

Aware of the continued regard of this malevolent pair, she rallied her forces. She must remember that their whole purpose was to induce her to marry Eustace. She must not allow anything they said—whatever its import—to affect her.

'Even if what you say is true,' she began, surprised at the steadiness of her own voice, 'it can avail Delagarde nothing if I choose to marry someone else.'

Eustace gave a jeering little laugh. 'Choose?'

Adela was openly scornful. 'What a fool you are, my dear Mary! You have placed yourself wholly in his power. You have only yourself to blame if he takes advantage of the situation.'

This was beyond Maidie. 'How could he do so? He has no control over me—over my decisions.' For to deny his control over her emotions would be futile and dishonest.

'Maidie, Maidie,' chided Eustace softly. 'You are living in his house!'

'Of course I am living in his house. What has that to say to anything?'

'It sets you at so great a disadvantage, my dear, that I doubt if even Lady Hester could save you.'

She stared at him, blank with incomprehension. Adela

positively sniggered, and Maidie's glance went quickly to her sharp-featured face.

'You are such an innocent, Mary,' said her cousin. 'Poor thing, it adds so greatly to your vulnerability. Thank heaven we are able to put you upon your guard!'

'But against what?' demanded Maidie frantically.

Eustace gave that secret smile that did not reach his eyes. 'Have you not yet understood? It will be easy enough for Delagarde to ensure his victory over you, Maidie. He has only to make you wholly his own—by seduction.'

Maidie gazed at him in shock, beset by a tide of warmth that seemed to spread throughout her body, causing a thrumming at her heart, and a most improper series of images to course through her mind. These last were so very unbecoming that she broke into hasty denial.

'Humdudgeon! I refuse to believe Delagarde to be so dishonourable. I know that he has no wish to marry me— and no need of my fortune besides.'

'Believe what you wish, then,' said Adela, adding slyly, 'but his true intentions will become obvious enough in time. Let us see how he conducts himself when you attempt to marry another!'

Chapter Nine

The interview with Adela and Eustace had left Maidie so discomposed that she had sought out the ladies' retiring room as soon as they left her. It had been some time before she was able to command herself sufficiently to return to the party, and for the rest of the evening she had been so abstracted that she could not afterwards recall anything other than the hideous consciousness of Delagarde's presence. He had not again approached her, much to her relief, but so aware of him was she that she could at any given moment have pointed out his whereabouts without looking.

How she had managed to talk so nonchalantly to Lady Hester in the carriage on the way home, or with what excuses she had staved off the inevitable eager questions of her duenna, she could not have said. But she found herself alone at last, and lay in bed, listening within the curtains for the door to close behind Trixie. The moment it did so, she let her breath go in a long sigh, and discovered that tears were trickling down her cheeks.

She lashed herself mentally for a fool, but the flow of tears refused to stop. She did not even know why she was crying—except for the cruelly hurtful remarks that had been addressed to her by those two horrid creatures. Of course, she knew how little fitted she was to be the wife of a fashionable peer. But need they have said so? Naturally she did not believe for one moment that their expressed fears on her behalf had the slightest foundation. Was she to accept that Delagarde would conduct himself in such an underhand way? As for the ridiculous delusion that he might seek to seduce her—!

But here, for some unfathomable reason, a pang, sharp and piercing, went through her, and the hot tears gathered momentum. Maidie clutched her pillows and buried her face in their comforting softness.

She slept late into Friday morning, the accumulated distresses, coming so soon after her recent illness, proving exhausting in her weakened state. Awaking with a slight headache, she was relieved to have an excuse to obey the decree of Lady Hester—summoned by an anxious Worm—that she remain in bed for the day.

Pampered and cared for, Maidie's natural resilience reasserted itself and she began to revive. She refused to give place to the intrusive thought that no message or inquiry about her condition came from the Viscount. And if she once or twice looked up rather eagerly at a knock upon the door, and then sank back at the entrance of Trixie or the Worm, it was not disappointment, but only a natural reaction to the boredom of seeing the same faces all day long.

She arose on Saturday, refreshed and ready—as she took care to inform Lady Hester as they set forth upon a drive in the park—to resume her interrupted search for a husband.

'I doubt if you need to search, Maidie,' said Lady Hester, amused. 'They are bound to come to you.'

She was found to be right. But, to Maidie's chagrin, it was not to her that the first one came. She had just entered the house with Lady Hester upon their return and was about to ascend the staircase, when a young gentleman was seen to be coming down it. Maidie had a vague recollection of his face, but Lady Hester hailed him in accents of some surprise.

'You are Selina's son, are you not?'

He ran down to the hall, and bowed. 'Yes, ma'am. I am Oliver, Lady Rankmiston's youngest.'

'Gracious me, what are you doing here?' Then her eye gleamed mischief and she glanced at Maidie. 'Can it be that you have come to call upon Lady Mary?'

Oliver flushed. 'Yes, I—well, I had hoped to do so. Only I have—I have seen Lord Delagarde, and—' He broke off, and coughed delicately.

Mystified, Maidie stared first at him, and then at Lady Hester. Discovering her ladyship's eyes to be brimful of amusement, she frowned in puzzlement.

'I do not understand you, sir. You came to see me?'

'Yes, Lady Mary. That is, I had something of a particular nature to ask you. Only of course I would not dream of applying directly to you, so—'

It was then that Maidie recalled Lady Hester telling her on the night of their party that this was the only one of Lady Rankmiston's sons still unmarried. Her eyes widened.

'A particular nature? Did you come to make me an offer?' she asked forthrightly.

Young Oliver reddened again, glancing from her to Lady Hester and back again. 'Well, yes, I did. Only Lord Delagarde has refused his permission, so I—'

'I *beg* your pardon?'

His jaw dropped perceptibly. 'Er—Lady Mary?'

'Dear me!' uttered Lady Hester amusedly.

Maidie paid no attention. She drew a ragged breath, demanding incredulously, 'Are you telling me that you asked Lord Delagarde's permission to marry me?'

'Yes, of course,' frowned the unfortunate young gentleman.

'But it has nothing to do with Delagarde!'

'But—but I was given to understand that he is your trustee. Naturally I had to ask him.'

Lady Hester's brows rose, but she said nothing. Maidie took on another cargo of air, and tried again. 'Did Delagarde tell you that he is my trustee?'

'Not precisely. I had heard it elsewhere. He did not deny it, however. To my dismay, he told me that I might not address you.'

Maidie was by now so furious that she could scarcely bring herself to ask the next question with any degree of composure. 'Did he give you any reason for his refusal?'

Oliver looked quite crestfallen. 'Lord Delagarde thinks I am too young for you.'

'Does he?' said Maidie flatly. 'Does he, indeed? Where did you leave him, may I ask? In the green saloon?'

'No, in his dressing-room. He had just come in from riding when I arrived and wished to change his clothes.'

Without another word, Maidie swept past him, running up the stairs. Behind her she heard Lady Hester calling to her to wait, but she did not stop. Reaching the main landing, she fairly ran past the doors to the three saloons and into the corridor beyond, where Lady Hester had pointed out the way to Delagarde's rooms on that first day. Grasping the handle of the first door she came to, she turned it without hesitation and threw it open. She took one pace into the room, and stopped dead.

Delagarde was standing at a dressing-table before a long pier-glass, clad only in his boots, buckskins and shirt-sleeves, and engaged in placing a fresh cravat about his throat. He paused, his startled glance flying to the door. Behind him, his valet hovered, holding in readiness several

more starched white cravats, on his face an expression of
severe disapproval.

'Oh!' uttered Maidie lamely.

'A somewhat inadequate expression, under the circumstances,' remarked Delagarde, his tone cooler than a natural embarrassment dictated.

Maidie's cheeks flamed, but she found herself unable to
move from the spot, her gaze riveted upon his *déshabillé*,
a slow pulse beating in her throat. Unconsciously, the tip
of her tongue ran over her lips, and her eyes rose, locking
with Delagarde's.

For a timeless moment, he could not drag his eyes away,
and the ruffle of his heartbeat threatened to choke him.
Then she spoke, and the breathy quality of her voice sent
heat fleeing down his veins.

'I wished—I wished to speak to you.'

Delagarde was scarcely aware of replying. 'Very well.
I will join you directly in the green saloon.'

'Yes…'

Maidie shut her eyes, turned quickly, and walked out of
the dressing-room, closing the door behind her. For a moment, she stood there, her breast heaving, unable to think
or move. Then, like an automaton, she at last shifted away,
her legs seeming of their own will to seek the relative
security of the green saloon.

For a few bemused moments she could not remember
why she had bearded Delagarde. She crossed to the window and stared out without seeing anything at all. Her
cheeks still felt hot, and she put up her hands to touch
them. Belatedly, it came to her that she had behaved with
a sad want of decorum.

What had possessed her? The vision of the Rankmiston
boy's face rose before her mind's eye, and memory came
flooding back. But gone was the righteous indignation that
had driven her to that disastrous impulse. She ought to be

angry, she had every right. She was indeed thrumming with emotion. Only it was far from anger.

Without thought, she reached out and her fingers came in contact with the cool glass of the window-pane. It stung. Oh, God, was she yet so hot inside? So hot—and *desperate*. For it came to her all at once that if there were any truth to the suspicions put into her head by Adela and Eustace, she had no defences. For if Delagarde chose to seduce her, he would find her resistless.

'I dare say I should have expected that I would be receiving a visit from you.'

His cool tones, coming unexpectedly from behind her, made her jump. A flush swept through her, and her pulse raced like a violin. Why had he to be so prompt? She needed a moment to compose herself. But there was no compassion of time. She must face him immediately. Drawing a breath, she turned.

He was fully dressed, and impeccable. His cravat was neatly tied, and the dark blue cloth coat over a silk waistcoat of brighter blue mercifully concealed the disturbing masculinity of his figure. The dark eyes, when Maidie dared to meet them, looked rueful.

'You met the Rankmiston boy, I take it?'

'Yes,' she agreed, and glanced away again, recognising that some sort of apology was in order. 'I—I did not think. I lost my temper, and—'

'And flew to find me so that you might instantly complain of my conduct.' He laughed lightly. 'As well that I had completed the preliminaries of my toilet!'

Maidie flushed again, and turned away, responding gruffly, 'You need not tease. I know it was not becoming conduct.'

Delagarde moved to the mantelpiece, wondering how he could ease her evident embarrassment. His own experience had shocked him, for he had felt acutely her response to his maleness. It had made him, for a few hideous moments, recall vividly Aunt Hes's assertion that he ought to consider marriage. But that was nonsense—merely a reaction to the discovery that Maidie had feminine instincts. He must not allow it to weigh with him. Nor with Maidie herself.

'Come, Maidie,' he said, with deliberate calm. 'It was not as bad as all that. We inhabit the same house. Such accidents are to be expected. After all, it is not so long since that I saw you in your dressing-robe.'

It was an unfortunate reminder. The last thing Maidie wanted was to recall that night: star-gazing with him in her bedchamber! More to deflect this line of conversation than anything else, she threw herself headlong into the protest that she had gone to his dressing-room to make.

'What do you mean by telling this Oliver that you are my trustee?'

'I did not tell him so,' Delagarde said calmly. 'But if you are asking whether I am responsible for his believing that I am your trustee, then, yes, I am.'

This confession succeeded in seizing Maidie's attention. She stared at him, moving into the centre of the room. 'How is that possible? What did you do?'

'I had my friends Riseley and Corringham put it about, with the proviso that you need my permission to marry.'

'You had them…' She faded out, shaken.

Delagarde eyed her. There was something in her face that he could not read. He had expected indignation and protest, that she might lose her temper. And she had, apparently, only to be taken aback by that unsettling encounter in his dressing-room. But now she was regarding him with—suspicion?

'What is the matter? It is only what you suggested at the outset. We could scarcely go on in the same way with your fortune known.'

Still she said nothing, only staring at him with that queer look in her eyes—as if she was repelled! He took an involuntary step towards her.

'Maidie, I have done it for your own protection. I know you think you can manage your own affairs, but believe me, your very innocence puts you in danger. In all honour, I cannot allow you to throw yourself away on some philandering wastrel, some worthless trifler who will fritter away your inheritance.'

At last Maidie withdrew her intent gaze from his face. She felt oppressed, beset by doubts. Finding her knees weak, she made her way to the little striped sofa and sat down, gripping her fingers tightly together in her lap. She could not look at him. She tried to gather her thoughts, and made the unpleasant discovery that it was as painful to believe him as it was to doubt him. In either case, Delagarde's concern was with her money, not with her.

Whichever it proved to be, there was one grievance which he could not justify. She recalled it with a slight resurgence of the indignation she had felt in the first place. She looked up at him again, lifting her chin.

'Whatever you may think of anyone who wishes to marry me, you have no right to refuse permission without even referring the matter to me. How could you know that I did not wish to marry this Oliver?'

Delagarde bent a disconcertingly penetrating gaze upon her. 'Do you?'

'I might. I don't yet know, I have barely met him,' Maidie said irritably. 'That is not the point.'

'I take the point,' he returned shortly, trying to suppress the rise of a sensation of wrath which he knew to be misplaced. 'Rest assured that when someone suitable does apply, I shall refer the offer to you.'

Maidie fairly gasped. 'Someone suitable? You are to judge their suitability, and I have nothing to say to it?'

'For God's sake, Maidie!' he exclaimed, losing patience. 'Get off your high ropes! Be glad that I rate your intelligence high enough not to suppose you so idiotic as to consent to marry a mere boy of twenty.'

'If that is the case,' said Maidie, jumping up, 'you ought to suppose me capable of making up my own mind.'

'No, because I don't trust you!' Delagarde threw at her. 'You are both impulsive and reckless, and your candour is a recipe for disaster.'

'Well, it is my disaster—not yours!'

Delagarde strode up to her and seized her by the shoulders. 'I am not going to let you ruin your life, so don't think it!'

'Let me go! It has nothing to do with you—as I have several times informed you.'

He shook her. 'You made me responsible for you, you obstinate little vixen! If you don't like the consequences, you have only yourself to blame.'

Maidie wrenched herself out of his hold, pulling away. 'You need not think you can go on in this high-handed fashion with me, for I won't bear it. You know very well I never wanted you to interfere in my life.'

'That is past praying for!' Delagarde flashed. 'And if anything was needed to demonstrate that I must interfere, it is that collection of freaks that you saw fit to encourage to dangle after you.'

'Freaks!'

'Yes, freaks. And let me warn you that if that clodpole Lugton takes it into his head to apply to me, he may look to have his ears boxed!'

'He will not apply to you because I will not let him. If I choose to marry him, nothing you could do or say would stop me, so don't think it!'

Delagarde laughed mirthlessly. 'You have a very poor understanding of my powers.'

An abrupt frisson jerked Maidie off balance. Adela's voice came back to her: 'You have placed yourself wholly in his power.' Her pulse missed a beat, and started up again unevenly. Her gaze widened, and she lost control over her voice.

'D-don't think I am un-unaware of what you intend by this. You m-may think you can m-make me do what you want, but you are m-mistaken. I am n-not afraid of you, Delagarde, and I know how to protect myself.'

There was a tumult of emotion in Delagarde's own breast: fire and fury, a devil of violence to which the wretch drove him, and that threatened every moment to overwhelm him. But these words threw bafflement into the pot.

'What are you talking about?'

Maidie saw the change in his face and was brought up short. That was stupid! She must not let him see her suspicion. As well blurt out at once that she believed he might be planning to trick her into matrimony! He was bound to deny it. She shifted away.

'It—it does not signify. Rest assured that I shall marry whomever I please, fortune-hunter or no, and you have nothing whatsoever to say about it.'

Delagarde fell back. The dark eyes burned, and he spoke in a voice of suppressed passion. 'If that is how you feel, I cannot think why you enlisted my help in the first place. You might as well have married Lady Shurland's brother. Do so, for all I care. Marry whomever you please—it is nothing to me!'

With which parting shot, he turned on his heel and walked quickly out of the saloon.

It was in a mood of great unease and tension that Maidie set forth to attend the Rankmiston ball early on the following week. It was set to be the high point of the Season, which was one of the reasons Lady Hester gave for refusing to allow Maidie to cry off. She had protested in vain.

'But only think how embarrassing, ma'am! Young Oliver will scarcely feel himself able to look me in the face.'

'Nonsense, child,' laughed her ladyship. 'If all young men who received a rejection were to abjure the society of the object of their affections, the rooms of most of our hostesses would be very thin of company.'

'I can scarcely claim to be the object of Oliver's affections,' Maidie pointed out.

Lady Hester smiled. 'No, I don't think even Selina would have the audacity to claim that.'

'And there is another thing, ma'am. Lady Rankmiston must have been much offended by the refusal. I am sure she could not wish to see me in her house.'

'On the contrary. She will be doubly anxious, for it will give Oliver an advantage over his rivals. As a son of the house, he may monopolise you with impunity.' She gave Maidie one of her mischievous looks. 'You cannot suppose that Selina is likely to be in the least put off by a first refusal. Besides, Oliver will undoubtedly have told her not only that Laurie turned him down, but that you knew nothing of the matter. She will welcome you with open arms, mark my words!'

Maidie soon discovered that Lady Hester had read her friend's mind only too well. She was greeted with much graciousness, and Lady Rankmiston herself insisted upon her accepting Oliver's hand for the opening country dance.

Maidie found him a little shy of her, and supposed vaguely that it was not altogether surprising, although it was all of three days since he had made his offer. But those three days had acquired a new significance for Maidie, since they also marked the time since her last quarrel with Delagarde, and the last time she had encountered him—until tonight.

She was wearing, for the first time, the cream gown with the huge black sprigs and a deep *décolletage*. A flutter at her breast as, accompanied by the Worm, she had presented herself in the drawing-room where Lady Hester and Delagarde were awaiting her, had accelerated suddenly into a racing pulse as she saw the Viscount's eyes widen at sight of her. His glance raked her, dwelled for a moment on her ginger locks, which Trixie had dressed high and ornamented with a string of pearls, and then fell again to the swell of her bosom. Maidie's heart thumped painfully, and warmth spread over her. She could not read his face, and tried to tell herself that it meant nothing to her whether or not he appreciated the picture she presented. His gaze moved up again, and he caught her glance.

For a moment or two, Maidie blanked out all thought. The unmistakable glow in his eyes touched off some spark within her, and a knowledge, deeper than consciousness, passed straight into her heart. The first wisp of perception came with the unwelcome remembrance of what Eustace and Adela had propounded. And she knew she could not do it. She had rather marry anyone else and live without Delagarde altogether, than live with him on those distant terms.

It was as well that Lady Hester had broken in upon these burgeoning ruminations; in the ensuing shower of compliments that fell about her head, she realised only later that Delagarde had not participated. The discovery she had made added nothing to her comfort, and it took all her resolution to appear normal. She reflected that even Great-uncle Reginald would not have detected the sham, and a pang smote her for what she had come to in these few short weeks.

When her dance with young Oliver ended, she was at once besieged by admirers, and within minutes had engaged herself for every further dance. As the gentlemen favoured moved away again, she found Eustace Silsoe at her elbow.

'Alas! I see I am to be unfortunate tonight. No dances left, I fear. Dear Maidie, walk with me a little instead.'

Maidie suppressed a shudder of distaste, and placed her hand on his arm. She could not make a scene at a function such as this. Besides, she had to marry, and she must remember that Eustace had been the most determined of her suitors. To be sure, she disliked him intensely, but the one thing she might be certain of was that as her husband, provided she handed him the use of her purse, he would leave her alone.

She allowed him to guide her to one end of the enormous ballroom where a number of sofas had been placed to enable the guests to rest between dances.

'You do not object to my company,' Eustace said smoothly, standing over her as she took a seat. 'I wonder what I have done to merit so great a change.'

Maidie looked up, and her heart sank at sight of his feline smile. 'I do not know what you mean.'

'Don't you?' he said, deceptively bland. 'Perhaps you suppose that Delagarde, having established his authority so publicly, will summarily nip my pretensions in the bud on your behalf.' A sneer crossed his features. 'Or don't you accept his authority?'

Maidie knew not how to reply to this. On the one hand, she wanted to repudiate his insinuations, but on the other, she did not wish him to suppose that she lent any credence to that hateful suggestion about Delagarde's intentions towards her. She was obliged to fall back upon compromise.

'You know me better than to suppose that I would tamely accept any man's authority.'

'Not even that of your prospective husband?'

'Meaning yourself?' Maidie returned swiftly, unable to help herself. 'Or Delagarde?'

His smile grew. 'Ah, so you have not warmed towards me at all. I could not quite believe in so rapid a change of heart. Then why, I ask myself, should you be behaving so strangely unlike yourself?'

'I am not unlike myself,' Maidie protested, annoyed to feel herself blushing. 'I am merely trying to be civil.'

'Come, come, Maidie, you can do better than that.' His eyes ran over her in a way that made her acutely uncomfortable. 'I believe I have it. For some unaccountable reason, you have decided that perhaps I may do after all. Now, why?' He laughed gently as Maidie threw an indignant look at him. 'Well, why should I cavil? My offer stands. I am not malignant. I harbour no thoughts of revenge for your unkind reception of me.'

'How generous!'

'Is it not? And remember, Maidie. Marry me, and you may do as you please—provided only that you agree to provide me with the lifestyle to which I aspire.' He smiled unctuously. 'Sadly, I do not think that forty-five thousand pounds will suffice.'

Maidie eyed him a moment. He was showing his true colours now. In the past, he had been content to pretend that the portion set aside for her marriage was all he wanted. She spoke with contempt in her heart.

'How much, then, will it cost me to marry you? I should like to know that, Eustace, before I make up my mind.'

'I am not interrupting, I trust?' said Delagarde's voice.

Maidie jumped, and she saw the chagrin spread over Eustace's face as he turned quickly with a muttered exclamation of annoyance. Her heart gave a bound, and then settled into an unsteady tattoo.

'You will forgive me if I remove my—protegée,' Delagarde continued, a veiled threat in the even tenor of his voice which Maidie at least recognised.

He reached down and took her arm above the elbow,

pulling her to her feet. Maidie's fingers shook as he placed
them within the crook of his arm. Without another word,
he walked her away from Eustace, but only a short distance
to one of the drapes that concealed an open French window. Delagarde stepped on to the little balcony beyond
and drew Maidie out.

The drapes closed, and Maidie was enveloped in semi-
darkness. She forced herself to look at Delagarde, who had
released her and was leaning back against the railing, his
eyes only just visible in the pale light of a partial moon.

'You have obviously taken leave of your senses,' he said
in conversational tones.

'Merely because I allowed Eustace to talk to me?' It
was hard to maintain her poise, but Maidie hoped that she
sounded quite normal.

'Don't be stupid. You were actively encouraging him to
suppose you are reconsidering his offer.'

Their last meeting came back to her. 'Why should you
care? You told me I might marry him with your good will.'

In one swift movement, he moved forward, grasping her
shoulders and pulling her towards him. His voice was
harsh.

'You know I didn't mean that!'

Maidie could not speak. His touch, his nearness were
causing the most unsettling sensations within her. Her
heartbeat was so flurried that she thought it must choke
her.

Something of her agitation communicated itself to him,
for he paused, and his grip loosened. 'You're trembling!'

'No, I'm n-not!' she protested helplessly.

One hand left her shoulder. She felt his fingers caress
her cheek and then he was pushing up her chin, scanning
her features in the dark.

'Maidie…' It was a whisper on his breath. He leaned
towards her, and his lips just brushed hers.

As he pulled away, Maidie felt her knees shaking. Faintness threatened to overcome her, and she reached out to seize the railing. He let her go and she turned to clutch the cold iron, catching at her breath to steady it. She heard him curse softly, but she could not look round.

'I'm sorry,' he said gutturally. 'I did not want—I did not mean—It is the fault of that gown! You look—God!—so alluring. And this confounded starlight! Oh, the devil! Maidie, I did not intend it. Think nothing of it. It was nothing—a mistake, that is all.'

He had said enough. More than enough. He had not meant to kiss her—a light, feathery kiss that had turned her limbs to water. But it was nothing. To him, it was nothing. Her eyes pricked.

Forcing down the surge of emotion, she gripped the railing. She must not be affected—must not appear to be affected. She turned her eyes heavenwards, and saw that the night was clear. The stars beckoned lovingly, and as of long habit, she searched for her winter base and began to pick out her friends. Rigel, then Betelgeuse. The pointer gave her Taurus, and peace began to seep back into her veins.

'Aldebaran.' Then down again to Canis Major. 'Sirius.'

She had been unaware of murmuring aloud. Delagarde's voice startled her.

'What are you saying?'

Without thought, she seized on the safety of her familiar territory. Pointing, she showed him Orion.

'Look along his belt—there. That bright one is Aldebaran. It has one of the strongest lights. Then, if you return to the Hunter, you must search for his feet. The brighter star is Rigel, but look!' Her pointing finger moved, drawing an arc. 'The lesser star, his other foot, will lead you to the Great Dog, and there you can find Sirius—see how bright he is?'

Delagarde had closed with her, was standing half behind her, perhaps in order to follow the correct angle of her pointing finger. His voice was a murmur close to her ear.

'Beautiful!'

If she had not buried herself in the comfort of her celestial world, she would have died inside with the force of his presence—so close: the arm that almost touched her breast as it encircled her to steady him with a hold on the railing; the warmth that emanated from him, burning the length of her back down one side; and his hand resting lightly on her shoulder, a heavy flame.

Delagarde heard her words, looked and saw the stars to which she directed his attention: Procyon, and the twins Castor and Pollux. With half his mind, he was drawn with growing interest. The other half wrestled only with the pull of his desire, as the tremble of her limbs gave answer. This was madness! Why had she not run from him, escaped? He could not see her face, but the memory of it, that night in her bedchamber, gave him the image that he must be glad was hidden from him at this moment: in this place, inflamed with a vision of what he might have done—could still do!—in that place, with Maidie and her starlight lure.

Sanity hit. 'My God, what the devil am I doing?'

He thrust away from her as she turned to look at him, startled. A sudden smile lit her features, and she laughed.

'You are asking me?'

Then consciousness returned, and she looked quickly away. The response had been involuntary. She could not think, now, why she had remained out in this seeming wilderness with Delagarde. Yet she did not move.

He could see the confusion even in the darkness, and a sudden urge seized him. Not to kiss her into submission—to the fate he had just been picturing—but to catch her up into his arms and simply hold her there.

The drapes moved, and Lady Hester stepped through

them. Without thought, both shifted swiftly away from each other, to the furthest points of the railing.

'Dear me,' said Lady Hester calmly. 'Has it occurred to either of you that you are setting tongues wagging?'

Maidie blushed in the darkness. 'Oh! I had not thought!'

'You had better go inside, Maidie,' advised her ladyship. 'The musicians are starting up, and I am sure you are engaged for the next dance.'

'Yes—yes, I am engaged for every dance,' Maidie agreed. She did not glance at Delagarde, but slipped quickly back into the ballroom, a prey to the most distressing reflections.

Delagarde saw his great-aunt turn to him, and threw up a hand. 'You need not say it, Aunt Hes. I am palpably to blame. I am fully aware of it.'

'I should think you might be,' said Lady Hester tartly. 'But I am going to say something, nevertheless. It is this. If you don't wish to find yourself obliged to marry the girl, I advise you to be more circumspect in future.'

With which, she left him, and turned to follow Maidie. Delagarde remained on the balcony for a moment or two, cursing himself, and Maidie—and Maidie's gown. He could not think what had come over him. Pray heaven the wench found herself a decent fellow before too long! Any more such encounters and he could not answer for what he might do. He pulled himself up. What the devil was he thinking? It was a mistake, that was all. A stupid mistake. It meant nothing. It was merely the heady combination of starlight and that abominable gown!

Maidie, meanwhile, re-entering the ballroom, had run straight into Eustace Silsoe. He was reinforced by the presence of Adela, and Maidie could not but wonder whether either, or perhaps both, had once again been witness to that illicit idyll on the balcony. Illicit? To her, perhaps, to her unsuspecting heart. But not to him. No, not to Delagarde.

'Excuse me,' Maidie said quickly, trying to forestall any conversation, 'but I am looking for my partner. I am engaged for the next dance with Wiveliscombe.'

'I am sure Wiveliscombe will come looking for you,' Adela said, helping her brother to crowd Maidie into a huddle against the wall.

'We will not detain you for more than a moment,' Eustace added, that unamiable smile creasing his mouth.

'What do you want?' Maidie asked tensely.

'I do not ask what occurred behind those closed curtains,' purred Adela smugly, 'but I dare say I can guess. But no matter for that. Remember, Mary, that we know the true circumstances.'

'What if,' added Eustace, taking up the thread, 'we are tempted to tell the world the truth?'

'That Delagarde has no real control over what you choose to do, and cannot in fact stop you from marrying anyone.'

'Then everyone will know for certain,' said Eustace softly, 'that he is after your money for himself.'

'He will be made to look a fool,' added Adela, with a malevolent look. 'What will people think of a man who deliberately lies to society for his own gain?'

Maidie had listened with the rise of a burning sense of injustice. Whether or not there was any truth in their accusations of Delagarde and his supposed intentions towards her had somehow lost its importance for the moment. Far more compelling was the horrid notion that these two could blacken his name, if they chose. Did they think she would stand by and let them do it?

'No one will think anything at all,' she stated in a steely voice, 'when they hear of my engagement to another.'

Adela blew scorn through her lips. 'Which other?'

'Save myself?' Eustace added.

That was a moot point. Maidie had no answer, but she saw rescue in the form of her partner, who had espied her despite these cousinly attempts to conceal her, and was coming across the ballroom to claim her.

'Excuse me, if you please,' Maidie said with dignity. 'I see Wiveliscombe approaching.'

She broke free and went towards him, with every evidence in her face and voice of pleasure at seeing him. She managed to keep up a lively conversation every time the movement of the dance brought her together with her partner. But her thoughts strayed back to the little scene on the balcony.

Why was she defending Delagarde? She knew that the sway of her emotions made her vulnerable. But what of his conduct? He had said that his actions were unintentional. But were they? Quick suspicion kindled, and she almost missed her step.

'Steady!' muttered Wiveliscombe, reaching out a hand.

'Don't trouble—an unevenness in the floor,' she said quickly, and moved on past him.

Could it be that Delagarde's whole action was feigned? Had he meant to discompose her? If it had been only that light kiss, she might not have thought so. Had he not swiftly apologised, explained it away as a mistake? But what of his subsequent actions? Why had he drawn close to her again? How, if his apology was earnest, could he have taken the opportunity afforded by her examination of the heavens to put her at so great a disadvantage once more? He must have meant it! It must have been deliberate. He had seen how he affected her, how successful was his first foray. And, pressing his advantage, he had done all he could to move her further. No doubt if Lady Hester had not interrupted them, there would have been another kiss.

To her dismay, the thought caused a flood of heat to sear her depths. She forced herself out of her imagination, and put all her concentration on Wiveliscombe. The dance, she found, was ending. He was bowing, and the music ceased.

'Thank you, sir,' she said with forced brightness. 'That was most pleasurable.'

'Was it, Lady Mary?' he asked, with a grin. 'Now I quite thought you had your attention elsewhere.'

'No, I assure you,' she uttered hastily, but with a betraying colour. She saw his lifted eyebrow, and gave a self-conscious laugh. 'Well, perhaps a little. Did I miss something of importance?'

'That depends.'

'On what?'

'On whose point of view we are considering.' He hailed a passing waiter. 'Some wine, Lady Mary?'

'Water, if you please.'

He took a glass from the proffered tray, and handed it to her. 'Lemonade, I think.'

She thanked him. 'You were saying—what I had missed?'

'Ah, yes. You did not respond to my request.'

'Oh? Forgive me. What was the request?'

He grinned. 'That you honour me with an answer in the affirmative.'

Maidie frowned. 'Don't say you made me an offer, and I did not hear you!'

Wiveliscombe gave his merry laugh. 'You did not hear me, and I certainly made you an offer—of a sort.'

The last phrase caught Maidie's attention. She recalled what Delagarde had said of this man, that he was unlikely to marry anyone. What, then, had he offered? Before she could think of alternatives, the plan sprang full-blown into her mind. Here was a perfect solution to both her difficulties. She could confound Delagarde—if she had read him aright—and also save him from the machinations of Eustace and Adela. And she need not hold Wiveliscombe to it. A discreet interval, to allow her to look about for someone else, and she would cry off. Forgetting that she had been reared to detest duplicity, she gave her suitor a bright smile.

'Very well then, Mr Wiveliscombe, I shall give you what you ask. Yes, I will marry you.'

If she had not determined on using him, Maidie would at once have retracted. Taken aback, Wiveliscombe stared at her blankly. Maidie hardened her heart. Let it be a lesson to him to be more careful in future!

But her reluctant suitor regained his poise in a moment. He smiled, and raised her hand to his lips, saying with all his usual grace, 'You have made me the happiest of men. But—er—should I not first obtain Delagarde's good wishes?'

A dangerous light entered Maidie's eye. She had not thought of that! Of course he must suppose there was that obstacle—hoped, no doubt, that Delagarde would refuse him. The whole black-hearted scheme of the Viscount's now burst in upon her. Why had she not believed it at once? Was it not proof enough that he had acted without her knowledge or consent to prevent her suitors from approaching her direct? Only she so much disliked Adela and Eustace that she had not wanted to believe it.

'You need have no fear,' she told Wiveliscombe flatly. 'There will be no opposition from that quarter. I shall tell Delagarde myself—and immediately.'

On the word, she turned from him, and her eyes searched the throng for the Viscount's figure. She caught sight of him, in the act of passing through the ballroom door, and hurried off after him. She caught him up in the corridor outside.

'Delagarde, I need a word with you.'

He looked at her with a frown in his eyes. There was no trace of the pretended amorousness he had displayed to her on the balcony. Of course there was not! Why would there be? He could hope for nothing from her in this public place.

'Certainly,' he said, and led the way back through the ballroom, to the far end, and into a small antechamber.

He left the door to the small room ajar, and turned to her. She appeared to be labouring under suppressed emotion. He had himself well in hand, determined not to indulge in a repetition of the idiotic passion that had attacked him earlier. He spoke curtly. 'What is it?'

Maidie lifted her chin. She was glad to find that her unruly emotions were tightly in her control. The harder he looked at her, the easier this was.

'I wished to tell you that you may consider yourself discharged of your duties towards me.'

Delagarde's brows snapped together, and a sliver of emotion shot through him. If this was what he instantly suspected—!

'Go on,' he said grimly.

'I am betrothed,' Maidie announced in a ringing tone.

A jolt struck at his chest. He drew his breath in sharply, and the dark eyes blazed. 'The devil you are! To whom, may I ask?'

Maidie's heart jarred uncontrollably as his eyes took fire. But she rallied, stiffening, and fairly threw the name at him. 'Wiveliscombe!'

Delagarde's gaze narrowed dangerously. 'We'll see that!'

He turned on his heel, and was gone. Maidie ran out, and saw him striding towards the ballroom door. She would have followed, but at this moment the musicians began tuning up again, and she saw hurrying towards her

Lady Pinmore's son, who hailed her as he approached. She was condemned to a further country dance, which she performed more or less automatically, answering her partner's sallies quite at random.

What Delagarde intended she did not know. That he had determined to interfere she could not doubt. Quite what he would do was a mystery that kept her on tenterhooks throughout the dance. She could not repress a feeling of elation at his reception of her news, even though it argued in favour of his diabolical plan to get her to himself. Almost she began to toy with the idea of allowing him to succeed with her—except when she recalled that the apparent jealous passion must be all pretence. Useless to dare to dream that he might be in earnest! If he were, what should stop him from declaring himself? He would not, had he any tender feelings for her, trouble with subterfuge. Why should he? He need do no more than announce his partiality, which would obviate the need to prevent her marrying anyone else.

But he would not do that, Maidie knew, abandoning the forlorn little hope. How could it be possible that Delagarde, who had the pick of the market, should fall for the wholly unsuitable Lady Mary Hope? No. The only explanation that fitted was the one that had been supplied by Adela and Eustace.

The dance at an end, she found herself face to face with Wiveliscombe. He gave her a conspiratorial look, and bowed to her partner.

'I must beg your pardon, Pinmore, and wrest Lady Mary away from you.'

'No, by God, you shall not!' protested the other.

'Ah, but I shall, my dear boy. Fear not, it is only for a moment. You may claim her again ere long.'

Maidie allowed Wiveliscombe to draw her a little aside,

and frowned at his look of dismay. 'You have seen De-lagarde?'

Wiveliscombe spread his hands. 'Alas, yes. He has for-bidden the banns. I am blighted, I am doomed.'

He looked rather to be relieved, Maidie thought fleet-ingly. But it was a momentary distraction. Delagarde had thwarted her. Of course Wiveliscombe meant to accept de-feat. He had never wanted to marry her in the first place. There was no more thought of duplicity. Sheer fury dic-tated her next actions. All her desire was to hit back—and immediately. She would show him—oh, she would show him! There was more than one fish in the sea.

Excusing herself as quickly as she could, Maidie went in search of Sholto Lugton. His was the next name on her dance card, and it happened that as he was also searching for her, she came upon him but a moment later, after pass-ing among a handful of couples awaiting their turn on the dance floor.

'Sholto!'

'Lady Mary, you have not forgotten me,' he cried joy-fully.

'Far from it. But come, Sholto. I wish to speak with you a moment before we dance. Come quickly!'

She fairly dragged the youth into the very antechamber to which Delagarde had taken her. Without preamble, she plunged recklessly in.

'Now, Sholto, is there nothing you wish to ask me?'

He stared for a moment in blank disbelief. Then stum-bled out his confusion. 'Lady Mary, I do not know how to say it!'

'Be frank, Sholto,' Maidie encouraged him. 'I prefer plain speaking.'

He looked at her, swallowed once or twice, and looked away again. Maidie began to be impatient. But before she could intervene, he tried again.

'Lady Mary…'

Maidie sighed inwardly. 'Yes, Sholto?'

'Lady Mary…'

'I am listening.'

He fell silent once more, staring at her as if he implored her understanding. Maidie heard the musicians tuning up again, and very nearly stamped her foot.

'Do get on, Sholto! We have very little time.'

Once more he hesitated. Then he drew a huge breath, and, to Maidie's intense astonishment, flung himself down upon one knee. 'Lady Mary, I must beg you to consent to marry me!'

With an exclamation of impatience, Maidie reached down her hands to him, with the intention of pulling him to his feet. But Sholto seized her hands, almost dragging her on top of him.

'Pray marry me!' he repeated, in frantic tones. 'For if you do not, I think I may put a pistol to my head!'

'Humdudgeon! I mean—' correcting herself hurriedly and trying to release her hands '—there is no need to go to such an extreme. Certainly I will marry you. Pray get up!'

But instead of complying, or expressing his delight at her acceptance, Sholto remained frozen in his position, and his horrified gaze shot to the doorway. Maidie turned her head, and very nearly cried aloud with vexation.

Delagarde stood on the threshold, surveying the scene with a sardonic expression spreading across his countenance.

Chapter Ten

Maidie drew herself up, trying to overcome the instant discomposure that attacked her at sight of the Viscount. She spoke in what she hoped was a repressive tone.

'This, sir, is a private interview.'

It had no effect whatsoever. Delagarde gave her one scorching glance and turned his attention to her suitor.

'Get up, Lugton,' he said in disgusted accents, 'and stop making a cake of yourself—or I shall be obliged to boot you out of the door!'

The boy released Maidie's hands, and got sheepishly to his feet. 'Your p-pardon, sir,' he managed, with what dignity he could muster, 'but you must know that Lady Mary has consented to—to marry me.'

'Yes, I have,' Maidie averred.

Delagarde did not even look at her. Instead, his glance ran from the youth's head to his heels and back again, and remained on the fiery blush at his cheeks.

'Perhaps you are not aware, Lugton, that Lady Mary cannot marry without my consent.'

'That is not—'

'And that consent,' he went on, speaking over the top of Maidie, 'I categorically refuse to give.'

'You have no right—' Maidie began.

'That will do!' he snapped, throwing a look at her that spoke volumes.

Her breath caught, and she subsided, quite unable to retain her spirits on the receiving end of such a look. Besides, what could she do? Sholto was looking terrified, as well he might, and, without him standing firm, she could scarcely hold him to a betrothal.

'Sir, I—I did not know,' Lugton said, rather faintly, and with a reproachful look at Maidie.

'In that case, I shall overlook your conduct,' said Delagarde, in a voice of such magnanimity that Maidie longed to hit him.

When Sholto did not move, he added, 'You need not wait.'

'But our dance! I mean, Lady Mary is—'

'Lady Mary will be sitting out the next dance.'

Maidie's fury shot straight through the emotional turmoil of the evening. She watched the youth make a disconsolate exit, and turned her fulminating gaze upon Delagarde.

'So now you are at liberty to dictate with whom I may dance, as well as whom I may marry?'

'I don't care who you dance with,' he returned, 'but I have not finished with you yet. If you think I am going to release you to go and find some other poor fool to inveigle into a subterfuge betrothal, you may think again.'

'Subterfuge? Do you suppose I did not mean it?'

'You meant, as I am perfectly aware, to set me at defiance.'

'What do you mean by this?' Maidie demanded rather desperately. 'What do you hope to gain?'

The brown eyes were hard. 'I might ask the same question of you. Why are you indulging in these idiotic engagements? To what end? And don't waste your breath telling me that you wish to marry either of those equally unsuitable pretenders, because I tell you now that I do not believe it.'

'I don't care what you believe!' Maidie returned, almost in tears. 'I told you I would marry whomever I chose.'

'And I told you that you underrated my power.'

Maidie regarded him impotently. Aware of the stinging sensation at her eyes, she withdrew her gaze, turning from him abruptly. Of what use to attack him? He would not confess his plot, of course he would not. For he must suppose that it would only end in her running away. Perhaps she would run away. Only would he not chase after her, and bring her back?

To her dismay, she felt him move behind her. His hand was at her shoulder, turning her. She felt its warmth but briefly, for he shifted back again, and she knew his eyes were on her, though she did not dare to look.

'Maidie,' he began on a more gentle note that put her at once on the alert, 'why are you behaving in this nonsensical fashion? There can be no need for you to rush into a betrothal like this. All I am trying to do is to prevent you from making a mistake that you will regret your life long.'

Was that all? Was that truly all? She could not forbear looking up into the dark gaze. It had softened, and her heart jerked. She longed to ask the question, but she could not—without revealing her reason for asking it. She found another instead.

'Do you mean to refuse every suitor?'

His lips compressed, and the gentler note vanished. 'Until you find the right man, yes.'

'Of whom you are to be the judge.' Flat, and dull.

'As you are obviously incapable of making any sensible judgement, yes.'

Maidie eyed him, trying to read his face. 'I see,' she said at length. 'There is no more to be said, then.'

For a moment, he surveyed her frowningly. 'What is it you are planning, Maidie? I warn you that I mean what I say. Don't try to outwit me!' She made no remark, and he sighed. 'I have no wish to act the tyrant, but you force me to it.'

She bit her lip against an automatic retort, and turned away again. 'If I am the goad, perhaps it would be best if I relieved you of my presence.'

He recognised the gruff little voice. It was the one she used to conceal her emotions, when she felt herself to have been taken at fault. At once Delagarde knew that, under all the defiance, she was deeply hurt. Remorse bit into him. He recalled his earlier conduct on the balcony with a good deal of self-reproach. He was conscious once again of a wish to put his arms about her—only for comfort. That was impossible. He must content himself with soft words. But when he spoke, what came out of his mouth was not at all what he had intended to say.

'I have no wish to be relieved of your presence, Maidie.'

Her glance flicked round, and he discerned wary suspicion in her eyes. Did she not believe him sincere? It was borne in upon him that a number of things she had said to him seemed to indicate as much. Puzzled, he frowned without intent.

'Why do you look at me like that?'

She shrugged, and looked away again. 'How should I look at you? In the way that you looked at me—on the balcony? Is that what you wish?'

'Of course not!' he burst out involuntarily. 'I told you—that was an accident.'

Maidie's wide-eyed gaze was turned back upon him. Her voice was flat. 'An accident. I see. Then believe it as much an accident that I became betrothed to Wivelis-combe.'

Maidie eyed the two elder ladies from her chair to one side of the fireplace in the green saloon, and tried to school her features to an expression of bewilderment.

'I do not know what you mean, Lady Hester. There is nothing the matter, I assure you.'

It was plain that she was not yet a master of duplicity, for her hostess exchanged a disbelieving glance with the Worm, seated next to her on the small sofa opposite, and then returned her gaze to Maidie's face.

'Then why has Ida reported that she heard you crying in the night?'

Maidie cast a glance of reproach at her duenna's face. That worthy looked guilty, and her unquiet fingers kneaded at a handkerchief held between them.

'Dearest Maidie,' she said imploringly, 'do not be angry with me! What else could I do but beg for dear Lady Hester's aid, when you refuse to confide in me?'

'There is nothing to confide, Worm,' Maidie said flatly.

She came under the sceptical eye of Lady Hester. 'Now that I know to be untrue. Do not imagine that I did not observe you go apart with Laurie a second time.'

'What has that to say to anything?' asked Maidie, annoyed to feel herself colouring up.

'What is more,' pursued Lady Hester inexorably, 'I saw you come away from that convenient little antechamber, and for the third time it was Laurie who followed you out.'

'Well, why don't you ask Delagarde what occurred?' Maidie demanded in a fretful tone. 'I am sure it is far more his doing than mine.'

'What is far more his doing?'

'That I am not yet betrothed!' Maidie burst out, unable

to help herself. 'If Delagarde has his way, I shall never be so.'

Lady Hester twinkled. 'I take leave to doubt that.'

She came under the beam of Maidie's wide-eyed gaze. 'Why? Are you in his confidence?'

A frown drove the twinkle away. 'You sound excessively suspicious, Maidie. What is in your mind?'

Maidie averted her eyes, annoyed with herself for having given so much away. 'Nothing.'

'If it is nothing,' put in her duenna in distress, 'why should you spend half the night weeping, Maidie?' She peered across at her charge, and evidently made a discovery. 'Good heavens, I believe you are in love!'

Maidie rose abruptly from her chair, and flew to the window, making valiant efforts to choke down the instant rush of sobs to her throat. There was silence in the room behind her, more significant than the concerned clucking that had begun this interview. She drew a painful breath. That had been foolish! She could not more surely have confirmed her duenna's intuitive guess. What now was she to do? Denial would be fruitless. But if she admitted it, would they not probe to discover the identity of the man upon whom she had bestowed her affections?

'Who is he, Maidie?' came from the Worm, as if she read her thought.

Maidie stiffened, rallied her defences, and turned to face them again. She found that both the elder ladies had risen, and so she kept her distance, as if by this she might better hold out against their curiosity.

'Is it one of those whom Lord Delagarde has dismissed?' pursued her duenna. She glanced at her cousin. 'If so, I am sure that Lady Hester might perhaps persuade him to alter his mind. Could you not?'

'I do not know that I wish to,' Lady Hester said slowly,

and Maidie was dismayed to see the comprehension in her eyes.

'But surely—' began the Worm, and was silenced by her cousin's lifted finger.

Lady Hester had not shifted her gaze from Maidie's face. She came slowly to the window embrasure, and Maidie watched her approach with a good deal of consternation. But when she reached her, Lady Hester put up her hands to Maidie's cheeks and held her so, scanning her face.

'You look drawn, Maidie,' she said gently. 'If I had thought that it would bring you this much unhappiness, I would never have encouraged it.'

Maidie did not pretend to misunderstand her. She winked away the wetness that rose to her eyes. 'He—he does not truly want me,' she said huskily.

Lady Hester's hands dropped. 'I am not at all sure that I agree with you.'

'You are thinking of his determination to refuse to see me married to another. But it is not what you think—what you might be pardoned for imagining.' A sudden irrational hope lit her breast, and she looked at Lady Hester in painful enquiry. 'Unless—has he said anything to you, ma'am?'

'Alas, no,' she admitted. 'At least, I have talked to him on the matter, but that was some days ago. His conduct has certainly borne out what I then suspected.'

'What—what did you suspect?' Maidie dared to ask.

Lady Hester smiled. 'That he is more drawn to you than he has himself any idea of.'

'Drawn to me,' Maidie repeated dully. 'Yes, perhaps. But that, Lady Hester, is not enough.'

By a supreme effort of will, Delagarde had managed to hold aloof from Maidie for two whole days since Tuesday's ball. He hoped that giving her a sensation of freedom, however illusory—for he had every intention of maintaining his strict guardianship—might induce her to refrain from engaging herself any further. He trusted that he had made it abundantly plain that he would not allow her to continue in such promises, even if she made them.

What was more, Riseley had reported that his prompt intervention on the night of the Rankmiston's ball had resulted in a falling off on the part of Maidie's would-be suitors. That Corringham had added a rider to the effect that Delagarde's conduct was rapidly earning him the reputation of having designs upon Maidie himself, he did not allow to disturb him. Let the world think what it might. He had little doubt that he had the Shurland faction to thank for such tattle. Maidie's safety meant more to him than the transitory tarnish of his own reputation. His integrity was at stake—and her whole life!

If there was a part of him that feared to be too much in Maidie's company, he firmly suppressed it. She plainly distrusted him. He did not wish to be provoked into giving her further reason. He was glad of the lack of engagements these two days, for it had given him all the excuse he needed to abjure her society. Tonight, however, there was a musical evening, and he braced himself to withstand any attempt by Maidie to provoke him into another quarrel.

When he had changed into appropriate raiment, and entered the drawing-room to await the announcement of dinner, however, he found only Lady Hester and Miss Wormley in possession.

'Where is Maidie?'

'She has gone to visit Sir Granville Wilberfoss again,' said Lady Hester.

'Is she not coming with us tonight?'

'Apparently not.'

Delagarde grunted, trying to will away a sensation of

disappointment. 'Well, I suppose she cannot come to any real harm there.'

'She is unlikely to engage herself to marry an old man, if that is what you mean,' said his great-aunt calmly.

He cast a quick glance at her. 'Do I detect a note of censure? I should have thought you would be glad that I am doing my best to prevent her from ruining her life.'

'Oh, yes.'

'What do you mean, "oh, yes"?' demanded Delagarde irritably.

'I beg of you to believe, my lord,' twittered the Worm nervously, 'that I am indeed very glad.'

He thanked her, and pointedly ignored the burgeoning mischief in his great-aunt's face.

Dinner was almost over when a note addressed to Lady Hester was brought in. She broke the seal and read it. Next moment, she half rose from her chair, exclaiming in a startled tone, 'Lord save us!'

Delagarde frowned across at her, aware that the Worm did likewise. 'What is it?'

Lady Hester raised troubled eyes from the missive. 'She has not gone to Sir Granville.'

'Maidie?' Instant alarm gripped Delagarde. 'Where then is she?'

'She has eloped with Sholto Lugton!'

'What?'

Delagarde was on his feet, only half aware that Miss Wormley's wineglass had clattered to her plate. Wholly ignoring her cluck-ing, he moved around the table and seized the note from his great-aunt's hand.

'What the devil—?' he uttered, running his eyes rapidly down the sheet. 'Has she run mad? By God, I'll murder her!'

'You will have to catch her first,' pointed out Lady Hester tartly. 'Can you do so? She has been gone at least three hours.'

'But where?' quavered the duenna, moving around the table and twitching the note from Delagarde's hand.

'North, I imagine,' he said.

Miss Wormley gaped at him. 'Not—not Gretna Green!'

'No, no, Ida, surely not,' Lady Hester soothed. 'She is of age.'

'But Lugton is not,' the Viscount said.

'Yes, but he will have his mother's permission. There is no need for them to take such an extreme step.'

'Oh, isn't there?' scoffed Delagarde. 'You don't suppose that looby has the faintest notion how to get himself a special licence, do you? As for Maidie, she would not even know that she needed one to get married in a hurry anywhere else. Of course they are heading for Scotland.'

'But this is dreadful!' cried Lady Hester, over the whimpers of the Worm. 'You must stop them, Laurie!'

Delagarde was already on the move. 'I intend to.'

The butler had been standing as if rooted to the spot, still holding the salver upon which he had brought the fatal note. Delagarde seized him by the shoulder.

'Lowick, tell Sampton to fig out my phaeton—instantly! And send Liss to my dressing-room!'

He was gone from the room on the words, running up the stairs two at a time. It took him less than five minutes to strip off his evening wear and drag on breeches, frock-coat and topboots, aided by his valet who flew to obey his barked commands. He was shrugging himself into his greatcoat even as he left his dressing-room, and rammed the hat on his head as he ran down the stairs, the valet puffing behind him.

At the bottom, he was detained by Lady Hester, the Worm weeping in her rear. He seized his driving gloves from Liss with an impatient hand, and began to drag them over his fingers.

'What is it, Aunt Hes?'

'A word, if you please, before you go,' she said, her tone more severe than he had ever heard it. 'In private.'

'Quickly, then.'

He moved to open the door to the little parlour. Lady Hester passed through. He went in and shut the rest of the household out.

'Well?'

'Do you have any idea why the child has chosen to run off in this way?' asked his great-aunt, fixing him with a steady regard.

Delagarde gave a short laugh. 'Am I supposed to be able to read her mind? She is determined to ruin herself!'

'Or to escape you, Laurie.'

He was brought up short. He stared at her, and sighed out his breath. 'Is she that much afraid of what I may do?'

Her brows rose. 'Why should she be afraid?'

'I wish I knew.' A frown creased his brow, as all the inconsistencies of Maidie's behaviour towards him suddenly coalesced into a definite whole. 'She suspects me of—what? Some design, not unconnected with her possible marriage, I think.'

'Have you any design?'

Delagarde looked at her. 'Only to see her happy. For that, I will do whatever is consistent with what I conceive to be my duty towards her.'

'Your duty. And that is all?'

All? What did she mean? He thought he detected a measure of disapproval in Aunt Hes's voice. Or was it disappointment? He shrugged it off. Time was pressing.

'What else? At this moment my sole concern is to save her from her own foolhardiness.' He went to the door and wrenched it open. 'I must go!'

Lady Hester followed him out into the passage, saying urgently, 'Deal gently with her, Laurie!'

'Gently?' he echoed, turning his head briefly as the porter swung open the front door. 'She may count herself fortunate to escape a throttling!'

But as the miles sped by beneath his horses' hooves, and anxiety overlaid the anger, he found himself gripped by the conviction that it was all his own fault. He had bullied her, taken high-handed action that she must feel to be an insult to her intelligence—and he had kissed her. The memory of it, fleeting though the kiss had been, came into sharp focus in his mind. His heart lurched.

Abruptly it came to him why he had so assiduously been avoiding her. Not for any of the reasons he had glibly given himself…but because he was afraid that he would be overcome by the desire to kiss her again! Through his head rattled a series of images—the entirety of his conduct towards her these last days, that he must now recognise to have been as eccentric as her own! Or, if not eccentric, to have only one sane basis. He could not tolerate her betrothal, that was certain. But it had nothing to do with the unsuitability of her choices—though they were ridiculous. He could laugh at himself, if his senses were not so ravaged by the discovery. For it afforded him no pleasure whatsoever to realise that the thought of her marriage to another had charged him with murderous jealousy!

He wanted Maidie. Flame whipped across his loins, and he jerked on the reins. There was an uneven ripple among his team, and his groom gave out an exclamation of concern. Delagarde dragged his attention to where it was needed, and became for some moments wholly intent upon controlling his horses.

'Would you wish me to take the reins?' Sampton asked him, when the team was once again steady.

'No, I have them in hand.'

But he had better command his thoughts if he did not
wish to endanger his cattle a second time. Command his
thoughts? Would that he could! What the devil was he to
do? A more misplaced desire he could not have contemplated. Should he marry her for it? Try to marry her! He
did not flatter himself that Maidie would accept him. Even
if she would have him, what would that avail him? A
somewhat grim despondency came over him. Was it to be
supposed that Maidie, of all women, might delight in am-
orous intrigue with her husband? She did not want a bed-
fellow! All she required of a man was that he should leave
her alone with her wretched stars. It was scarcely compli-
mentary to one's pride to know that one must come a poor
second in importance to the planets!

But she had responded to him, he recalled, with a resurgence of warmth that he fought down, forcing his attention back to the road ahead. On the balcony, he had felt
how she was affected. He could win her, were he to make
the attempt. There was the nub. Win her to what? There
could only be marriage. Anything else was out of the question. And marriage to Maidie was not a proposition that
he could readily contemplate. Apart from the heady attraction of her sensual allure, her attributes were quite opposite to those suitable to his wife.

Delagarde found that he was slowing his horses. Why
was he chasing after her like this? Why stop her from
marrying Lugton? It was what she wanted. The boy would
offer her no opposition. He was unlikely to wish for anything more than the forty-five thousand pounds that would
be his due. He would not trouble her, and she might observe the heavens to her heart's content—and welcome.

That she would be heartily bored by his youth and in-
experience was quite unimportant. As was the fact that she
would never know what it was to give herself in exquisite

surrender to a man who would take delight in pleasuring her, in acquainting himself with every secret—

He pulled himself up, realising where his thoughts were tending. He discovered that his breath had shortened, and the outrageous images in his head were heating his blood to fever pitch. No, he could not endure it! A savage determination gripped him. Whatever else, Maidie was not going to marry Sholto Lugton!

Delagarde caught up with the runaways some miles north of Welwyn. He'd had news of them at the posting-house, in a chaise and two that had changed horses there less than two hours before. A chaise and two! No wonder he had readily gained upon them. The description was unmistakable. There could not be more than one couple on the road where both lady and gentleman were endowed with so distinctive a head of hair! They were travelling as brother and sister, it seemed, and had spoken of pushing on for another stage before stopping for the night. It was past eleven when Delagarde's phaeton swept into the village of Knebworth and halted by the single inn while Sampton ran inside to make the usual enquiries.

'They are here, my lord,' he reported when he came out. 'I understand that Lady Mary has just retired. The young gentleman is in the coffee room.'

Delagarde was already descending from the vehicle, and his groom went to the horses' heads.

'See them watered and rested, Sampton.'

'Will your lordship be remaining here for the night?'

'I doubt it. We can get another change back at Welwyn.'

He walked into the inn, and the landlord, who had already come bustling out after the groom's enquiry, led him to the coffee room and opened the door.

It was a small apartment, with a fireplace and a single large round table in the centre, surrounded by a number of

chairs, at one of which Delagarde spied the red head of
Mr Sholto Lugton. The boy was in the act of drinking from
a tumbler as he looked up. Seeing Delagarde, he leapt from
his seat, choked violently and fell into a fit of coughing.

Delagarde was obliged to thump him on the back several
times before he recovered. By the time he had pushed the
boy back into his chair and handed him some water, the
whole situation seemed to him to have taken on the nature
of a farce. Lugton sipped at the water, looking altogether
ready to burst into tears. Amusement drove away Delagarde's resentment.

'You need not imagine that I am going to call you out,'
he said sardonically. 'I don't for a moment suppose that
the notion for this escapade came out of your head. Which
is Lady Mary's room?'

'I—I don't know, sir,' said Sholto unhappily. 'She went
up with the landlady but a few moments ago.'

'Very well.' He went to the door, and turned there. 'You
stay put, Lugton. I am not yet done with you!'

An expression of deep foreboding crept across the
young man's face, but Delagarde hid a grin and went into
the hall. A fright would do him no harm—even though he
had undoubtedly been dragooned into his shocking conduct by Maidie. Let it be a lesson to him not to hang about
eccentric heiresses.

It did not take Delagarde long to find the landlady and
send her up to Maidie's room with a curt message. In a
very short space of time, she came running down the stairs.
She stopped short at sight of him standing in the hall, and
eyed him in silence for a moment.

The sight of her held him equally silent. Whether it was
an effect of the dimly lit hall, he did not know. But she
looked pale and drawn, and he thought he detected a distinct unhappiness in her features. Something gave in his

chest. He had no chance to think about it, for Maidie spoke at last—dully, without expression.

'What have you done to Sholto?'

Delagarde drew a breath, and found it ragged. 'Nothing at all. Unless you blame me for his choking on his drink when he saw me.'

Concern entered her eyes, and turning, she went into the coffee room. Following, Delagarde saw that the youth had risen, and as she reached him, Maidie took his hand and held it between both her own.

'Are you all right, Sholto? Did he frighten you?'

The boy flushed. 'No, I—that is—' He seemed to pull himself together a little. 'His lordship has been most—most understanding.'

Maidie did not look at Delagarde. She reached up and held the back of one hand to the young man's cheek. 'I am truly sorry, dear Sholto. I should not have led you into this. Can you forgive me?'

'No, no—I mean—only too happy!' He seized her hand and held it rather tightly, casting an apprehensive though challenging glance at Delagarde. 'Lady Mary, I will come with you, if you still wish it. Only—only I don't think you should, you know.' He swallowed. 'It ain't the thing.'

'No, I know it is not,' Maidie agreed.

Her smile, Delagarde thought, was a little tremulous. A shiver went through him, as of an ill wind. This was not the Maidie he knew. The life seemed quite to have gone out of her. She had not at all the appearance of a female frustrated in an elopement. She was—yes, passionless.

Delagarde was beset by a feeling of unreality. In a situation which would have thrown most young ladies into hysterics, Maidie behaved in a prosaic fashion that was distinctly out of place. Instead of upbraiding the marplot who had interrupted her flight, and declaring her intention of flouting him at the first opportunity—a reaction that

Delagarde had every reason to anticipate—she politely requested him to wait while she arranged for the disposal of her erstwhile suitor.

'I have paid for the hire of the chaise, Sholto, so you may use it to have yourself driven back to town,' she told him kindly, adding in a motherly way, 'I think you should set forward at once. It will be better to wake in your own bed, and then the events of today will seem very much like a horrid dream and you may readily forget them.'

Not content with this recommendation, she sent Delagarde to request the landlord to have the horses put to upon the hired vehicle, and herself helped Sholto into his coat, pressed his hat and gloves upon him, and went out to see him into the coach.

From the doorway of the inn, a bemused Delagarde watched her wave Lugton off, and stand for a moment in the inn yard as the chaise bowled away down the road. Then she turned and came up to Delagarde, still speaking in that toneless voice.

'Are you tired? Do you wish to take some refreshment before we go?'

'Do you?' Delagarde asked.

'I will drink a glass of wine, perhaps, if you are having something.'

She might have been on a morning call! Feeling baffled, Delagarde bowed her back into the inn, and ordered wine and cakes for Maidie, and ale with a sandwich for himself. He was tired, but there could be no question of remaining here for the night, with Maidie unchaperoned. He had as well have left her here with Lugton as stay with her himself!

'I will fetch my things,' she said, and went on up the stairs.

By the time she returned, burdened with a small portmanteau and a hooded travelling cloak, the refreshments were on the table. Delagarde put down his tankard and rose, relieving her of the portmanteau. He surveyed her narrowly in the light of the two extra candelabra which the landlord had thoughtfully provided and placed on the mantelpiece. Maidie looked paler than ever, and the oddest sensation struck Delagarde when he noted her reddened eyelids and realised that she had been crying. His heart seemed to wish to rise up and choke him, and it was a moment or two before he could command himself sufficiently to hand her to a seat at the table.

They sat in silence for a while. Maidie sipped at her wine, and crumbled a cake in her fingers, her gaze averted from Delagarde's. He did not know if she was even aware of his steady regard, and at length he could no longer tolerate her seeming indifference.

'For pity's sake, Maidie!' She jumped slightly, and looked across at him. 'Reproach me! Revile me, if you will—scream, cry! But say *something*.'

He was treated to her wide-eyed look. 'What should I say? Thank you for rescuing me from my own folly? I am sure that is what you believe you have done.'

Delagarde felt his chest go hollow. 'Are you telling me that I have not?' He drew a breath. 'Are you in love with the fellow?'

A tiny smile appeared fleetingly upon her lips. 'With Sholto? Oh, Delagarde, really!'

Relief made him want to laugh out, but he bit it back, saying with a faintly mocking air, 'I am glad that your heart is not broken.'

Maidie made a queer little noise, like a gasping sob, and put a hand to her mouth. She regained control swiftly, seizing her wineglass and sipping at its contents with dedicated concentration.

Delagarde caught it all with a growing feeling of dismay. He stared at her, wondering whether or not to voice the thought in his mind. But he found that he could not. She was in love! Hopelessly, it would seem. If not with Lugton, then with whom? Not—surely not with Wiveliscombe? Tightness gripped his chest, and he dwelled with savage satisfaction upon a vision of his hands about that gentleman's throat.

Just then Maidie looked at him again. 'Should we not be setting off?'

He agreed, glad of the distraction. In the bustle of departure, he had no leisure to think any further upon the hideous notion that had come to him. But the phaeton was soon bowling along, the road clearly visible under a moonlit sky, and once he had assured himself that Maidie was wrapped up warmly enough against the cold night air, he found his thoughts straying back.

Maidie would not by any means be the first female to have fallen for Wiveliscombe's charms. His amours were notoriously successful. Delagarde remembered, with uncomfortable clarity, Maidie's expression when they had that first argument over him. He had suspected then that she more than half liked the fellow. An unpleasant possibility occurred to him: perhaps she had not been throwing down the gauntlet when she became entangled in that engagement. It had been obvious to him both that Wiveliscombe was only too delighted to be rescued from the betrothal, and that it had been Maidie who had engineered it. He would not put it past her to defy convention and ask the gentleman to marry her! What he had not supposed, and now began to fear may well have been the case, was that she had done it because she had formed an attachment to Wiveliscombe. She was far too intelligent not to have recognised his reluctance—which would account for her present depression of spirits. Had she taken Lugton because she felt her case to be hopeless?

He glanced down at Maidie by his side, and discovered

that she had fallen asleep. Her head had slipped forward, jogging uncomfortably. Delagarde transferred the reins to one hand, and gently shifted her head to rest against his shoulder, pulling the hood more closely about her against the wind.

By the time he stopped for the last change, it was nearly four in the morning. Sampton was obliged to get down and go through the yard of the posting-house to wake the ostlers in the stable. Maidie's head had slipped again, and Delagarde placed an arm about her, trying to make her more comfortable. Glancing up, he saw that the stars were out in force, and was smitten with a sudden unbearable sense of loss.

In a moment, it was borne in upon him that Maidie was awake, and then that she was crying. His arm tightened about her involuntarily, and he dipped his head to hers.

'Maidie, Maidie,' he murmured softly. 'Don't weep... don't.'

Without thinking what he was doing, he found her lips with his own and mouthed them gently, tasting the salt of her tears. Her lips moved under his. His blood warmed swiftly. Her mouth was tender, trembling at his touch. He pressed her lips closer, and she answered. Heat quickened within him. The kiss deepened, and the soft moan that escaped her throat drove him to force her lips apart. The touch of velvet there shot fire into his loins and he groaned.

And then the sound of footsteps and the clatter of hooves penetrated his absorption. He felt Maidie struggle in his hold, and reluctantly broke away. He glanced round to see his groom returning with a couple of ostlers and a team of horses, and gave up the reins into his groom's hands for the change.

By the time he was at leisure to turn back to Maidie, she had huddled away from him to the other side of the carriage seat, her face averted.

Oh, good God! What the devil had he done? He had
entirely forgotten her distressed state of mind. To take advantage of her vulnerability was the act of a blackguard.
He toyed with the notion of making an apology, and decided that she had been upset enough. What explanation
could he give? Scarcely, under the circumstances, that he
could not resist her! When the phaeton was underway
again, he initiated a light discussion about the stars, which
in no way reflected his own state of mind, but which lasted
until they arrived back in Charles Street.

The household had been roused upon instructions Lady
Hester had given before she had retired. In fact neither she
nor the Worm, as they had told Maidie, had been able to
do more than doze lightly now and then. Maidie had dissolved into tears again at their concern, and had sobbed
out her story and apologies while she was whisked to her
room and put to bed. Before exhaustion claimed her, she
knew herself to be forgiven.

Unsurprisingly, when she woke at last next day, the hour
was considerably advanced.

She learned, as Trixie helped her to dress, that Lady
Hester and Miss Wormley had risen some time ago and
had given directions that Maidie was not to be disturbed.
Both ladies, it appeared, had gone out for a drive in the
park, information which Maidie received with equanimity.
Trixie's next piece of news was less welcome.

'His lordship give me his orders, too, m'lady.'

'Oh?' said Maidie, with less nonchalance than she felt.
'What were they?'

'He's waiting to see you as soon as ever you've breakfasted.'

This disclosure effectively killed Maidie's appetite. She
felt quite sick, wondering what Delagarde could have to

say to her that he had not said last night. The memory of events added nothing to her comfort.

The depression of spirits that had gradually crept over her during her abortive elopement had worsened with the intervention of Delagarde. If he had only thundered at her, she might have revived. Useless to pretend that she had not expected—even hoped?—for his chasing after her to fetch her back. Indeed, she had pictured a very different scene—one in which Delagarde's indignation was a demonstration of a warmer feeling towards her than she knew him to harbour. He had not been in the least indignant! Indeed, he had conducted himself quite as if he was indifferent to her fate—so long as he had carried out what he conceived to be his *duty*.

Maidie could feel resentment now, when the protestations of Lady Hester and the lamentations of the Worm had shown her what behaviour was to be expected from those who did care what happened to her. And then that hateful, that *exquisite* kiss. How could he do it? Was it to make her realise that her escapade had in no way jeopardised his plans? Then, having reduced her to a quivering jelly, all he could find to talk about was the subject of astronomy. For once in her life, the heavens had been the last thing Maidie had wanted to discuss. If she was not so very much in love with Delagarde, she might have hated him for that!

'What constellations can you direct me to tonight?' he had asked, as lightly as if she had not eloped at all.

Fortunately, it was second nature to her to pick something out merely by glancing at the heavens. With spring approaching, the Great Bear was rising high overhead, and Maidie had rather listlessly begun there. Delagarde knew that one, as most people must, and she had led him star by star down to the brightly glowing Arcturus.

'Do you know every one by heart?' he had asked, on a note of awe.

'Hardly. There are millions, and some too far distant and thus too small to be worthy of note. One learns to find a path about the celestial map by star pointers, though it is the shapes of the constellations and the brightest stars that guide the way.'

Delagarde had let out a laugh. 'You have it all so pat.'

'I have been doing it since I was eight.'

For some reason, he had remained silent for several moments after that. Maidie had felt herself tensing up again, and sought at random for some innocuous remark lest she again gave way to her overwhelming emotions. She found one.

'The eastern astronomers say that they can foretell the future by the stars.'

She thought Delagarde started. But he answered readily enough, 'So I believe.' She felt him move beside her, and turned her head to find him looking down at her, his face a pale oval in the gloom. 'Can you? Foretell the future, I mean.'

She met his eyes briefly and quickly turned away. 'How should I be able to?'

'I thought you might hazard a guess at mine,' he said lightly. 'What do the stars foretell for me, Maidie?'

Maidie had been unable to answer. After a while, he had laughed, a harsh sound in the night. To her relief, they had arrived back at Charles Street a short time later.

She approached with trepidation the saloon where she had been told he was awaiting her, and steeled herself to withstand the promptings of her own heart which might give her away. Softly opening the door, she entered and saw him standing at the window looking out, his back to the room. Something in his stance recalled that very first day when he had been bemused by her coming and unable to concentrate for his morning head. It was a wistful memory, for she had been heartwhole then.

Delagarde must have felt her presence, for he turned sharply. He was pale, she thought. From lack of sleep? He seemed older somehow, his voice and manner overly formal. Maidie felt distanced.

'I trust you are rested?'

'Yes, thank you.'

'Thank you for coming.' He moved into the room and gestured towards a chair. 'Sit down.'

She took the chair to one side of the fireplace, and Delagarde seated himself on the little sofa opposite. There was silence for a moment or two. Delagarde crossed one shapely leg over the other and contemplated his boot. Maidie surveyed the gilt overmantel with intense interest.

'Devil take it, this is absurd!' burst from him suddenly.

He got up and took a hasty turn about the room. Maidie watched him. He caught her eye, and sat down again, leaning forward slightly.

'Maidie, I have thought and thought about all this. Have I been too restrictive?' He looked away. 'Why do I ask you? Of course I have!'

Maidie forced herself to speak, but she could not conceal the gruffness in her voice. 'I know that you have only had my interests at heart.'

'I wish that were true,' he said involuntarily.

She cast her wide-eyed gaze upon him. 'Haven't you?'

'No—yes! At least, I—' He broke off, drew a hasty breath, and began again. 'All I wanted to say to you was that I withdraw my objections. You have been right all along. It is no concern of mine. You can be the only judge of what will suit you. Marry whomever you wish!'

Chapter Eleven

Maidie gazed at him. Of what possible use was it to tell her to marry whomever she wished? She had run away with Sholto Lugton because she could not bear the thought of marriage with the only man whom she did wish to wed. At least not the kind of marriage she had believed he wanted. Now it appeared that he did not wish for a union with her at all!

'If you mean that, why did you stop my elopement?' she demanded, out of the despair that rushed in on her.

Delagarde threw up his hands. 'It was your elopement that made me realise how wrong I had been. I cannot be sorry that I interfered, if you are not in love with Lugton.' He paused, looked away briefly, and back again. 'I only hope your fancy has alighted—will alight—on someone worthy.'

Maidie clasped her fingers tightly together in her lap, and did not look at him. Her voice was low. 'I have no fancy.'

There was a pause. Then Delagarde's voice came again, harsh. 'I don't believe you.'

Her head came up. 'Why should I lie?' she demanded

in a stronger voice. 'And why would I elope with one man if I were in love—had a fancy for another?'

'Perhaps because he had not a fancy for you,' Delagarde answered deliberately.

She flinched, and he thought again, with venom, of Wiveliscombe. Maidie got up, and he automatically rose as well. She looked at him, and the hurt in her eyes pierced him.

'If you really mean to leave me free to make a choice, I am glad of it, and must thank you. I am sorry to have given you so much trouble.'

Delagarde stopped her as she reached the door. 'There is one more thing.'

Maidie turned. 'Yes?'

He appeared to have difficulty in meeting her eyes. 'I forgot myself last night. I should not have—' He broke off, glanced at her and away again.

'Another accident?' Maidie suggested.

'Oh, the devil!' He swept to the window, and spoke without turning. 'Accept my apologies.'

Maidie said nothing. She waited a moment, but he did not speak. There seemed nothing more to say. As Maidie passed through the door, she thought she heard him call her name. If he had, she ignored it. She could bear no more.

By the time she next emerged from the seclusion of her bedchamber, an hour or so later, the elder ladies had returned and Delagarde had evidently gone out. She invited Lady Hester and Miss Wormley to congratulate her on having won the withdrawal of Delagarde's opposition.

'I beg your pardon?' said Lady Hester blankly.

'Delagarde has said I may marry whomever I please,' Maidie repeated stonily, moving to stand before the fireplace.

Her duenna, seated as usual next to Lady Hester on the little sofa from where Delagarde had announced his change of mind, looked at that lady, and then back at Maidie, clearly unable to decide whether this was to be regarded as good news.

'Well, that is—that is very well done of him,' she twittered. 'I think. Do you agree, Lady Hester?'

'My dear Ida, it entirely depends upon his motive.' Her brows rose at Maidie. 'Did he give one?'

'He says that my elopement made him realise that he was wrong, and that he hopes my fancy has alighted upon someone worthy,' Maidie reported evenly.

'Ah, I see,' said the elder lady, and Maidie stiffened as she saw the twinkle. Lady Hester put up a restraining hand. 'Don't poker up! You did not, I do sincerely trust, give him to understand that your affections are engaged.'

Maidie whisked restlessly away. 'He guessed it—I think. I denied it—or I think I did.' She turned to look back at them. 'He said he did not believe me.' She frowned direfully at Lady Hester. 'Is that funny?'

'It is delightful!' But the elder lady muffled her amusement and rose to come and put an arm about her young friend's shoulders. 'Come, dear child, don't look daggers at me. Save them for Laurie. I declare, I have a very good mind to box his ears for him!'

Mystified, Maidie opened her eyes at Lady Hester. 'I cannot think what you would be at.'

'I know, but never mind. When you are my age, you will have the same privilege of laughing at the blind folly of your fellows.' She kissed Maidie's cheek. 'Would you care for some advice?'

'Very much indeed,' said Maidie sighing.

Lady Hester gave her a hug and let her go. 'Abandon these die-away airs, my dear, and bury yourself in that hobby you love so much. Leave your future to take care of itself, and the right man will very soon find you out.'

It was sound sense, and Maidie resolved to do her best to carry out the first part of this programme at least. For Lady Hester's sake, if nothing else. She had not thought how poor a companion she must be, wearing her heart on her sleeve in this melancholy fashion. Besides, it was a foolish waste of time and energy, moping about after a man who plainly did not return her affection. Great-uncle would have heartily disapproved.

Besides, it was important not to appear in the least conscious tonight, for their engagement was at the Shurland house in Hanover Square. One of the reasons Maidie had chosen to elope the previous day was in the hopes of avoiding the necessity of attending this event. But this was now inevitable, and she could only hope that Eustace and Adela would have too much to do to trouble her.

So it proved, although she was frequently aware of Eustace watching her. But Maidie was hard put to carry out the rest of Lady Hester's advice, for her suitors were as assiduous as ever. Even Sholto Lugton came up to her, with a sheepish grimace.

Under cover of some idle chatter, he whispered, 'Lord Delagarde has just told me I should appear to favour you still, so that no one may suspect anything.'

She thanked him, casting an involuntary glance about for the Viscount. She could not see him, and suppressed a sense of disappointment at his failing to intervene in her affairs. He had promised he would not, and she had besides refrained from going apart with any of her attendant cicisbeos. She had no desire to be tête-à-tête with any of them, and was unable now to imagine how she had ever contemplated matrimony even with the amusing Wiveliscombe. As well, perhaps. There were new faces, but although Hampford, Bulkeley and the Rankmiston son had not given up, Wiveliscombe was conspicuously absent from her circle.

A fact which Delagarde had noted with scarcely veiled satisfaction. 'Better a wounded heart, than a lifetime of slights and betrayal.'

'What was that, old fellow?' asked Corringham.

Lord Riseley snorted. 'Muttering again, is he?' He moved to stand by Delagarde, laying a hand on his shoulder. 'No use glowering at them, dear boy. Either you forbid the banns, or you leave her be.'

Delagarde turned his head. 'I have given my word, Peter.'

'I know you have,' said his friend, shaking his head. 'Stupid thing to do, if you ask me. Only look at the collection of riff-raff she has about her!'

'Thank you, I have seen them,' Delagarde said shortly. 'And you are adding nothing to my comfort.'

'Well, what in Hades possessed you to back down, old fellow?' protested Corringham reasonably.

Delagarde had no reply to make to this, but Riseley answered for him.

'Taken leave of his senses!' He laughed. 'Mind you, I've a notion he did that a few weeks back.'

'What the devil do you mean, Peter?'

Riseley clapped Delagarde on the back. 'Never mind!' He grinned. 'Lay you odds she takes the Rankmiston boy.'

'Oliver?' uttered the Viscount scoffingly. 'She will not. If for no other reason than that she can't wish for that old cat as a mother-in-law.'

'There is something in that,' Corringham conceded. 'For my money, it will be Hampford.'

Delagarde uttered a short laugh. 'Are you mad? Maidie can't abide him! He was out of the running at the start.'

'Well, she can't take Bulkeley, that is sure,' Corringham argued. 'So who else is there?'

Delagarde caught a glance exchanged between his two friends, and frowned. 'What are you two at? There are plenty of prospects. She does not have to choose among these.'

'No, no,' agreed Corringham soothingly. 'She might meet anyone at any time. There's no saying.'

Riseley let out another snort. 'Oh, isn't there, by God! She don't need to meet anyone new. What about Wiveliscombe?'

Delagarde's breath shortened. He glared at his friend. 'What about Wiveliscombe?'

'Well, look at it, dear boy. Fellow has to settle down some time. May as well do so with someone who can provide him with the ready.'

'He has a point, Laurie,' Corringham agreed. 'The fellow seems deucedly attractive to the fair sex.'

'Oh yes, devil of a fellow! Tell you what, Laurie. If I were one of your Maidie's court, I'd snap her up sharpish—before Wiveliscombe gets to thinking too deeply about letting her slip through his fingers.'

It had been difficult enough to stand aside while Maidie basked in the adulation of as ineligible a set of potential marriage partners as one could imagine. After this hideous conversation, it was well-nigh impossible. Delagarde found himself disinclined to linger in the company of his friends, and curtly excused himself, withdrawing to a more secluded vantage point from where he could watch who approached Maidie. If that abominable reprobate dared to go anywhere near her, there would be nothing for it but to break his word!

To his relief, Wiveliscombe kept his distance. But he was no better pleased to see Eustace Silsoe move in and take Maidie aside for a moment or two. He was half inclined to go across and rescue her, but he had done so in the past, and the results were not happy. She would do better without his intervention.

But Maidie was never more sorry that Delagarde had withdrawn his protection.

'Now, how have you persuaded your scrupulous champion to relax his officious guardianship, my dear Maidie?'

She lifted her chin, determined that Eustace should not guess her state of mind. 'There was no persuasion. He has merely recognised that I am capable of judging for myself.'

The feline smile appeared. 'But how very clever of him!'

A wisp of disquiet flitted through Maidie's heart. 'Why do you say that?'

'Your naivety never ceases to amaze me,' said Eustace, laughing gently. 'I suppose it is one of the drawbacks of being yourself so very frank. You are the easiest of dupes, Maidie.'

Resentment burgeoned within her. She might be a novice in the fashionable world, but she knew Delagarde—or at least, she had thought she knew him. Unease stirred again.

'How am I duped?' she asked forthrightly.

Eustace leaned closer that his words would reach her ears alone. 'You have been lulled into a false sense of security. It is a good ploy, but an obvious one. Delagarde's recognition has more to do with your rebellious spirit than your judgement, I fear.'

'How so?' asked Maidie, but recalling her many quarrels with the Viscount, his words had an ominous ring of truth.

'He sees that the more he intervenes, the readier you will be to throw yourself into matrimony—however unsuitable the match. He steps back, and you desist.' Eustace drew away and smiled again, though his voice was cold. 'Delagarde must be congratulating himself on the success of his tactics. Your conduct tonight has been most prudent. You are all unsuspecting, Maidie. He may pounce at his leisure.'

Seated on her stool before the telescope, her eye to the piece, Maidie shifted the stem in a slow but comprehensive sweep until she found her marker. If her calculations were correct, the comet should be at a point within inches of this spot. The mapped-out path was on the open chart on the whatnot at her side, and she came away momentarily to check exactly where the comet last had been.

It was nearly three in the morning, and she had abandoned any attempt to sleep. Recalling Lady Hester's advice, Maidie rose out of her bed, dragged on her dressing-robe, and set about star-gazing in earnest. She must do something to distract her mind! Anything to unburden herself of the incoherent mutterings of her heart. All the fault of that hateful Eustace, with his insidious murmurings.

If the exercise of comet chasing did not quite banish the distressing effects of the thoughts Eustace had set in motion, the meticulous nature of the task of recording her findings proved sufficiently engrossing to dull them. She checked through the eyepiece again. Yes, there it was! Precisely where her amended calculations, made after the visit with Sir Granville, had predicted. She drew up the circle that was created by the telescopic frame, and began to chart in the pattern of stars that would fix the comet's current location.

Her concentration intensified, for she had to check, come away to draw, and check again, several times over. Great-uncle Reginald had been strict about the necessity for accuracy. He would not accept shoddy work, and doing tasks over again had taught Maidie to be meticulous.

The click of the door latch did not penetrate her absorption. Delagarde stood for several moments in the doorway, watching her in silence. Sleep had proved elusive, and he had been walking the corridors. Was it mere accident that he found himself outside her bedchamber door? He did not think so. Stealthy sounds from within had told him that she was also awake. He had not knocked. He had not meant to disturb her at all. He'd had no notion of coming in! Yet here he was, and the sight of her stargazing caught at him with unbearable poignancy.

Delagarde felt shut out, and the desire to be part of it, to be one with her obsession, possessed him to the exclusion of discretion or forethought. He moved softly forward.

Maidie felt him as a presence only seconds before he reached her. She turned her head on a gasp, saw him, and would have cried out. But Delagarde slipped so swiftly on to the stool behind her, his arms encircling her body, and the fingers of one hand pressing silence on her lips, that the cry died in her throat.

'Hush! It is only I,' came the whisper directly into her ear, and the lips there brushed at her cheek and her hair, his chin snuggling into her neck.

Maidie did not know that her hands were clasping tightly to his arms, for the shock had been so instantly overlaid with sensation that she was powerless to think, let alone consider her own actions. Warmth enveloped her everywhere his body touched with hers: at her back, at her upper limbs, and within seconds at her breasts as his tight hold loosened enough that he could cup one heavy softness in his hand.

'Maidie, Maidie…God, my Maidie!' he groaned beneath his breath, and the fingers at her mouth moved to turn her head so he might find her lips with his own.

Flame coursed through her as the soft mouthing pressed her lips apart and Delagarde tasted deeply of the wine within. Maidie's hands flailed wildly, and then gripped down either side, seizing on his limbs for purchase. Delagarde moaned at her touch, and instinct sent her fingers rippling down the hard flesh of his thighs. He kissed her deeper still, and his own hands moved: one to press her womb, pulling her hard against him, the other to drag away the bulk of her dressing-robe, that he might caress the inner softness of her thigh through the thin silk of her night-gown.

Afire, clutching helplessly wherever her fingers rested, Maidie came from his kiss to gasp in air, and frenzied, unable to help herself, as he nuzzled into her shoulder, she sought desperately with her lips for his again, kissing across the hard line of his jaw, and murmuring his name.

'Laurie…oh, Laurie!'

His hold tightened, strengthened by a deep sense of intimacy engendered by her use of his name. He answered her need, and for some moments the kiss became all. She twisted a little in his hold, and her fingers came up, seizing at his face, twisting and turning in his hair, as the fierce intensity of his passion burned into her bones.

Delagarde released her mouth, and she fell limply against him, weak and quivering with the aftermath of this wild assault. But there was no diminution of his feverish pursuit. While his lips tantalised at her neck and shoulder, his hands went down, and his fingers moved to draw away the silken folds, all that lay between his tempestuous desires and the intimate lair of their fulfilment.

'Shall I keep you, Maidie?' he murmured darkly into the ardour of her dreams. 'Shall I make you mine?'

The words grazed the contours of her clouded mind, but his fingers, streaking across the flesh he was laying bare, spoke louder. The stark flash of sanity threw her hand into uncontrollable reflex. She seized on his larger one with vicious force, halting it dead. Every muscle in her body strained to rock hard power, and Delagarde froze.

'Stop!' It was guttural, and tense. 'Get away from me!'

Shock sobered him, and he shifted slightly, creating space enough to enable Maidie to slip from his hold. She stood up, whirled, and backed away from him, clutching at the edge of one French door.

With dawning horror, Delagarde watched the concealing folds of her disarranged garments falling back into place, and faced the hideous recognition of what he had so nearly done. He got up slowly from the stool, his gaze on the livid pallor of her starlit features, the enormous depths of her haunted eyes. He had no words.

His hand came up in a gesture not yet formed, and was halted by the quick shake of her head.

'Go!' It was a plea, breathless and deathly still. 'Leave me—*pray*.'

In that instant it came to Delagarde that in all the world there was nothing she could have asked of him that he wanted less to do. But that very knowledge commanded him. One last glance, searing him to the core, and he turned from her, and departed.

It was long before Maidie slept. She did not weep, for it was a despair too deep for tears. Painstakingly, she went through the routine to put aside her work and to close up the telescope. Shutting the French windows, she prepared herself again for bed, and lay staring sightlessly into the dark.

It was a heavy thing to have one's faith shattered. In the man one loved, it was almost too great a burden to be borne. She knew now that, despite everything, she had never truly believed in the slanders of Eustace Silsoe. To have them proved, and in a manner that had torn down her defences, laying her soul bare for Delagarde to read, was a blow from which she would not readily recover. She had given her heart to a cheat!

She must have slept at last, she realised, for she woke to a sunlit dawn that crept in through the gaps in the curtains that she had improperly shut about her bed. Groaning at the heaviness of her head, she turned back into her pillows and tried to recapture sleep. It would not come.

At length Maidie grew too frustrated to remain in bed. Throwing aside the bed-curtains, she got up and rang for her maid, and then stood staring blankly at the empty stool before the shut-up telescope, vainly trying to make herself believe that the entire episode was a figment of her fevered imagination. The betraying kindle at her loins belied her, and she wished fervently that she had never conceived that ludicrous scheme to foil Adela's plans. At this distance in time and events, it appeared to her the madness that Delagarde had called it. Would that he had not allowed Lady Hester to overbear his rejection!

Trixie's entrance gave her occupation to keep the thoughts at bay, and tidings that threw her into considerable disorder.

'Early, m'lady?' she said, upon Maidie's apologising for calling her at such an hour. 'Why, bless you, Miss Maidie, what are you thinking of?'

'Well, it is barely past dawn, Trixie.'

The maid trilled with laughter, and went to fling aside the heavy drapes. 'It ain't dawn, not by a long way. Look! It's after noon.'

'After *noon*?' Hastening to the French windows, Maidie stared aghast. The sun was indeed high overhead. 'Oh, Trixie, no! Why did you not wake me?'

'I would have, m'lady, only his lordship ups and tells me on no account to disturb you.'

'His lordship?' repeated Maidie faintly.

'And,' added Trixie, with round-eyed emphasis, 'if he ain't gone and said the same to her ladyship and Miss Wormley both! ''Don't you trouble the wench,'' says he.

''I happen to know,'' says he, ''as she ain't slept nowise well last night.'''

'What?' squeaked Maidie.

'Yes, miss,' nodded the girl fervently. 'Then his lordship comes right out and says as you didn't get no sleep in his carriage t'other night to speak of when he fetched you back from running off to Gretna, and losing sleep two nights in a row ain't good for you, and I don't know what more besides. Then her ladyship—' answering the startled question in Maidie's own mind '—arst him how come he knows as you never slept last night, and his lordship colours up something horrible!'

So indeed did Maidie upon receipt of this alarming information. What in the world was Lady Hester to think? And the Worm would be scandalised! How could Delagarde be so mad? Or was it merely carelessness? No— worse. She had responded to him with so much abandon that he must feel certain of her—despite her belated but violent rejection. Was he still determined to pursue his design to woo her into marriage? Of course he was! The words he had whispered, that had only touched her consciousness last night, came back to her with startling clarity. *Shall I keep you?* Then he had only pretended to let her go! *Shall I make you mine?* What, seduce her into submission? Oh, so sure of her as he was, he did not scruple to speak so openly before the household.

Maidie quivered with consciousness. She could not face the inevitable questions. How would she reply? How speak to her hostess of her great-nephew with the disparagement that she must use? Could she bear to disillusion Lady Hester as she had been stripped of illusion? Not after her kind affection. And there was no confiding in the Worm. Not any more. For the two had become such bosom friends that it was but a short whisper from the ears of the Worm to those of Lady Hester. She could not see either of them until she had better command of her emotions. Yet she knew not how to avoid them.

Providence intervened, in the guise of an unexpected letter among the pile of correspondence that Trixie had brought in. For want of anything else to do, while she waited for her maid to fetch up some sort of light refreshment for her from the kitchens, she flipped disinterestedly through the several invitations and a few tradesmen's accounts. Then she came across the sealed missive and picked it up.

The handwriting was unknown to her. Faintly intrigued, she broke the seal and unfolded the letter. It was from one of the assistants at the Royal Observatory, extending a flattering invitation from the Astronomer Royal himself—who had heard of her through the instrumentation of Sir Granville Wilberfoss—to visit at Greenwich. He had been acquainted with her great-uncle Reginald, and he looked forward to meeting her. A few weeks earlier such a letter would have thrown Maidie into transports. As it was, she read in it only a hope of salvation as she took in that the invitation was for that day.

A carriage would call for her at two o'clock, trusting that it was convenient. If not, she had only to send a note with the coachman and the visit would be rearranged for another occasion.

Maidie fairly leapt at Trixie the instant she returned, demanding to know the precise time. Discovering that it was but twenty minutes to the appointed hour, Maidie began quickly to eat. She learned, upon inquiry, that Lady Hester and the Worm were in the green saloon, and that Delagarde was out. Relieved, Maidie directed Trixie to go down and ask Lowick to send to her bedchamber immediately upon arrival of the chaise.

She wrote a brief note for Lady Hester and, placing it with the letter, told Trixie to deliver it after she had left the house. When the footman tapped on the door, Maidie was ready. She slipped noiselessly down the three flights of stairs, the footman in attendance, and was out of the house and away in the carriage so thoughtfully provided before anyone other than the servants even suspected that she had woken up.

Delagarde stared at the two letters in his hand, beset by a hideous feeling of incapacity. Something was not right, but the exact point eluded him. Maidie's own note to Aunt Hes had obviously been written in agitation—that he could comprehend. He had himself been conscious all day of a like sensation. That, and the obtrusive and unshakeable desire to experience it all again—and more! The impossibility of it had kept him away from Charles Street until close upon the dinner hour.

Now he wished fervently that he had given in to temptation, and come home sooner. Soon enough to have prevented this ill-considered flight. Flight? A memory clicked into place. He looked up.

'This must be a blind!'

'What can you mean, Laurie?' demanded his aunt. 'I own I have been anxious myself, but—'

'The Astronomer Royal is away,' Delagarde broke in, the urgency that was rising up inside him finding expression in the curtness of his tone. 'I saw it in the *Morning Post* the other day. The paragraph caught my eye—because of Maidie's obsession, I must suppose. He is gone upon a matter of business—to Italy, I believe.'

Lady Hester was already rising from the little green-striped sofa, consternation in her eyes. 'But that would indicate that—'

'That the letter is a forgery!' finished Delagarde grimly.

'But who would write such a—?' She stopped, a dawning comprehension in her countenance that made Delagarde's jawline harden. 'Eustace Silsoe!'

'My thought exactly.'

Lady Hester came up to him, tightly grasping his arm. 'Laurie, you do not suppose that Maidie herself has written it? Is it yet another attempt at escape?'

'From me, you mean,' Delagarde said bitterly. But he brought up the letters again, intently surveying them both. After a moment, he shook his head. 'It is not the same hand. Even were one of them disguised, some slight resemblance must have been discerned.'

The saloon door opened, and Delagarde turned as one with Lady Hester. The sudden hope was instantly dispelled as Miss Wormley walked quickly into the room. She was holding out yet another sealed missive.

'This has just come for you, Lord Delagarde. I ventured to bring it, for—'

'Give it to me!' He snatched it from her hand, breaking the seal with fingers that were not quite steady, and spreading open the sheet.

'Delagarde—' the note abruptly ran '—I am gone to Scotland with the man I truly love. It is useless to attempt to follow me, for I am determined on this course—Mary Hope.'

The world spun briefly. Unaware that the note fell from his hand, along with the other two letters he had been holding, Delagarde swung to the window embrasure, and stood there, supporting himself with a hand gripping one of the straight-backed Chippendale chairs. In a moment the dizziness receded, but it was succeeded by an emotion no less distressing. A sensation of loss so intense that Delagarde thought his heart must crack. The man she truly loved! Not then Eustace Silsoe, but Wiveliscombe! And he had driven her to this. The memory of last night came back to him—a torment then, an agony now! How blind he had been! Even then, fool enough to mistake his own heart.

'But this is not Maidie's hand!'

The Worm's voice, raised in shocked protest, penetrated his inward absorption. He turned to discover Aunt Hes close behind him, an echo of his own pain in her eyes. He looked past her to where Miss Wormley stood, peering closely at the note she had brought to him. She looked up.

'My lord, I know this writing, for all she has attempted to pass it off as Maidie's.'

'She?' said Lady Hester, echoing the question in Delagarde's mind as they both moved swiftly back to the centre of the room.

'Lady Shurland—Adela,' explained the Worm. 'It is her hand, I am sure of it.' She ventured to touch Delagarde's arm. 'And Maidie would never sign herself so, my lord. Not to you.'

The faintest of hopes began to struggle out of the black despair in Delagarde's heart. 'No,' he said slowly, taking the letter and staring at the signature, 'you are right. She would not.' His eyes clouded again. 'But she is in love!'

'Lord save us!' uttered Lady Hester in exasperated accents. 'Are you still so blinkered, Laurie? Of course she is in love—with you!'

Delagarde's heart stopped. He gazed at his great-aunt, poised between hope and stupefaction.

'Oh, dear!' broke from the Worm. 'Oh, dear Lady Hester, pray, do you think—?'

'Nonsense, Ida. The matter is far too urgent for concealment now. Besides, cannot you see that Laurie has at last come to his senses?'

But Delagarde was still too dazed to be affected by the lurking twinkle. 'Aunt Hes, don't trifle with me, I beg of you! If this is the truth—'

'My dear boy, why in the world do you suppose she ran

off with Lugton? Because she believed you to be indifferent.'

'Indifferent! Good God, I was never that! Only I did not realise—' He broke off, suddenly regarding the letter again. 'This Adela would have us believe that Maidie has run off again to Gretna. Only Lady Shurland cannot know that an attempt has already been frustrated. Not even Maidie would be so idiotic twice in the same week!'

'Then Ida's fears have not been groundless,' said Lady Hester, with an unaccustomed grimness in her face. 'Eustace Silsoe has indeed kidnapped her, aided and abetted by Adela.'

'Yes, for she would never have gone with him willingly,' said the Worm, anxiety spreading across her features. 'Pray, my lord, go after them!'

'You may be sure I will,' said Delagarde, all the heat of his emotions coiling into rage. 'But I am not going north this time. A little too clever, these pretty schemers.'

'You think they are laying a false scent?'

'I am sure of it, Aunt Hes.'

'But you will not go to Greenwich?' objected Miss Wormley.

'I must begin on that route. The coach must have gone some way towards Greenwich or Maidie would suspect the cheat,' Delagarde said, crossing to the bell-pull and tugging it with violence.

'Gracious, yes!' exclaimed Lady Hester. 'Besides, what need of his taking Maidie north? They are both of age. As long as he has a special licence, he may wed her at any time.'

'But she is not willing!' protested the Worm despairingly. 'How could he persuade her to marry him?'

Delagarde's eyes burned, and his voice was roughened at the edges. 'Very easily. If he succeeded in holding her somewhere for a day or two, she would have no choice but to wed him, for she would have not a shred of reputation left.'

Both ladies gazed at him in horror. Lady Hester sank on to the sofa, a stricken look in her eyes. Delagarde strode to the door, and turned.

'You need have no fear, either of you. If Eustace Silsoe marries Maidie, it will be over my dead body!'

Maidie trudged wearily into the yard of the Cross Keys inn in the village of Charlton Wood. The farm hand who had allowed her to ride in his cart had assured her that she was now but four or five miles from Greenwich. Mr Tupham of the Cross Keys would, the lad was sure, help her to reach her goal, and at Greenwich she was certain to be able to hire a conveyance to take her back to London.

She was chilled, hungry and dishevelled, but the welcoming lights of the Cross Keys put heart into her as she walked past the single vehicle standing in the yard. The glance she gave it was cursory. But that single look swept light into her heart. A phaeton and four! Surely she knew those horses? An ostler was at their heads, talking to a groom in livery, who turned at that instant.

'Sampton!' cried Maidie joyfully.

'Lordy, miss, is it you?' returned the groom, in equal delight. 'If that don't beat all! We've been searching for you all over.'

'Where is Lord Delagarde?' she demanded eagerly, hardly aware of the instant tattoo that flittered through her pulse.

'Inside, m'lady. Asking after you! Shall I fetch him?'

But Maidie was already halfway to the door of the inn, calling out, breathless with need, 'Delagarde! Delagarde!'

An exclamation sounded from within. Then came hasty footsteps, and the Viscount erupted from the doorway just as Maidie reached it. He paused on the threshold, stared for several seconds in a suspension of belief, and then swept her up into a smothering embrace.

It was as if the shattering events of the day had blasted the barriers apart. Maidie's despair of last night, and Delagarde's wicked scheme were alike forgotten, dispelled by the balm of the passionate murmur in her ear.

'Maidie…Maidie…I thought you were lost to me!'

For some moments the violence of Delagarde's feelings made it impossible for him to release her. But at length he became aware of the sob in her throat, and his arms loosened so that he could look into her face.

'You are safe! Good God, what you have put me through!' He saw her tears, and instantly reached up to brush them away. 'Don't weep, my dearest love.'

The endearment only caused Maidie's tears to flow the faster. 'Oh, don't call me that! You cannot mean it.'

Delagarde grinned. 'Can I not? We'll see that!' He put an arm about her, and threw a command over his shoulder to his groom. 'Stable them, Sampton! We will be dining here.'

The next moments passed for Maidie like a dream. Delagarde issued instructions left and right as he drew her into the inn. But in a very short space of time she found herself alone with him in a little parlour, with the door closed, and his dark eyes burning down into her own as he held her by the shoulders, much too close for comfort.

'Of all the occasions on which I have wanted to strangle you, Maidie, I believe this to be the worst!'

'Why should you wish to strangle me?' Maidie demanded indignantly. 'If you strangle anyone, let it be Eustace!'

'That goes without saying,' he said shortly, and shook her. 'But you—abominable little wretch! Do you know what you have done to me? You have turned my life upside-down, and you have made it impossible for me to live without you!'

Maidie had been upon the point of retorting in kind, but this last utterance wiped that response from her lips. She gazed up at him, mute.

He read the shock in her eyes, and remembered the suspicion she had shown him. 'Why do you look at me like that? Don't you believe me?'

'I don't know,' Maidie said truthfully, her voice a trifle hoarse. 'You might make me believe anything—try to.'

Delagarde released her, swept with instant hurt. 'Why? Why should I do that?'

Maidie's heart sank at his tone, and she had all to do not to fling herself back into his arms. She must know the truth, she *must*. She forced herself to say it.

'To gain my trust. If you had always meant to—to marry me. For convenience only.'

'Whose convenience?' he asked sardonically. 'Yours, or mine?'

'Both?' Maidie ventured. 'You know that I meant to marry only to be spared further importunities. Why should you not make use of that?' Suddenly the pent-up emotions of the last few days broke free, and it all tumbled out. 'It is not as if you could wish me to be with you, to be a companion to you. I am not a fit wife for a fashionable peer, I know that well enough. But you need an heir. My portion must be useful, though I acquit you of outright fortune-hunting—'

'I thank you!'

'—but it would be convenient, would it not—' hardly hearing his ironic interruption '—to have a wife who wished only to be let alone to spend her time star-gazing? Who would not importune you in any way, but let you alone to continue in your present way of life, and—'

'Let me tell you,' Delagarde broke in, his voice tight

with suppressed violence, 'that I am far more likely to interfere with your star-gazing than to let you alone at it. Nothing arouses me more than the way you look in star-light!'

Maidie's lip trembled, and her heart hammered in her chest. 'I know—and you could so easily seduce me in those circumstances. It is what made me half believe what Eustace and Adela said.'

Delagarde's face changed. '*They* said it? And you believed them!'

'It is of no use to look at me so hatefully, Delagarde,' Maidie uttered forcefully. 'I tried not to believe it, but everything you said to me—everything you did—'

'Made you suspect me all the more?'

'Yes,' she admitted. 'I felt that you wanted me—'

'Desperately, God help me!'

'—but you gave no sign that you felt—that there was anything more than that.'

'Because I did not know it myself!' He seized hold of her again. 'Maidie, I did not want to love you! It has happened entirely against my will—which is why I have refused to recognise it. You drive me demented!' He laughed suddenly, and pulled her closer. 'And I know very well that I have much the same effect on you. As for *this*—'

With which, his lips came down on hers in a kiss so intense that Maidie half-swooned in his arms. But as he came away and loosened his hold, she threw her own arms up around his neck and kissed him back. Delagarde dragged her hungrily against him, exchanging with her a deep caress that drove fire down his loins. He felt Maidie's response, and groaned his despair, for he knew he must stop before fulfilment.

Maidie's skin was flaming where his body met hers, her pulse rioting wildly, her limbs crushing tightly against Delagarde's. She sagged when he put her firmly away from him, holding her at arm's length.

'Will you marry me, wretch?' he demanded gutturally.

'For love alone?'

'Devil take it, do you doubt me still?'

'But, Delagarde, I am so very much *not* the wife for you.'

'Which is all the proof you need, simpleton,' he said smilingly as he dragged her close again. 'You cannot suppose there is any inducement other than love which could persuade me to make such a sacrifice!'

Maidie dissolved into giggles. 'Nor I, indeed, for I had no mind to give myself to so temperamental a creature as you. As well marry a bear!'

Delagarde laughed, and kissed her again, deeply. 'God!' he groaned, with difficulty withdrawing his mouth from hers. 'You need not imagine I will wait for the marriage bed—of that I warn you now.'

'Is it eccentric in me to answer that I do not wish you to wait?' Maidie asked breathlessly.

'Delightfully eccentric,' Delagarde murmured against her mouth. 'And I will take that for a yes.' He brushed her lips in a way that left her weak, adding, 'Not that it matters, for you are going to marry me, if I have to drag you to the altar.'

Maidie was in no condition to reply to this, for her lips were otherwise engaged, and her bones threatened to abandon the struggle to hold her up. But at length Delagarde finally disengaged himself, declaring that if he was not to take her there and then—and if, moreover, they were to get any dinner!—they must restrain themselves for a time.

In very short order, Maidie found herself in a bedchamber, with the landlady pouring hot water from a jug into a basin, and hovering with an offer of combs and brushes. Maidie did what she might to tidy herself from the further

dishevelment caused by Delagarde's assaults. The cool water did much to revive her, and she began to have leisure
to reflect on the extraordinary coincidence that had brought
Delagarde to this place at just the right moment.

Back in the private parlour, she discovered that covers
had been laid for them, together with a number of interesting silver dishes awaiting their pleasure. Joining Delagarde at the table, Maidie realised that it was many hours
since she had eaten. As they consumed a light repast, she
gave him an account of her escape.

Eustace's advent had been the most dreadful shock.
Upon the carriage entering Greenwich, it had begun to
slow down. Looking from the let-down window, Maidie
had seen the signpost, expecting the Royal Observatory to
come presently into view. Instead, the coach had paused
by the village green. The door had opened, and Eustace
Silsoe had leapt into the coach, which had started up again
immediately, and had gained a furious pace before Maidie
had been able to gather her wits.

'He made no secret of his intentions,' she told Delagarde. 'He meant to take me back to East Dean. He has a
small house about fifteen miles from the Shurland home.'

'He meant to hold you there?'

'Yes, for he planned for us to be married quite respect-
ably in the East Dean parish. There is a new incumbent in
the rectory, who is in a string with Firmin.'

'The rectory is in Shurland's gift?'

'Exactly. But I had no mind to fall in with his scheme.'
She perceived that Delagarde was looking murderous, and
her heart leapt. 'Why do you look like that?'

'Because I would like to kill him!' Delagarde announced
fiercely. 'He may count himself fortunate that you have
prevented me from coming up with him—tonight, in any
event.'

'What do you mean to do?' Maidie asked, a throb of

emotion in her breast. It was a heady sensation to discover that the man one loved was intent upon avenging one's honour!

Delagarde's eyes narrowed, and he sipped his wine. 'That need not concern you. Tell me how you got away.'

'But it does concern me, Laurie,' Maidie protested. 'I do not want—'

'Maidie,' he warned, 'don't imagine that my partiality will prevent me from quarrelling with you! Will you have the goodness to answer my question?'

Maidie twinkled with sudden merriment. 'I hit Eustace on the head with my reticule, and he fell unconscious.'

'Your reticule?' scoffed Delagarde. 'Don't be stupid. Tell me the truth at once!'

'It is the truth. Only you see, I had my hand telescope inside it. I had taken it with me, for I wanted to ask for some advice about replacing it.' She saw that Delagarde was looking sceptical, and took up the reticule that she had laid beside her on the table. She handed it across to him. 'See for yourself.'

Delagarde took it, opened it, and brought out a squat brass tube that readily telescoped out. He closed it again, and glanced across at her, one eyebrow raised.

'I begin almost to feel sorry for the fellow! Where did you perpetrate this daring escape?'

'Just past Lewisham,' Maidie answered. 'I saw a lad with a cart going the opposite way, and seized the opportunity. I hit Eustace, and jumped out of the coach, and then bribed the farm boy to take me up. He was but the first of three, who brought me by stages to this place.'

She might have kept to the main post road, but she believed that Eustace, once he regained consciousness, would scour for her on that route. He would hardly guess that she would return by a circuitous way to Greenwich.

'And you would not have met me so fortuitously,' Delagarde pointed out. 'I had been asking for you at every inn in every village round about Greenwich for the past hour and more, only to try to discover which way he had taken you.' He told her about the letter that Adela must have forged, and explained why he had opted for Greenwich.

Maidie eyed him a little uncertainly. 'Did you believe that I had run away with Eustace?'

'No, I thought you had run away with Wiveliscombe.'

Maidie stared. 'How came you to think of him?'

Delagarde took a painful breath, as the memory of that hideous suspicion returned. 'I believed that you were in love with him.'

'With Wiveliscombe? Oh, no!'

'Is it any more ridiculous than the suspicions you have harboured of me?' he demanded. He eyed her bodingly. 'By the by, Maidie, do you know what strikes me?'

'No, what?'

'There is one thing you have not said. I have said it, more than once. But you, Lady Mary Hope, have not.'

Maidie opened her eyes at him. 'But what is it?'

Delagarde rose from his chair and went around the table. Catching her hands, he pulled her up, holding her so. 'In all this tender talk, you have not once mentioned your own feelings—about me.'

'But you know how I feel,' Maidie protested, colouring up.

'Do I, indeed? Allow me to point out to you that I am no mind reader.'

'You wish me to say it?'

'No, I wish you to fly to the moon!' Delagarde snapped. 'Of course I wish you to say it, simpleton! And you had better, with frequency and tenderness, if you know what is good for you.'

Maidie gazed at him wide-eyed. 'Is this your idea of love talk?'

'No. It is my idea of bringing you to heel.' He shook her. 'The devil take you, wench—say it!'

Maidie smiled at him, and Delagarde's heart melted. He could not resist kissing her. She drew away a little, and reaching up her fingers, delicately touched his face.

'This,' she said softly, 'is my brightest star. If I had to choose but one to gaze upon throughout my life, I would forsake all others for this one.' She reached up to him and her lips brushed his. 'Does that answer you?'

Delagarde's dark eyes glowed. 'Yes, star-gazer, that answers me indeed. And yet you claimed you could not foretell the future!'

Maidie's widening gaze searched his. 'Meaning?'

'Oh, I will not have you abandon the heavens entirely,' he assured her, drawing her into his arms. 'Merely at interludes throughout the night—for refreshment such as this.'

And Maidie, giving herself up to his passion, was moved to approve this very agreeable compromise.

*   *   *   *   *

MILLS & BOON®

Makes any time special

Enjoy a romantic novel from
Mills & Boon®

Presents...™   *Enchanted*™   TEMPTATION.

Historical Romance™   ✚ MEDICAL ROMANCE™

THE
Regency
COLLECTION

Where rogues find romance

Look out for the eighth volume in this limited collection of Regency Romances from Mills & Boon® in December.

Featuring:

Fair Juno
by Stephanie Laurens

and

Serafina
by Sylvia Andrew

Still only £4.99

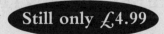

MILLS & BOON®

Makes any time special™

MILLS & BOON®

MISTLETOE *Magic*

Three favourite Enchanted™ authors
bring you romance at Christmas.

Three stories in one volume:

A Christmas Romance
BETTY NEELS

Outback Christmas
MARGARET WAY

Sarah's First Christmas
REBECCA WINTERS

Published 19th November 1999

FREE!

2 Books
and a surprise gift!

We would like to take this opportunity to thank you for reading this Mills & Boon® book by offering you the chance to take TWO more specially selected titles from the Historical Romance™ series absolutely FREE! We're also making this offer to introduce you to the benefits of the Reader Service™—

- ★ FREE home delivery
- ★ FREE gifts and competitions
- ★ FREE monthly Newsletter
- ★ Books available before they're in the shops
- ★ Exclusive Reader Service discounts

Accepting these FREE books and gift places you under no obligation to buy; you may cancel at any time, even after receiving your free shipment. Simply complete your details below and return the entire page to the address below. *You don't even need a stamp!*

YES! Please send me 2 free Historical Romance books and a surprise gift. I understand that unless you hear from me, I will receive 4 superb new titles every month for just £2.99 each, postage and packing free. I am under no obligation to purchase any books and may cancel my subscription at any time. The free books and gift will be mine to keep in any case.

H9EB

Ms/Mrs/Miss/Mr ....Initials...............................
BLOCK CAPITALS PLEASE

Surname..

Address..

....

....Postcode ....

Send this whole page to:
UK: The Reader Service, FREEPOST CN81, Croydon, CR9 3WZ
EIRE: The Reader Service, PO Box 4546, Kilcock, County Kildare (stamp required)

Offer not valid to current Reader Service subscribers to this series. We reserve the right to refuse an application and applicants must be aged 18 years or over. Only one application per household. Terms and prices subject to change without notice. Offer expires 31st May 2000. As a result of this application, you may receive further offers from Harlequin Mills & Boon Limited and other carefully selected companies. If you would prefer not to share in this opportunity please write to The Data Manager at the address above.

Mills & Boon is a registered trademark owned by Harlequin Mills & Boon Limited.
Historical Romance is being used as a trademark.

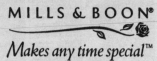